JIMMY, MRS FISHER AND ME

Eric Bishop-Potter

Matador
5 Weir Road
Kibworth Beauchamp
Leicester LE8 0LQ, UK
Tel: (+44) 116 279 2299
Fax: (+44) 116 279 2277
Email: books@troubador.co.uk
Web: www.troubador.co.uk/matador

ISBN 978 1848767 379

British Library Cataloguing in Publication Data.
A catalogue record for this book is available from the British Library.

Typeset in 11pt Palatino by Troubador Publishing Ltd, Leicester, UK

Matador is an imprint of Troubador Publishing Ltd

Eric Bishop-Potter has worked as a journalist for the Daily Mirror, the Mail on Sunday, the Press Association and the Sporting Life. He has also been employed as a public relations executive, a builder's labourer, and a merchant seaman. Born and educated in London and now living in Sussex, Eric Bishop-Potter is the author of *Dear Popsy: Collected Postcards of a Private Schoolboy to his Father*, about which Michael Palin wrote: '...wonderful turns of phrase...carries on where *Decline and Fall* left off...I think I am jealous.' *Dear Popsy* was published (under the name E. Bishop-Potter) by *Andre Deutsch* and *Penguin*.

The day had been long and hot. It had been many hours since anyone had looked up at the clear blue sky. It was still summertime and there were many more hot days to come.
- Hubert Selby jr

I am with you kid. Let's go.
- Maya Angelou

CHAPTER 1

Seeing that my pre-pube years were nothing out of the ordinary – like, I wasn't a child genius or the victim of one of those diseases where your mother goes, *'Oh, no doctor, not that!'* and starts packing for Lourdes – I'll skip them and pick up with me at the age of seventeen, which is the age I'm at now, the age, I read somewhere, when a person grabs life by the balls. Or was it the tail … ? I forget.

Anyway, I've just left Jimmy's bed and am now in my room, pulling on some threads. White T-shirt, pale blue jeans, orange-leather moccasins. No socks; socks are out. I run long, slim, suntanned fingers – nice fingers – through plenty of light brown hair and go downstairs. I'm feeling good, on the edge of great. Up until recently, up until we got the news, the bad news that had me – and I'm not exaggerating here – that had me howling like a dog, banging my head against walls – up until then, I *always* felt this good. Now there are days when I feel – well – shitty.

Downstairs I make for the kitchen, where I know I'll find the old lady. It's where she spends most of her time – when she's at home, that is.

She's standing with her back to the cooker, gazing out the window at our let-go rear garden, or at the tower block beyond it. She's wearing a white housecoat with a yellow rose and thorns pattern (a birthday present from Jimmy and me) and yellow terrycloth mules open at the toe. A few strands of naturally blonde hair have escaped from the stone-coloured comb she wears and hang from her temple. (An aunt of mine – Aunt Dolly – once told me that the old lady looks a lot like a forties' movie actress named Veronica Lake, but never having seen a Veronica Lake movie I can't corroborate that. All I can say is, if Aunt Dolly is right, then Veronica Lake must have been a real head-turner.)

"Morning," I say. My voice has a husky note. Very sexy. I like my voice a lot. The sound of it, I mean. Not many people can say that, I bet.

The old lady's head comes around and she flashes me a smile. "Morning," she says back. Then, "There's hot coffee in the pot."

I catch a whiff of cardboard as she says this. In summer the old lady tends to have a cardboardy smell.

None of us is perfect – right?

I pour myself coffee and sit at the scarred oak table we bought second-hand. The only sounds: the silvery gurgling of the beat-up refrigerator, and the faint buzzing of the clock on the wall. Saturday. Eight a.m.

As I drink my coffee I sense the old lady watching me. I look at her and drowsily grin.

The old lady smiles again. "Going out?" she asks. She means later, after I've washed.

"Yeah," I say.

"Where're you going? Anywhere nice?"

Anywhere nice? What, around here?

"Not really."

Silence.

"Centrepoint."

"Centrepoint?"

"That's where I'm going."

"Oh."

More silence.

I drink off what's left of my coffee and get to my feet. The fridge is making a twittering sound now. It's on its last legs, no question. I carry the mug I've been drinking from to the sink, rinse it under hot water, and place it on the steel drainboard, one corner of which is stained with yesterday's curry. (Twice a week the old lady makes curry. Hot. It blisters the tongue. And the taste … Ronseal tastes better, I bet. A genius in the kitchen, the old lady ain't.) I start for the door.

"Take care," the old lady says. She means on the roads, when I go out. You'd think I was about five or something. "You know me," I say.

Back upstairs I brush my teeth and wash. When I've rinsed and dried off, I look in the mirror above the basin and see a face that recalls James Dean. Eyes, eyebrows, nose, mouth – James Dean. If Dean could be brought back to life (looking as he did in *East of Eden*, say) and I was to stand next to him, we'd be taken for twins. There's no doubt about that. Not identical twins, since I'd be taller than Dean. Dean, I read somewhere, was practically a midget – a little over five-feet-seven. I'm five-feet-nine-and-a-half, which for a guy of seventeen is a pretty respectable height. By the time I'm twenty, I expect to be at least six one.

A six-foot-one James Dean …

Think about it.

I wink at myself in the mirror, then go to Jimmy's room and poke my head round the door.

He's in bed still. His hands are clasped under his

neck and he's looking at the poster he's taped to the ceiling. The poster is of the Grand Canyon. Jimmy is hooked on the Grand Canyon. He has a scrapbook filled with articles and information about it. A rock from it – a gift from a friend of a friend – stands on his chest of drawers. I once asked him (this was when we were kids and he'd just started his scrapbook): "What's so special about the Grand Canyon?" Jimmy looked at me and grinned. "It's the ultimate thumbprint," he said. "The ultimate thumbprint?" I said. "What's that supposed to mean?" "God's thumbprint," Jimmy said. I gave him a long look. "Yeah," I said, "and I'm Zoltan the Terrible."

Jimmy is my half-brother and is part Nigerian. No shit, that's what he is, part Nigerian. Here's Jimmy:

Frizzy black hair – make that *tightly-curled* black hair – a small, slim nose with a chiselled tip; high cheekbones; a wide-ish mouth (the lower lip slightly fuller than the upper (double sexy); big black liquid-y eyes; a clean-cut jaw; and golden brown skin. I tell you, you've never seen anyone so beautiful. You look at Jimmy and your heart takes off. That's how beautiful he is. Jimmy is eighteen and is suffering from – it breaks my heart to tell you this – is suffering from retinitis pigmentosa, which, as you may know, is a cause of blindness. His eyesight is OK *now*, but come December …

"Seeyalater," I say.

Jimmy unlocks his eyes from the poster and raises himself on his elbows. "Where you going?" he asks.

I smile mysteriously.

Jimmy smiles back, showing me perfect teeth (he's got these perfect teeth).

"Stay loose," I tell him. I quietly close the door on him and start out of the house.

Our house is a grey-brick, three-storied Victorian pile (flaking paint, loose plaster, leaking roof) that stands with five others on Jessup Street, a street of small attached houses in the East End of London. Jessup Street, you may be interested to know, gets its name from Bertram Jessup, a big-time businessman who owned a shoe factory in the area. Jessup, so the story goes, gave a lot of money to local welfare groups, so the council named a street after him. He's dead now. He died about sixty years ago. Bertram Archibald Jessup. You may've heard of him.

At one end of Jessup Street, running left and right of it, is Ferndale Avenue (Jessup Street all over again only longer), and at the other end, within spitting distance of our house, Albion Street – a narrow, mile-long main road restricted to buses and light traffic. On both sides of Albion Street, rubbing shoulders with mini-marts and furniture stores, are small brightly painted shops, seventy per cent of which are owned and staffed by Pakistanis. And before you start getting it into your head that I'm racially prejudiced, let me tell you: I couldn't give a fossil-fuelled fuck if *every* shop on Albion Street was owned and staffed by Pakistanis.

Excuse my language, please.

Outside – I'm out of the house now – the sun breaks from behind clouds and dapples the leaves of the plane tree that grows from the pavement outside the house two up from ours. As kids, me and Jimmy must have spent half our lives up this tree. Our initials are carved on practically every one of its branches. J.M. S.S. Jimmy

Murphy, Simon Sixsmith. Murphy was the name of the old lady's first husband, Jimmy's father. Crazy name for a Nigerian, though not as crazy as that of a Sudanese family I know: Wagstaff. Can you beat that – Wagstaff. The father, Abdi Wagstaff (Abdi Wagstaff!), was adopted by a white couple, as was Jimmy's old man. Jimmy has a photograph of his old man which he keeps in a wallet I bought for him at Christmas one year. A tall, lean guy with kind eyes and a mouth like a woman's. Very black. Like black coffee. I sometimes picture the old lady making it with him and get turned on. I can't help it, I just do.

Incidentally, if my words have an American flavour it's because trans-speak is in – 'trans' being short for transatlantic, of course.

Trans-speak is here to stay.

Believe it.

I make my way to Albion Street and there see a bus that will take me to Sarah Jane's. I run for it, and, as I do, an idea forms in my head – this crazy idea that I know won't let go of me.

CHAPTER 2

Sarah Jane's is a boutique, and the reason for my going there is to buy Jimmy a dress. No shit. A fact. The dress is gold-coloured, sleeveless and has a Chinese-style collar – a mandarin collar I think it's called. Jimmy'll look terrific in it. Really terrific. Sensational in fact.

The dress costs twenty-nine-ninety-nine – a snip at twice the price, in my opinion – and I raised the money for it by cleaning cars for Harry Haynes, a used-car dealer with a showroom (Big H For Value) on Portway, which is at the northern end of Albion Street.

Now, I guess you're thinking Jimmy's gay or something. Well, he's not. Neither am I. Okay, we occasionally – all right, *frequently* – get physical with one another, but we're not gay. You can make what you like of that. Anyway, what if we were, the world'd come to an end?

As soon as I saw the dress, I knew I had to see Jimmy in it. More than see him in it, be *seen* with him in it – like at a dance. That's what I've got planned for tonight, a dance. Tonight I'll be dancing with Jimmy in a dance hall, Jimmy shining like a beacon in a gold dress. It's what I wanna do. It's what I *have* to do. Why? Who knows why? Maybe I'm fucked up in the head. Or maybe it's the romantic in me. I'm a pretty romantic person. I sometimes picture myself dining by candlelight with a beautiful woman. We're on a moonlit verandah somewhere. Just the two of us. Palm trees, and a band playing in the distance. The sound of waves hitting a shore ...

There's Simon Sixsmith the streeter, and there's Simon Sixsmith the romantic.

We've all got another side to us, right?

But back to the dress: Jimmy's in the dark about it. It'll come as a total surprise. As will the sandals and the make-up and the Diana Ross wig – this wild Diana Ross wig – I intend getting him. Some surprise! I can just hear him when I hit him with it, when I tell him what I've got planned for tonight. *No way*, he'll say. *No-o-o-o-o way*. But he'll come around. He always does. Jimmy'd do anything for me. Jimmy'd do anything for anyone. That's the kind of person he is. A really special person. Let me give you an example of the special person Jimmy is:

Two weeks ago, on our way home from a movie, we saw in the street a bunch of slimes. There were maybe ten of them and they were beating up on a tall skinny guy in glasses. The guy's face was streaked with blood and he was crying. Sobbing. It turned out the guy was Laurie Parkes, who lives a few doors along from where *we* live, but that's not important – Jimmy would have done what he did even if he hadn't known him. What Jimmy did, he went up to the slimes, went up to Laurie Parkes, and, not saying a word, put an arm round Laurie's shoulders and led him away. Just like that. And the slimes didn't say shit, didn't move. It was as if they were mesmerized or zonked out or something. Really weird. I've never seen anything like it. Never. It was kind of ... well, it was just kind of weird. Later, over a coffee – this was after we'd wiped blood from

Laurie's face and walked him to his door – I said to Jimmy, "You know, what you did tonight wasn't clever. You could've been killed – knifed to death or something." Jimmy looked at his coffee. Then he gave me this kind of sad, you-don't-understand smile that went on for a long time. I had to look away. I felt uncomfortable. I felt I'd failed him somehow, that I'd somehow let him down.

But wasn't that something – Jimmy taking on those slimes like that. Like I said, Jimmy's special. Every day of the week.

I get off the bus and cross the street.

Sarah Jane's is in the west wing of Centrepoint, a run-down shopping mall shaped like a crucifix. Yellow strip-lighting, a cement floor strewn with junk food wrappers, piss stains, the smell of disinfectant, graffiti you wouldn't want your mother to see, stray dogs, screaming kids.

It's not Gold Card territory, Centrepoint.

Today the smell of disinfectant is stronger than it usually is; it takes your breath away. And there's a busker here today.

The answer my friend is blowin' in the wind …

He's murdering it.

I skirt a dropped portion of French fries, pass two black guys in Brasher boots and hiked-up-high jeans, and come to Sarah Jane's, standing in the doorway of which is one of those screaming kids I mentioned. His eyes are shut tight and there's snot running into his mouth. He's screaming like he's on fire. I tap him on his head. "Give it a rest, Rodrigo," I say, and the kid bares his teeth and screams even louder.

In Sarah Jane's I stand at a glass-topped counter, and after not too long a wait a fem in a yellowy two-piece with floppy shoulders comes up and says, "Can I be of assistance?" She's about five-feet-six, slimly built and has short, blonde hair. Her face is small and oval and her skin clear and creamy. A paper bag job, she's not. "Yes," I say, "I'd like to see a dress like the one in the window – the gold one."

"Certainly," the fem says. I see her eyes go from my face to my hair and back to my face, which tells me I've tapped into her interest system. "What size?"

I look at her cool. "I dunno," I say. "What size would you say I am?"

This knocks the fem for six, and it's a while before she can say, "Size ten."

"Size ten, eh?" I say.

"I'll see if we have one," the fem says and goes off.

While she's away, I look around me – and find I'm being clocked by two twentysomethings in mini-skirts. They're standing by a rail of tank tops. One has a potato-looking nose, and the other black furry eyebrows that grow together in a straight line. Both have vampire-white faces, and nose rings. I tell you, I wouldn't want to meet them in an alley on a dark night. Like I said, they're giving me earnest attention, so I wave to them.

I might as well've waved to the man in the moon.

The fem gets back to me and says, "You're in luck; this is the last size ten."

She has the dress draped over her arm, and close up it looks metallic. I touch it and it *feels* metallic. I picture Jimmy in it and my heart flips over. "Where can I try it on?" I ask.

"Oh ..." the fem says, and twists and turns like she's in urgent need of bladder relief. "Um," she goes.

I look at her cool again. "I haven't got all day," I say.

"Well, ah ... " the fem says.

I give her a slow smile, raising my right eyebrow. Very James Bond. "I don't have this trouble at Miss Selfridge," I say.

The fem likes that, I can tell. She nods towards Potato Nose and Eyebrows. "There's a cubicle over there you can use," she says, and hands me the dress – carefully, like it's precious. A woman glides by carrying a blouse on a hanger.

"Thanks," I tell the fem.

The cubicle is small and hot and I'm glad I'm not trying on a ball gown. I draw the curtain, hang the dress on a hook, and strip.

There are two full-length mirrors in the cubicle, so I waste a minute admiring my body – specifically my arse (I'm not wearing underpants; underpants, like socks, are out), which is neat and firm, and my dick, which is very capable-looking – a good size. I'm really proud of my dick. (More about my dick later.) I dimple my arse a couple of times, then take the dress off the hook and pull it on.

Except for the places where the tits go, it's a perfect fit, or it appears to be; I can't tell for sure until I get the back zippered, and this I'm unable to do without help.

You need help, you look for it. I draw back the curtain and step outside.

And put on a look of surprise.

Why I do this is because every face in the shop is pointed in my direction; I'm the focus of attention –

which is OK by me. Being the focus of attention is something I can stand. I camp it up. To keep the attention on me that's what I do. Why not? I give a coy smile and flutter my lashes. I pout, and shake my hips. I execute a rolling bump, flap a hand. I even break into song:

The boys are back in town
The boys are back in tow-ow-ow-ow -

"It looks wonderful."

It's the fem who's serving me. Trailed by five or six punters and eyeing the dress and smiling, she's coming towards me. She walks with a lot of energy, I notice. Plenty of shoulder movement. I shoot a look at Potato Nose and Eyebrows, who haven't moved since I entered the shop. They're looking at me like they'd like to fuck my brains out. "I need something to shove down the front," I tell the fem, and a middle-ager with hair like brown glass steps up to me and hands me a bunch of silk squares. She must've pulled them from a rail or something. "Thanks, Coach," I tell her, and start to pad myself out.

"Here, let *me* do that," the fem says. She makes a grab for the squares, and I move them back, playing with her. "No tickling," I tell her.

"No tickling," the fem says.

She pads me out and zips me up. Then she looks me over, tilting her head to get an impression. "He looks gorgeous," one of the punters says. A woman at the door is beckoning to someone to come in. She glances at me, then beckons again. *Quick! Get a load of this!* "Wait here," the fem says, and hurries off. In less than a minute she's back with a red shoulder-length wig. "Let's see if *this* works," she says. Her eyes are shining.

She fits the wig on me, and a big sigh goes up. "Cute as shit," I hear someone (it could be Eyebrows) say. "Does anyone have a lipstick I could borrow?" the fem asks, and I think, 'This is getting out of hand.' But then I think, 'What the fuck, she's having fun.'

On goes lipstick.

"Now," says the fem, "just a little eye shadow. Eye shadow, anyone? You've got wonderful lashes, do you know that?"

"Of course," I say, and everyone cracks a rib laughing. I'm making their day. They've never had such a good time.

On goes eye shadow.

"Come," the fem says, and, to applause (no shit, people are putting their hands together), takes me to a standing swing-mirror. "There," she says, "what do you think?"

I study my reflection.

I tell you, I look so fantastic I could slip it to myself. "I'll take it," I say, meaning the dress.

I also take a coat – a white shaggy number with a tie belt and a high collar – which, according to the fem, had "just come in".

While I'm settling the bill, a woman who looks like she could punch out a rhinoceros comes up and says – get this – "How would you like to work here?"

This throws me, I have to admit, and I don't answer immediately. Instead I wipe lipstick from my mouth with a Kleenex I've dug from my jeans. Eventually I say, "Doing what?"

"What you just did," the woman says.

"What, dress up, d'you mean?"

The woman smiles and looks around the shop.

I look around with her ... and catch on. The place is practically full, and I was the draw.

"One day a week," the woman says. "Saturday. Five pounds an hour."

"You the owner?" I ask.

"Yes," the woman answers. "Mrs Hollis."

"Six," I say.

"Five-fifty," Mrs Hollis says.

I laugh. "I'll think about it," I say and, after I've smiled and winked at Potato Nose and Eyebrows and got nothing back, exit the shop, carrying two bags with *Sarah Jane's* printed on them in red lettering. I'm full of electric energy.

I head for Dolcis, which is in the east wing of the mall. My mind is on Mrs Hollis and the five-fifty-an-hour she offered me. 'Not bad,' I tell myself, 'not bad at all. A lot better than what I'm getting from Haynes.' For a split second I see myself cleaning one of Haynes's shitty cars. There's sweat running down my back and I'm covered with grease. 'You arsehole, Haynes,' I think. Then I fade out all thoughts of work and money and concentrate on the moment.

In Dolcis I approach an assistant and ask to see a pair of gold-coloured sandals; size eight.

The assistant doesn't bat an eye.

It's the same when she brings me the sandals and I try them on and do a test walk across the floor. Plenty of *other* people bat an eye, but the assistant – nothing. A very cool lady. Cool, she's liquid nitrogen.

For fun, I ask to see a pair of high heels in the same

colour, and the assistant says, "Are they for you?"

"My brother," I say.

The assistant says, "If he's never worn highs before, he'll find them awfully difficult to walk in."

"Is that right?" I say.

The assistant nods.

"You're the expert," I tell her. I turn to a customer, a big-jawed oldie with feet like tree roots, and stick out a foot. "These do anything for me?" I ask.

The oldie gives me the fisheye. "Do what?" she says.

"These sandals," I wriggle my toes, pink nailed and clean, "they do anything for me?" I give her a smile that must be beautiful to see.

The oldie turns her head away.

I shrug. It's the way of the world.

I pay for the sandals, then head for Boots, which is four doors along from Dolcis, set between a bookie's and a florist's. The florist's is where I once bought a bunch of daffodils for the old lady (this was when I was about thirteen). I just went in there and bought them – with the last of my pocket money. I was that kind of kid.

In Boots, after checking out the singles' chart and giving myself a squirt of something – aftershave or something – from a 'tester', I step up to the cosmetics' counter and get involved with a saleslady (a really beautiful woman of about forty with carrot-coloured hair) who, after I've asked her why it is that all the best-looking women work for Boots, helps me choose make-up – lipstick, blusher, eye shadow. No mascara. Jimmy needs mascara like the Queen needs somewhere to live.

"Go easy on the blusher," the saleslady tells me, handing me my change.

"I will," I say, flipping her a wink. Then, "Moderation in all things – right?"

The saleslady laughs. "Have a nice day," she says.

"Count on it," I tell her, and she laughs again. A really nice woman.

When I come out, I make my way to The Strandz Palace, a unisex hairdresser's whose owner, Big Maria, is a major friend of mine. Big Maria's been cutting my hair since I was a kid.

"Simuhn!" she yells as I walk in the door. She leaves what she's doing and comes up to me.

"H-e-e-e-e-y!" I say, and as we give each other a high five I smell the coconut oil she massages into her hands – to keep them, so she once told me, smooth and sweet-smelling – *sm-o-o-o-o-th and sweet-smellin'*. "I want a favour, Maria," I say.

"You're my man," Maria says. "Whatever you want you got."

"The wig in the window: I'd like to borrow it. I'll let you have it back first thing Monday."

Maria looks at me with wide eyes for a few seconds, looks at the bags I've dumped on the floor. "Simuhn," she says, "you ain't cross dressin', are you? You ain't a tee vee?" And then she laughs. She laughs like she's just been told the world's funniest joke. Her whole body shakes. She rocks back and forth, slapping huge thighs. She doubles over, hands on knees, and pounds the floor with her foot. *Ha, ha, ha, ha.* She grabs hold of a chair to keep from falling over. *Ha, ha, ha, ha.* She's entirely out of control.

When she's back on track and after she's said "Jeeeeezus!" a couple of times, she goes to the display window, lifts out the wig, shakes it, and puts it in a Sainsbury bag taken from a cupboard above a hair-wash basin. "Now … gimme a kiss." She comes up close to me, smiling.

"Girl of my dreams," I say.

She draws me to her and very gently kisses me on the mouth. "Mmmmm," she goes. "Mmmmm." I can feel the heat of her body through the black silk dress she's wearing and I get a little horny (I sometimes think that sex is taking me over. I do). "Mmmmm," I go.

After a while, after about two hours, Maria stops kissing me and looks into my eyes, kind of adoringly. "When we gonna cut your hair?" she murmurs. She strokes my cheek with fat, shiny fingers.

"I'll swing by in a week or two," I say.

"You better," Maria says.

On my way out, she calls, "How's that beautiful brother of yours?"

"Impressive," I call back.

"Impress-i-i-i-i-ve!" Maria repeats. "Impress-i-i-i-i-ve!"

I hear her laughter two doors away.

A really hysterical character.

I wander around Centrepoint for a bit, and then, after I've laid some silver on the busker (a young sad-looking guy in black jeans and a white sweatshirt with a drawstring hood), I take a bus to Toni's Tea Room, a greasy spoon on Albion Street where most Saturdays I hook up with a couple of guys I know: Wally and Stan. We went through school together. Wally is tall and thin with ginger hair, and Stan is tall and thin with fair hair. Both are nuts about football. It's all they ever talk about. Wally wants to be a lorry driver and Stan is thinking of joining the army.

Pathetic, both of them. But I like them a lot.

Toni's Tea Room is owned by Toni Goulandris, or Toni the Greek as he's known locally; a fat little guy who wears – make that *douses* himself with – Brut aftershave – to kill, so the joke goes, the stink of the place. Toni's wife, Carla, does the cooking, and Toni serves and takes the money. Nobody – apart from Toni – has ever seen Carla. The only part of Carla anyone's ever seen is a hand that comes through the serving hatch – this bony hand with hooked, yellow nails; a really disgusting-looking hand. I've never had any of Carla's food, but I've had her tea, and it tastes like pig piss. Her coffee is better. Her coffee tastes like dog piss.

Toni is wiping down the counter, his face and the had-it singlet he's wearing wet with sweat. Toni sweats a lot, even in winter. He always looks as if he's in meltdown. Seeing me, he lets go the filthy piece of rag he's using as a wiper and, without my asking, pours me a cup of dog piss.

"Wally or Stan been in?" I ask.

"Wally was in yesterday," Toni says. "I ain't seen Stan." He slides the cup – no saucer – across the counter to me – slop, slop – and I hand him a thick one. "How's business?" I ask.

"No fuckin' good," Toni says. "Nobody got no fuckin' money, ain't they?"

I shrug.

"Fuckin' government," Toni says. "They fuckin' killin' business."

"You were one of those voted 'em in," I point out.

"No more I fuckin' don't," Toni says. He hands me

my change, and I take my dog piss and bags to a table by a wall.

"Next time I vote Conservative," Toni says."

"We need Livingstone in charge of things," I say. And mean it. Livingstone is one of my heroes. It's my belief he cares about people, and by people I mean those that ain't got.

"Livingstone's a fuckin' lunatic," Toni says.

"Don't believe all you read in the Tory press," I say.

"What Tory press?" Toni says. "I buy *The Star*."

End of convo.

At the table I take a swallow of dog piss, then open one of the *Sarah Jane's* bags – the one with the dress inside; I wanna see it again.

Under Toni's strip lighting it looks kind of greenish, and I wonder how it will look under the lights of the Paramount. The Paramount is where I'm taking Jimmy tonight. It's our local dancehall. I go to there every Saturday. I go there alone, but I'm never alone when I leave – like, I've always got a fem with me. Fems want me badly. That's the truth. As soon as I walk through the doors of the Paramount they make a bee-line for me. I can have my pick.

I'm not kidding.

Incidentally, why I go to the Paramount alone and not, as you might expect, with Wally or Stan, or both, is because Wally and Stan can't pass for eighteen. The Paramount is for eighteens to twenty-fives only. I've been going to the Paramount for four months now and never once been asked my age – something I'm proud of.

I wait for Wally and Stan to show, and when they don't, I finish my dog piss, say So long to Toni, and pretty soon I'm in my room unbagging the stuff I bought Jimmy.

I lay it out on the bed and stand looking at it, admiring it. I do this for a long time. Then I pick up the wig. As with the other stuff, if it fits *me*, it'll fit Jimmy. Jimmy and me take the same size in everything – shoes, headwear, everything. I keep telling him to get some decent threads so I can borrow them, but Jimmy's not interested in clothes. They're just not important to him. Me, I love clothes. A dedicated follower of fashion, you might say.

I pull on the wig, and because it's a little screwed up from its stay in the Sainsbury bag I look as if I've been hurricaned. But it fits. It's elasticated. It'd fit the Elephant Man. I play around with it for a while, then, feeling a need to see Jimmy, go to his room.

He's sitting in a chair, wearing headphones. He's dressed in faded brown cords, a red and black check shirt, beat up brown brogues, and red woollen socks. He looks terrific. I sit in the chair facing him – *my* chair – and he takes off the headphones. There's a faint sound coming from them: Mahler. Mahler is the only music Jimmy plays. He's nuts about him.

"We're going out tonight," I announce.

"We are?" Jimmy says. "Where're we going?"

I open my eyes wide to convey mystery. "I'll tell you later."

Jimmy gives me a big smile. "Big secret, eh?"

I give him a big smile back. "Right," I say. A silence then, until I say, "So what've you been doing?"

Jimmy shrugs and says, "Listening to music. Reading. Helping Mother put up a shelf." Jimmy always refers to the old lady as 'Mother', something I do only when I'm in Jimmy's company. Why I do that, I don't know.

"It's a nice day, you should be out," I say. There's a note of – what? – concern – there's a note of concern in my voice.

Jimmy doesn't reply, just looks at me like he's saying, "Look, bro, don't worry. It's no big deal, I can handle it."

No big deal. Retinitis pigmentosa. Blindness.

He switches channels: "What've *you* been doing?"

I grin. "Buying a few things."

"Such as?"

I do the wide-eyed bit again. "No can tell." I get to my feet and move towards the door.

At the door I pause and look back. Jimmy has his headphones back on and his eyes are closed. I leave him with Mahler and go downstairs.

The old lady is in the kitchen, ironing. If the old lady's not cleaning the house, she's ironing. Or cooking. Or, if she's not doing any of those things, she's breaking her back at an old people's home (something I'll get to later). I don't know how she stands it. The drudgery. If *I* was the old lady, I'd say fuck it and go on the game. I would.

"Hi," I say.

The old lady comes out of the dream she slips into whenever she irons, smiles, and says, "*You* look pleased with yourself."

"You think so?"

"Like the cat that's swallowed the canary."

"Speaking of canaries," I say, "how about a coffee?"

"Why not?" the old lady says.

21

I make and pour coffee that won't taste like dog piss and sit at the table, most of which is covered with piles of neatly ironed laundry. One of the piles is topped with a pair of Jimmy's boxers (the fact that boxers are out doesn't bother Jimmy) and looking at them I see my fingers hooked onto their waistband, lowering them. Before I can get seriously aroused, the old lady says, "Going out tonight?" (Every Saturday it's: "Going out tonight?")

"Yes," I say, "I'm taking Jimmy dancing."

The old lady stops ironing. "Dancing?" she says. "I didn't know Jimmy danced."

"He will tonight," I say.

The old lady gives me a smile that makes her look about nineteen. "Oh, Simon," she says, "how nice."

For some reason, her saying this embarrasses me, so to cover my embarrassment I say, "We're gonna knock their socks off."

Corny, I know.

The old lady's eyes mist over and she can't speak. She wants to, but she can't, I can tell. I see her swallow, and at this point *my* eyes mist over. The old lady and me get easily upset these days. It's to do with Jimmy's condition. We haven't come to terms with it yet.

I let a few seconds tick by, then, to get us both on track, say, "Is there a clean shirt for me tonight?"

The old lady fights back tears and nods at one of the piles on the table. In an American accent, sending me up, she says, "Whaddaya think *they* are, airhead?"

After that we don't say anything. I sip my coffee and the old lady works at her ironing, her expression gradually becoming dreamy again. I ask myself what it is she's dreaming about and guess it must be something very personal, something she wouldn't wanna talk about.

I finish my coffee and get to my feet. The old lady looks at me dreamily – without, it seems, really seeing me. I wanna say something special to her, tell her she looks terrific or something, but am unable to on account of the emotional stoppage in my throat. "Take it easy," I manage to get out.

Back upstairs, I go into the bathroom, blub into a towel for a few minutes (you can't be cool *all* the time), and then run the bath water.

I like to have music playing when I take a bath, so I fetch a portable radio from my room and tune in to Jazz FM.

> *And we'll be pleeeeased to be caaaaaaalled*
> *What we have always been caaaaaaalled*

It's Peggy Lee. *The Folks Who Live On The Hill*. It's not jazz but it'll do. I peel off my clothes and step into the bath, recalling the time I saw Lee on TV. She came on stage in a wheelchair. She was about eighty but had the face of a young girl – the result of her latest lift. Dead eyes in a young girl's face. Very spooky.

In the bath I look at myself in the full-length mirror that's fixed to the wall back of the taps. I look first at my chest and shoulders, and then let my eyes go to my dick. As is always the case when I see my dick I'm struck by its colour; like, whereas my legs and torso are white, my dick is brown. Not brown, exactly – swarthy. A swarthy dick ... Weird, but OK. Pretty nice, in fact.

On the subject of dicks: I once saw Wally's, and it was maggot white. A real throw-up job. I'd hate to be the woman who gets to marry him. I mean, imagine having to be nice to a maggot-white dick every night.

No thank you.

Looking at myself in the mirror, I get horny and in no time at all I'm jerking away for dear life. I have to admit: I jerk off a lot. You do when you're seventeen, right?

Afterwards, when I've wiped myself off with a Kleenex taken from a box on the windowsill, I lower myself into the bath and soak for a while. Then I get on my knees and submerge my head. I'm one of those people who wash their hair in the bath. Saves time. The shampoo I use is called Orange Blossom. The old lady gets it from Boots; it's their own brand. The old lady also gets Boots' Orange Blossom soap. Everybody in our house smells faintly of orange blossom. A pretty delightful smell.

When I've washed my hair, I soak for the duration of a Quincey Jones' number – *The Places You Find Love* – a really terrific number – then soap all over, rinse, and release the bath water. I towel down, part dry my hair, wipe around the bath, and pull on my blue terrycloth bathrobe taken from a hook in the bathroom door. Then I turn off the radio, go to my room, and lie on my bed. As I drift towards sleep, the idea I had when running for the bus this morning comes back to me and I make a giant decision.

CHAPTER 3

I wake at four-thirty and straight-off dress: cream polo shirt; beige summer-weight trousers; highly polished chestnut loafers with fringed tongues. The jacket that matches the trousers I'll put on later. I gather up the stuff I bought Jimmy and go to his room.

He's stretched out on his bed, his eyes on the Grand Canyon poster. He seems lost in it. "Yo," I say. There's the smell of orange blossom in the air, so I figure he's recently bathed – or it could *me* I'm smelling.

Seeing me, Jimmy swings his legs over the side of the bed and sits up. "What've you got there?" he asks.

I grin. "Your outfit for the night. We're going dancing." I dump the stuff down next to him, and he looks at like it's diseased or something. "Are you serious?" he says.

"C'mon," I say, "get it on." I take hold of his wrists and pull him to his feet.

"You *are* serious," he says.

"You know me, bro," I say.

"Hey, wait a minute," he says.

"Come on, Jimmy," I say, "do this for me."

Jimmy looks at me with solemn eyes, and I try not to laugh. 'No way,' I say to myself. 'No-o-o-o-o way.'

"No way," Jimmy says. "No-o-o-o-o way."

"Please, Jimmy," I say. "I promise you, you do this for me and that'll be it – I'll never ask another thing of you."

"Hey, come *on*," he says. He makes no attempt to unbutton his shirt, so I unbutton it for him. "Please, bro," I say. "It'd mean a lot to me."

There's a long silence while he thinks. Finally, looking at the dress, he says, "Where'd you get it?"

He's given in. I've won.

"Bought it, you dope. Where d'you think I got it?"

I get his shirt off, then take down his cords. For some reason he's not wearing boxers, and catching sight of his crotch I'm tempted to bury my face in it. Instead I pick up the dress, make a circle of its opening, and drop it over his head. He slips his feet out of the Jesus sandals he's wearing (he's ditched the brogues and's wearing Jesus sandals now) and says, "You know you're crazy, don't you?" He steps out of his cords.

"Arms," I say.

He raises his arms, and I work them into the dress's armholes. The air around us is filled with the smell of orange blossom.

I work the dress over his hips and smooth out the wrinkles. "Turn around."

He turns around, and I zipper the dress. Then I get the wig. This is the bit I've been waiting for. "Lower your head."

He lowers his head, and, with big bubbles of excitement exploding inside me, I fit the wig on him. "Okay, look up."

He looks up.

He's so beautiful it's not true.

I sit him in a chair and start making up his face.

The blusher is bronze-coloured, and I use it sparingly, the way I've seen the old lady use blusher – a few brushstrokes on the cheekbones and forehead, a dab on the nose and chin. I hope you're seeing this: bronze on golden brown skin ... I tell you, there's nothing like it.

The lipstick I'm not sure about. It's kind of purply. I apply it, and it's exactly right.

The eye shadow is a couple of shades lighter than the blusher, and this also is exactly right.

I get him to his feet and take him to the mirror that hangs above the fireplace. "Am I good, or am I good?" I ask. I'm smiling.

Jimmy looks at his reflection for a minute, and then looks at mine. He shakes his head. "Crazy," he says. I put an arm round his shoulders. "You look sensational," I say.

I notice he needs tits, so I go to the chest of drawers for a pair of the thick woollen socks he wears.

As I pad him out, he says, "What's this all about?"

I try to find words, but can't. "Later," I tell him. "Put the sandals on."

I return to my room, finish dressing, and, when I've run a comb through my hair and called a cab from downstairs, get back to Jimmy.

He's sitting in a chair, staring into space.

"Come on," I say, "get the coat on." I check out his feet. He has the sandals on – the gold ones – and they look terrific. He gets the coat and slips his arms into the sleeves.

"Tie the belt."

He ties the belt

I look him up and down, and, as I do and without warning, these words come into my head, words I didn't know I had in me: "A black orchid in a bank of snow." (The coat's white, remember.)

"How about a drink?" I suggest. My voice sounds hoarse.

"I think I'm gonna need one," Jimmy says.

I go to the bathroom and return with two tumblers, into which I pour scotch from the hip flask I've started carrying. I have to confess: I'm a secret drinker. I usually drink in my room while listening to music. Springsteen. Velvet Underground. That kind of stuff. Jimmy hardly ever drinks. A glass of wine at Christmas, maybe.

"Cheers," he says.

"Don't smudge your lipstick," I tell him, and at this moment a car horn sounds. It's the cab I ordered. We finish our drinks and leave the house.

From the cab, as it turns into Albion Street, I see Mrs Fisher pushing our kid – mine and Mrs Fisher's, that is – in a pushchair.

CHAPTER 4

It happened like this, when I was fourteen and Mrs Fisher about thirty-three:

I was thirsty from all the running around I'd been doing at school, so, thinking 7-Up, I ducked into Fisher's news-and-food shop on Albion Street. It was closing time Friday and Mr Fisher was just going off somewhere (to his weekly Chamber of Commerce meeting, I found out later), leaving Mrs Fisher to lock up. Mrs Fisher, I should tell you, is a very beautiful Jewish woman. Tall, with coal-black hair. Skin the colour of eggshells. Terrific figure. People follow her with their eyes as she walks along the street. Why she married Mr Fisher is a mystery. Mr Fisher's a nice guy, but he's not what you'd call good-looking; a small, fat guy with doorknob eyes and lips that are always wet. Old Fishface, the kids around here call him.

Anyway, I paid for the 7-Up, and as I made to leave, Mrs Fisher went to the door, bolted it, and said, "Simon, will you do something for me?" I was surprised she knew my name.

"OK," I said.

"Come this way," Mrs Fisher said and led me through the back of the shop and up a flight of stairs. As she climbed the stairs she ran her hands over her hips, and seeing her do this I got a bad case of dirty thoughts. For a second I had the manic notion to put my hand up her dress. But of course I didn't. It's not something you do.

Also, Mrs Fisher is a big woman; she could've knocked nine kinds out of me.

At the top of the stairs, Mrs Fisher stopped. "How old are you, Simon?" she asked.

"Fourteen and two weeks," I said.

Mrs Fisher looked at me with quiet eyes for a moment, and then moved to a room that I could straight-off see was a bedroom – like, there was a king-sized bed in it. Bedroom! My heart started to beat fast.

Mrs Fisher sat on the edge of the bed, took the 7-Up from my hand and placed it on the floor.

"What is it you want me to do?" I asked. My voice sounded weird, sort of hollow and far off.

"Do you have a girlfriend, Simon?" Mrs Fisher asked.

"No," I said, which was the truth. I could've if I'd wanted to: girls were – still are – crazy for me. There was one, Angela Cummings, who was always feeling me up.

Which is what Mrs Fisher did.

I couldn't believe it was happening. She didn't feel me up, exactly, more she stroked my crotch with the tips of her fingers. Jesus, it was terrific. I was on fire. The whole of my body was on fire.

She stroked my crotch and with the other hand unbuttoned her dress – a pink and white number – I can see it now – that buttoned all the way down the front. Then she stood up and the dress parted and I could see that under it she was wearing pale-yellow pants and a white bra. "Have you ever seen a naked woman, Simon?" she asked. She removed the dress and tossed it onto a chair like it was nothing.

"Only in books," I said. *One* book, to be precise. Not

a book, a magazine. One of the kids at school got hold of a copy of *Penthouse*. In it were pictures of a naked blonde doing housework. Vacuum hose. That kind of stuff. Pathetic, really.

Mrs Fisher undid her bra and let it slide over her arms.

Her tits were huge, totally huge. I never realised tits could be that big. World-class tits. With terracotta-coloured nipples.

She sat on the bed again, took off her shoes, and eased down her pants. The pants had a small stain at the front, and I worried that I might have a stain at the front of mine (I had the feeling I'd be seeing them pretty soon!).

"You're a beautiful boy, Simon," Mrs Fisher said, and took hold of my hands. "I suppose you know that, don't you?"

I didn't answer. I couldn't. I was too fazed by what was happening.

She parted her legs, drew me to her, and placed my hands on her tits. A second later she was unfastening my jeans. "Don't you?" she asked again. She smelled kind of appley.

"Don't I what?" I said. I'd forgotten the question.

"Know that you're beautiful," Mrs Fisher said.

"No," I said. My heart was racing so fast I could hear my pulse in my ears.

"Well, you are," Mrs Fisher said. And then she smiled like someone apologizing. "If you want me to stop, I will," she said.

'No!' I thought. 'Keep going! Keep going!' "It's okay," I said. I could feel her nipples on my palms, but I didn't play around with them like I wanted to. I didn't have the nerve to. I just stood there getting hornier and hornier.

She lowered my jeans and pants – giant stain on pants – and suddenly I was looking at her holding my dick. Of course, being only fourteen it wasn't too big – attractive-looking but not too big – and I felt a little ashamed of it. I half expected Mrs Fisher to poke fun at it, but she didn't, she seemed pretty pleased with it, and it occurred to me that maybe Mr Fisher's was smaller.

"Take your shirt off while I untie your shoes," Mrs Fisher said. She bent down, and the next thing I knew she had it – my boyhood – in her mouth.

Wow, what an experience! I can't tell you – all you ladies and sexually inexperienced guys – how wonderful it was. It was like – I dunno – like wetting the bed. Remember when you were a kid and you wet the bed – how warm and liquid and beautiful it was? Well, it was like that only a hundred times better. I can remember thinking, 'Wait till I tell the guys on the street about this.' But then I thought, 'Screw the guys on the street. I tell the guys on the street, they're all gonna want some.' I wanted Mrs Fisher to myself.

With an empty mouth, Mrs Fisher said, "Let's get on the bed", and I breathed a sigh of relief: in another couple of seconds I'd've squirted off, and all the good feelings I was having, all the *extra-terrestrial* feelings I was having, would, if you'll excuse the pun, have come to an end. I wanted them to go on for ever.

Mrs Fisher stretched out on the bed, and it was then that I got my first good look at her pubes. They were an orangey-yellow colour – not, as you might expect, black like her hair, but orangey-yellow – and looked very wiry, very industrial.

I lay down, naked, beside her and she started kissing me, gently at first, then hungrily, as if my mouth was delicious food and she hadn't eaten in a month. In between kisses, she said, "You're beautiful. You're so beautiful. Do you think *I'm* beautiful? Do you? Tell me I'm beautiful, Simon."

"You're beautiful," I told her, and almost before I knew it I was inside her and she was riding me in the astride position.

When it was over we stayed on the bed, Mrs Fisher propped on an elbow and looking down at me and occasionally drifting her fingers over my body. We got off the bed after I'd said, "Can I have my 7-Up, please?" and Mrs Fisher had laughed.

And so I became Mrs Fisher's boy lover. Every Friday at 6.30 I'd be outside Fisher's news-and-food shop waiting for Mr Fisher to leave for his Chamber of Commerce meeting. I guess you could say I was Mrs Fisher's Boy Friday.

I stopped being Mrs Fisher's Boy Friday when she told me she was pregnant and I was the father.

The kid was born two summers ago and was named Benjamin.

Benjie Fisher. Some name.

A couple of weeks after Benjamin was born I saw Mrs Fisher in the street pushing him in a pushchair. There was nobody about, so I went up to her.

"This is your son," she said, and I thought, 'Why can't she keep her voice down!' I could feel my face start to burn. "He has your eyes," she said.

"How about Mr Fisher," I said. "He suspect anything?"

"No," she said, "he's very happy."

I looked in the pushchair and saw this beautiful kid. He was so beautiful my heart went all still inside me. I couldn't take my eyes off him.

"Would you like to hold him?" Mrs Fisher asked.

"No thanks," I said.

Mrs Fisher smiled. "He won't bite," she said softly. And then she gave me this long, quiet look, the kind of look you give someone to tell them they're special. "Goodbye," she said at last, and walked off.

I wave to her now from the cab, but she doesn't see me.

CHAPTER 5

The Paramount (you may be interested in knowing this) stands on a cheap-stored main road that gives direct access to the City. A big yellow building with a plain windowless front and a roof with a notched edge that makes you think of a battlement. Up until a few years ago it was a cinema, and before that a music hall. When it was a cinema it was called The Granada. It was the first cinema I ever went to. The first movie I saw there was *Pinnochio* (I was a kid at the time), which I liked a lot. The last movie I saw there was *Top Gun*, starring Tom Cruise. Total crap.

The cab comes to a halt, and the driver – a pale, round-shouldered guy who shed dandruff every time we hit a bump in the road – lowers the sound of the Englebert Humperdinck tape he's playing and waits to be paid.

I pay him off on the pavement, and, as he pulls away, say to Jimmy, "Englebert Humperdinck … Anaesthesia." (Englebert Humperdinck's voice is not something I think is essential to my life on this planet. Please Release Me Let Me fucking Go.)

The Paramount has three dance-floors – Dance-floor One for funk trippers, Dance-floor Two for smoochers, and Dance-floor Three for rap freaks. (Four words on rap: You can have it.) Dancing starts at seven and, providing nobody gets knifed, goes on till midnight.

I get two tickets for Dance-floor Two, and then, since it's only 6.30, suggest we go for a drink.

We make our way to a pub called The Horseshoe, a small out-of-the-way Truman's house with cement planters and coach lamps at the door. Legend has it that it was the haunt of one of the Kray twins – Ronnie, I think – the one who was sexually involved with Lord Boothby. Unlike most of the pubs in the area, The Horseshoe is pretty quiet. No Kill The Giant games and no loudmouthed slimes throwing drink around. None of that shit.

As we walk through the door, every eye goes to Jimmy. It's as if the latest Miss Venezuela or the newest Hollywood dish has just walked in. You've no idea how proud I feel. "What'll you have, bro?" I ask, when we're at the bar.

"A fruit juice with ice'd hit the spot," Jimmy says, and I smile. I do this because I know he's sending me up. It doesn't bother me that Jimmy and the old lady send me up; I find it amusing.

Jimmy's voice doesn't go with the outfit he's wearing, and the guy who's waiting to serve us – a youngish guy with baby-shit-coloured hair – gives him a look that says, "What-the-fuck've-we-got-here?" and for a second I wanna punch him out. I don't know about you, but people who think it's smart to be snide, who take the piss, as we say on Albion Street – and the guy who's waiting to serve us definitely comes into that category, you can tell he does – make my blood boil. It's my belief that we should take trouble with people, show them a little respect, a little consideration.

Am I right, or am I right?

I talk Jimmy out of having a fruit juice and order two vodka and tonics. Large ones. Vodka is my favourite drink.

While we're waiting for the drinks to arrive, I glance at Jimmy and notice he looks a little out of it, a little lost. "You okay, bro?" I ask.

Jimmy looks at me with bright eyes. "Great," he says, smiling. "Why d'you ask?"

"I dunno," I say.

I feel stupid saying this.

Eventually our drinks arrive and we take them to a table that's placed against a wall, and sit facing each other. There's a shaded yellow wall light above Jimmy's head, and the rays from it make his face glow and gleam like maple syrup. Beautiful. I can't help wondering how *my* face'd look under that light. Pretty good, I wouldn't mind betting. I swallow some vodka and glance round the bar. We're still getting a lot of attention – or, rather, *Jimmy's* still getting a lot of attention – one guy, a blond guy with a crew-cut, can't keep his eyes off him – and I wonder if Jimmy is aware of the impression he's making, if he knows just how mind-blowingly, balls-achingly beautiful he is, and I come to the conclusion that he isn't and doesn't, that in one respect he's like a kid: he can't see his own beauty. "How about some music?" I say. I get to my feet. "Anything special you'd like to hear?"

"Put what *you* want on," Jimmy says

"If you say so, James," I say, and roll my eyes and grin (it's what I sometimes say and do to make Jimmy laugh).

Jimmy laughs, and I go to a box on the wall and choose a selection of Bruce Springsteen numbers, one of which is *The Streets of Philadelphia* – a favourite of mine. In my opinion, *The Streets of Philadelphia* is the best thing

Springsteen's done. His *Hard Land* is pretty good too.

I return to the table, and after a while, after I've made a few hilarious remarks, *The Streets of Philadelphia* comes on, and Jimmy says, "You play this a lot, don't you? I've heard it coming from your room."

"I've got a Springsteen tape," I point out.

"You play *a lot* of sad music, I've noticed," Jimmy says.

"That's rich coming from you," I say. "What about that Mahler stuff you're always listening to?"

As a matter of fact Jimmy is right, I *do* play a lot of sad music. Vocals mainly. I *like* sad music. My favourite piece of sad music is Oleta Adams's *Many Rivers to Cross*. Whenever I hear it I get all choked up. I wouldn't mind having *Many Rivers to Cross* played at my funeral. That and *Everybody's Talkin'*. The Nilsson version.

We listen to Springsteen, and then decide to leave. As we rise from the table, I cut a look at the blond guy with the crew-cut and see that he's still clocking Jimmy. I catch his eye and look him out of existence.

In the Paramount Jimmy checks his coat, and we make our way up stairs to a wooden-railed bar that looks onto the dance-floor, Jimmy in his gold dress shining like a torch. No, that's wrong: he's not shining, he's radiating. He's a fucking masterpiece.

The place is beginning to fill, and the DJ for the night, a youngish guy with hair like my old bike's saddlebag straps, is inviting couples to dance. "It's lurve time," he drawls. "It's time for lurve."

Pathetic.

I get drinks – a beer for Jimmy, a vodka and tonic for me – and we find a table and sit down. The table overlooks the dance-floor, so we're able to see the dancers.

They move in a misty blue light to Ben Webster's *Easy Come, Easy Go*, Webster's sax sighing and panting like a great animal brought down. I see a couple – a willowy blonde and an Asian guy with a Gino haircut – stop moving and kiss lingeringly. Another couple whisper to each other. To our right, a guy flicks out his tongue and his partner flicks out hers. I see hips slowly rotate and mouths brush necks. I see hands find bare flesh. The whole scene is loaded with sex.

A half-minute goes by, then Jimmy turns to me and in a gentle voice says, "Now, suppose you tell me why I'm dressed like this." He must have been biding his time, waiting for the right moment.

"Um," I go. I'm finding this entirely embarrassing. I give a quick smile and look away for a second.

"Well?" Jimmy says.

"You'll think I'm nuts," I say.

"Tell me," Jimmy says.

I take a deep breath and hit him with the heavy truth: "I wanna dance with you." My voice sounds thick. You've no idea how stupid I feel.

There's a small silence before Jimmy says, "We could've danced in the house. Why go to all this trouble?"

"It wouldn't be the same," I say. "Dancing in the house."

Jimmy looks at me with quiet eyes for a long time, then gets to his feet. "You lead," he says.

Going down the stairs, my legs shake and my heart bangs against my chest. I hear Webster panting into his sax, and pant with him. I'm on heat.

On the dance-floor I take hold of Jimmy, and we move into a slow shuffle. My legs are still shaking. They're shaking so much I can hardly move. Jimmy has to notice this, but doesn't say anything. A girl would. A girl'd say, "You're shaking."

As we dance I feel Jimmy's hair – or rather the wild Diana Ross wig – against my face, and get a faint whiff of Big Maria's coconut oil. I move closer to him so that our pelvises touch, and immediately get a hard-on – a real wilder. I apologise, and Jimmy laughs and says, "It's okay. Don't worry about it." I move my face closer to his. My heart is pounding and I'm having difficulty with my breathing. "Ah Christ, Jimmy," I say. I let my mouth brush his cheek.

* * *

We leave the Paramount at eleven-thirty and cab it home.

There are lights on in the house, and parked out front is Uncle George's beat-up Escort. Uncle George is the husband of the old lady's sister, Dolly, a highly-strung individual who's got just about everything wrong with her – or so she says. Uncle George and Aunt Dolly visit us once a month and we're always pleased to see them.

I pay off the cab, and, after it's pulled away, say to Jimmy, "Don't make a noise. If Aunt Dolly sees you dressed like that it'll be coronary time."

The idea of Aunt Dolly seeing Jimmy in drag tickles me, and entering the house I'm falling about laughing. Jimmy is falling about too, but for a different reason –

he's two parts cut. Bang! He collides with the coat stand and knocks it flying. I hear a scream (Aunt Dolly, no question), and a second later the living-room door opens and the old lady appears.

"Simon?" she says. Then, "Jimmy? *J-i-m-m-y*?" She puts a hand to her mouth and opens her eyes wide. "Jimmy, what on earth ...?" And then she smiles; she gives this big, bright-as-a-diamond smile. Not taking her eyes off Jimmy, she calls, "Dolly! Dolly, come here a minute."

"Terrific, eh?" I say, my eyes going from the old lady to Jimmy and back to the old lady again. I'm grinning.

The old lady cuts me a look. "Oh, Simon ..." she says.

Aunt Dolly appears, and the old lady says, "Dolly, look ... Look at Jimmy." Her voice has a kind of stunned wonder to it.

Aunt Dolly looks at Jimmy, screws up her face and says, "That's not Jimmy, is it?"

"Yes," the old lady says.

She pauses.

"Doesn't he look fabulous? Doesn't he look absolutely fabulous?"

"Oh, my God!" Aunt Dolly says, and for a minute I think she's gonna have a seizure or something. But she doesn't. She just stands there gawking.

I get Jimmy to his room, sit him in a chair, and go back downstairs for coffee. The old lady is in the kitchen fixing some. I stand in the doorway watching her. I notice how clean and neat she looks and how trim her figure is. I notice her perfect features.

She must have sensed my presence, because, without looking at me, she says, "What am I going to do with you?" Her voice is soft saying this.

"We knocked their socks off," I say. (That corny line again.)

The old lady looks at me, and beams. "I bet you did," she says. She pours coffee into two mugs and stirs in milk.

"Correction," I add. "*Jimmy* knocked their socks off."

The old lady beams again, but this time without looking at me. I expect her to ask questions, but she doesn't, and I wonder if she knows what Jimmy and me get up to. It's my guess she does.

She hands me the mugs. "Be careful, it's very hot," she says.

"G'night," I say.

The old lady plants one on my cheek. "'night," she says.

Going upstairs again I feel suddenly depressed.

Jimmy is as I left him. He looks tired but OK, sort of contented. "Here, drink this," I say, and hand him a coffee.

"How's Aunt Dolly?" he asks. "Still standing? I must've given her quite a fright."

"*She'll* survive," I say. I sit facing him, and we drink our coffee in silence. I can't understand why I feel so depressed: I've had a terrific time.

After a while the silence gets to me, and I say, "Let's have some music."

"Good idea," Jimmy says.

I set down my coffee and go to a tape deck that sits on a shelf behind Jimmy's chair. There's a tape ready to play, so I press a couple of buttons and pretty soon we're hearing Mahler's *Fifth*. It's Jimmy's all-time favourite piece of music. He never stops playing it.

"Take your coat off," I tell him. I feel really shitty.

Jimmy gets to his feet, and I help him off with the coat. I wonder what I'm gonna do with it now that it's served its purpose. Maybe the old lady would like it. I doubt she'd want the dress – too glitzy. The sandals'd be too big for her. I hang the coat on a hook in the door and return to my chair. As I sit down, Jimmy pulls out one of his sock tits and throws it at me. I catch it and crack a feeble joke: "They felt like the real thing." My voice sounds flat. Mahler's not doing much for the way I feel. A big mistake putting him on.

"How would *you* know?" Jimmy asks. He's smiling.

"I've felt *hundreds*," I reply. "All sizes."

Jimmy laughs and throws the second sock, but because I'm all torn up inside, I ignore it. Him laughing has torn me up. Why'd he have to laugh? I ask myself. Why couldn't he have reacted differently, shown me, with a look or something, that he was jealous – of my having been physically involved with someone other than himself, I mean. But Jimmy, I remind myself, is not a jealous person. I could tell him I was running with Miss California and that we planned to set up home together, and he'd be speechless with happiness for me. That kind of attitude in someone you're nuts about is hard to deal with.

Mahler and everything is turning me inside out; I'm ready to crack. "The music's a little loud," I say, and go to the tape deck – anything to keep Jimmy from seeing my eyes fill. I lower the volume and don't move from the spot. I tell myself to stop being a prick, but it doesn't work: I feel a tear track down my cheek. Hang on, I tell myself.

A half a minute goes by, and then Jimmy comes and stands beside me.

In a gentle, understanding voice, he says, "Come on, help me get this dress off."

I shake my head no. "Wash the make-up off first," I say. I want him out of the room.

"Okay," he says and squeezes my arm. I hear the door close behind him, and then I lose it: I sob my guts up.

When he gets back, the light is out and I'm in his bed, with the covers drawn up to my ears. I hear a soft rustling as he takes off the dress, and a few seconds later feel the bed move as he climbs in. The bed's a single, but even so our bodies don't touch. I'm on my side, facing the wall, and Jimmy's on his back. Mahler's *Fifth* is still playing, and listening to it I get a picture of black hills with dark clouds passing over them. I want to turn to Jimmy, but a little voice in my head tells me, "Wait".

After a while Jimmy says softly, "You all right, Si?"

"I'm okay," I say.

"You sure?"

Now I turn – quickly, moving my body into his and throwing an arm across his chest. "I'm okay," I repeat. I smell orange blossom and Gibbs SR.

"You're crazy," he says.

"I'm sorry," I say.

"For what?"

I pull him round to face me. "For having you dress up like that. It was a lousy thing to've done."

"Si," Jimmy says, "I enjoyed myself. I had a really good time." I feel his breath on my face and I drink it in.

I can't get enough of it.

"You mean that?"

"Yes."

"You really had a good time?"

"Yes."

I slide my hand under his arm and draw him closer. Except for our faces, the whole front of us is touching. I try to stop myself, but can't. "I love you, Jimmy," I whisper.

Jimmy places a hand on my shoulder. "I know," he whispers back. "I love you too."

I ought to feel terrific when he says this, but I don't, I only feel very good. Why I don't feel terrific is because I know that if a skinhead slime or some old bird with handles down to her knees was to say to Jimmy, "I love you, Jimmy", he'd say the same to them as he said to me.

CHAPTER 6

This is Harry Haynes, the shitcake I work for: About 40 years of age, of medium height, balding, has a big gut, is loudmouthed, wears a shirt and tie with a black-leather zipper jacket, drinks beer from the bottle, sports two heavy gold chains on each wrist, drives a white Jaguar X16 with personalised number plates, calls his wife 'Babe', thinks the sun shines out of Margaret Thatcher's arse, never misses a Spurs midweek home match, and hates blacks.

I've been working for the moron now for six months. I work for him to supplement the unemployment benefit I receive. Because I'm registered as unemployed, I receive £39 a week unemployment benefit, which, if you'll pardon my French, is not a fuck of a lot of money. Haynes pays me – wait for it – £25. For ten hours work. That's £2.50 an hour. Repeat: £2.50 an hour.

Think about it, please.

As you probably know, a person who works while claiming unemployment benefit should, by law, declare his earnings. Me, I don't declare my earnings. Which makes me a criminal. So go ahead somebody and report me. There are people who would, you know. Oh yes. If there's one thing I've learnt in my seventeen years it's this:

There's always someone ready to fuck you over.

Anyone who wants to quote me on that, can.

Of the £39 I get from the Unemployment Office, I

give thirty to the old lady. That may seem over-generous, but the old lady has some hefty bills to meet. For example, she's just had to fork out £200 for work done to the house. Repair work. A ceiling came down. It just came down. Prior to the ceiling coming down, a window fell out. Now we've got a blocked drain. *More* expense. With a bit of luck, we'll get through the week without the roof caving in.

Anyway, back to Haynes:

"You're late," he yells as I push through the showroom door. He's wearing a blue and white striped shirt, a navy tie, and navy trousers. His shoes are grey-patent loafers with little gold chains at their sides. Dire shoes. You wouldn't like his shoes.

"I had some business to take care of," I say, which is the truth – like, I returned the Diana Ross wig to Big Maria ("Simuhn! How'd your cross dressin' go? You have all the boys hittin' on you?" Seismic laughter).

"Don't give me that crap," Haynes says, and I see his eyes go to my crotch – something they're *always* doing. Haynes comes on macho, but in reality he's queer. He has to be, otherwise he wouldn't keep grabbing my arse (he keeps grabbing my arse) and eyeing my crotch. "You're late because you couldn't get off your fuckin' back. You wanna keep this job, fuckin' get in on time."

"S'the truth," I say, and make a big show of re-arranging my balls. Not that they need re-arranging; I do it to bring Haynes on – like sex him up. Remember after taking a bath I made a giant decision? Remember that? Well, what I decided was that I would take Jimmy to the Grand Canyon – the one place I figure he'd wanna see before he loses his sight. Haynes, if he's as hot for my arse as I think he is, will, without his realising it, help fund the trip.

"Bullshit," he says. Then, "Come on, get your fuckin' jacket off and clean that Datsun that came in on Friday."

"Certainly, Harold," I say (Haynes hates being called Harold), and, singing to myself *I'm not wild about Harry*, go to his office and pull open the door. And – phew! – get a whiff of the cheap cigars he smokes. That's something I forgot to mention: Haynes smokes cheap cigars. Something else I forgot to mention: he has BO. I get a whiff of this also.

The office is not what you'd call lavishly furnished; a formica-topped desk with angled aluminium legs, three chairs – one a recliner that Haynes uses – and a metal filing cabinet. No carpet. Lino. On the desk is a blotter and a stand-up calendar, and at the side of the filing cabinet, out of sight of ripped-off customers, a heavy metal bucket containing car polish, wash-rags and a packet of Daz.

I remove my jacket (a cream-coloured cotton number that I got from a charity shop (off-the-peg clothes are out of my financial orbit), place it on top of the filing cabinet, and, after I've admired the nipple that peeps (for Haynes's benefit) through a tear I've made in the had-it T-shirt I'm wearing, pick up the bucket and exit the office.

The Datsun stands in a fenced-off yard back of the showroom, where Haynes does tricky things to cars he buys second-hand; things which if you were a Trading Standards' Officer you'd be interested in knowing about. Behind and to the left of the Datsun is a brick-built washhouse-cum-craphouse, the hanging-off door of which has Private written on it in white paint. In here I three-quarters fill the bucket with water, and pour in Daz. I pour in *a lot* of Daz. You could do a week's laundry with the amount of Daz I pour in. Haynes, when he sees how low on powder the packet is, will, to use one of his quaint expressions, come his guts. That's another thing about Haynes: he's a tightarse. He hates putting his hand in his pocket – even for a packet of Daz. This'll give you an idea of just how tight Haynes is:

One day his wife – 'Babe' – came into the showroom with their six-year-old daughter Sharon, Babe loaded with shopping and looking pissed off. She was wearing six-inch highs, flesh-tight leopard-print pants, a knee-length bronze leather jacket with shoulders out here, a floppy orange shirt, and enough junk jewellery to weight a tarpaulin in a high wind – chains, rings, bracelets, big hoops in her ears … you name it. Stuck in her hair was a white paper flower. That's the way Babe dresses when she shops. I once saw her coming out of Tesco's. She was wearing an ankle-length fur coat, suede pirate boots, gold lamé hotpants, and a Nike baseball cap. You've never seen anything like it.

Anyway, Babe in the showroom:

"Harry, gimme some money," she said.

"What!" Haynes said.

"Gimme some money, I wanna get a taxi."

"What happened to the money you took out with you this morning?"

"I've spent it."

"Whaddaya mean, you've spent it?"

"I've spent it. I bought a few things."

"Three hundred quid! You spent three hundred quid!"

"Look," Babe said, "I don't wanna stand here arguing with you, I'm tired. Just give me some fucking money so I can get home."

"Mum ...." the kid said.

"Shut up," Babe said. "Shut, fucking, up."

"How can you spend three hundred quid just like that?" Haynes wanted to know.

"It was *my* money, I spent it."

Haynes shook his head. "I don't fuckin' believe it," he said. "Three hundred quid!"

"Are you gonna give me the fucking money?" Babe said.

"No I'm fuckin' *not*," Haynes said. "You wanna throw money away, get a bus home."

"*I haven't got any money,*" Babe said.

"Tough," Haynes said. "Fuckin' walk."

That's Haynes for you. His own wife ....

Okay, I get to work on the Datsun. I work hard. After twenty minutes there's sweat running down my face and back. Two-fifty an hour, I think. Slave labour. It's shitballs like Haynes who keep people in poverty. *Minimum wage! Three-forty an hour! Are you kidding! How'm I gonna pay for my holidays in Bermuda and the kid's riding lessons and the wife's nose job and the new set of golf clubs I've just gotta have? Minimum wage! Are you on this planet!*

People like Haynes: they suck the life out of you.

After a while I wipe sweat from my face and glance at the showroom. Haynes is looking at me through his office window. His eyes have a fixed look, and it takes him a few seconds to hook on to the fact that I've clocked him. Then he turns away. I smile to myself and wonder how long it'll be before he comes out. I give him ten minutes, fifteen at the most.

He's out in five.

I make a ball of the washrag I'm using and toss it into the bucket. Plop! Haynes comes up, and I nod at the Datsun. "You need a blowtorch to get that stuff off," I say.

Not looking at the Datsun, looking at my exposed nipple, Haynes says, "It's good underneath."

I play around with my balls again. "If you say so, Harry."

Haynes is silent; he's concentrating on my crotch.

"There's rust on one of the doors," I tell him. (There's not, but I tell him there is. Piss him off.)

Haynes stays silent.

"You with me, Harry?"

"What?" He looks into my face, and I lay a dynamite smile on him (phoney, of course). "Rust," I say. "On one of the doors." I'm still smiling.

Haynes sticks his hands in his pockets and jingles coins. It's what he does when he's on edge. "Do the best you can," he says and walks off.

A half hour later he's back, saying, "You're getting there, Simon." *Simon*. He's coming on to me.

"You think so?" I say. I'm stretched across the Datsun's bonnet, cleaning the windscreen. Haynes is standing behind me. He's smoking one of his cheapo cigars; I can smell it.

"It's looking good, son," he says, and pats my arse. In a lower voice, he says, "You're doing a good job,

Simon – a first class job." He strokes it now – my arse.

Normally when he touches my arse I tell him to fuck off, but I want Jimmy to see the Grand Canyon, so I let him have fun. Not for too long. Long enough for his groin area to come alive. Then I'm in there with this: "How much?"

"How much for what?" His voice is dreamy now, as if his mind is somewhere else, which, of course, it is.

"My arse."

"What?"

"My arse."

"Your arse …?"

I straighten up and turn and face him. My hair is over my forehead and sweat is running down my face and neck. I must look terrific. Sultry. "It's what you want, isn't it?"

Haynes fixes me with a stare. He's wondering if I'm putting him on.

When he sees that I'm not, he says: "A tenner."

I look at him like he's a bucket of shit.

"A score," he says.

I shake my head, no.

"How much then?"

"Fifty."

Haynes's eyes pop. "Fifty!"

"Take it or leave it," I say. I'm full of determination.

There's a long silence while Haynes considers my nipple, from which, with my middle finger – a nice touch this – I carefully brush imaginary dirt.

Finally Haynes, breathing heavy, says, "Okay – where?"

"Your office."

"Let me lock up first."

He locks up in nothing flat.

In his office, I say, "Don't forget, Harry, fifty."

Haynes doesn't reply; he closes the door.

"Fifty, Harry."

Haynes clears his throat (not a pleasant sound). "All right, don't go on about it."

"Just so's you won't forget."

"I won't forget." He nods at my jeans (I'm wearing faded blue jeans). "Come on then," he says. He means get them off. He's hurting to see what they're hiding. There's sweat on his upper lip.

I unfasten my jeans and let them drop to the floor. I do this, thinking, 'What I'm doing I'm doing for Jimmy. It's not as if I'm doing it for kicks.' And then I think, 'So what if I was?'

Haynes, when he sees my dick, can't keep his eyes off it. He's looking at it like it's a ticket to the World Cup. In an admiring voice, he says, "You've got a big 'un", and hearing him say this I get a good feeling inside. Nobody's ever said that to me before. "Satisfaction guaranteed," I say.

Haynes, still breathing heavy, unhooks and lowers his trousers, lowers his Y-fronts (Y-fronts!)

His dick is a real gross-out: lily white, with a pink, wet-looking head. Small. Does 'Babe' go down on him? I wonder. I turn around, place my hands on the desk and spread my legs. To take my mind off what's about to happen, I try to picture something pleasant. I picture Jimmy and me boarding a plane for America.

It's over very quickly. Eight seconds max. I do a rapid calculation: Six-pounds-twenty-five a second. Not bad. That's more than the chairman of British Gas gets. I hoist and buckle my jeans, thinking, 'Let's hope he enjoyed it, let's hope he'll want it on a *regular* basis – like twice a week.' I swing round to face him.

His mouth is open and his eyes are bulging. He looks a lot like a beached fish.

I give him time to fix his clothes, then hold out my hand. "Fifty," I say.

Haynes doesn't move, doesn't say anything; he just looks at me. I can read his mind. He's thinking: Fifty – that's a lot of dough.

"Fifty," I repeat. My voice has a threatening note.

Haynes reaches into his back pocket and brings out a wad.

'Pay time, Sixsmith,' I tell myself. 'You've got a nice piece of change coming here.'

Haynes peels off a ten and points it at me.

I stare at it. This is not a happy moment.

"What's that?" I say.

"Ten," Haynes says.

I fight back anger and say, "This is you being a wag, right, Harry?"

"Ten," he says.

A big knot forms in my stomach. "Fuck off," I say. "Fifty. We had a deal."

"Fuck the deal," Haynes says. "Ten, that's all you're getting. Take it or leave it."

I want to throttle the scumbag, beat piss out of him. Instead I appeal to him: "Come on, Harry, " I use one of his cute expressions, "play the white man."

"Ten," Haynes says.

I look at him without speaking. I feel humiliated,

wiped out. I grab the ten and stuff it in my pocket. My voice shakes a little, saying, "You know something, Harry, you're a germ – a full-time fucking germ."

Haynes grins and shrugs.

I snatch my jacket off the filing cabinet, walk to the door and, before leaving, crook my little finger and wave it at him. Weeny, weeny.

Haynes doesn't like that: his face goes red. "Fuck off, you cunt," he says.

I give him a tight smile. All at once I'm fired up, I'm all fire-power. "Okay, Harry," I say.

I go outside to the Datsun, pick up the bucket I've been working with, and – try to picture me doing this, please – and swing it at the Datsun's windscreen. Then I return to the showroom and swing the bucket again – this time at Haynes's showpiece – a dark blue Merc he wants sixteen grand for. I swing the bucket maybe half a dozen times. *Then* I fuck off.

* * *

Because of my exertions, I'm thirsty. Also, I need to sit down and think, so I head for Toni's Tea Room.

The sun is slamming down and Albion Street is crowded with shoppers and unemployed teenagers and groups of pushing and pulling schoolkids out on their lunch break. Everywhere I look I see dark-skinned women in saris, and old dark-skinned guys in long white gowns and little white caps: sweet, beautiful people with soft, gentle mouths and eyes there seems no bottom to. From some of the shops comes the sound of Indian music and from others warm gusts of spicy food being cooked. I could be on a street in Bombay or Calcutta.

I get to Toni's just in time to hear a conversation he's having with a customer, a cruddy-looking guy in a greasy cap and suit and a shirt with no collar. The conversation goes something like this:

Toni: You see in the paper this mornin' how much they askin' for a cup a British Rail tea?

Customer: I ain't seen a paper today.

Toni: Eighdy fuckin' pence.

Customer: Eighty pence!

Toni: Eighdy fuckin' pence. (A pause.) For a cheese sanwidge they wan' two powns twenny – two powns fuckin' twenny for a cheese sanwidge. An' they reckon they losin' money. How can they be losin' money they chargin' eighdy pence for a cup a tea an' two powns twenny for a cheese sanwidge? It don' make fuckin' sense.

Customer: Give us one of your sausage rolls, Toni.

Toni: Eighdy fuckin' pence for a cup a tea. I was to charge tha' amown', I have no fuckin' customers.

I pay fifty pence for a cup of dog piss and take it to a table that doesn't look like a bad accident. I should be feeling shitty, but I'm not, I'm feeling pretty good. Why I'm feeling pretty good is because I know that the damage I inflicted on Haynes's Merc and Datsun will cost him at least, at *least*, seven hundred to put right – and that pleases me: Mr Tightarse having to shell out seven hundred pounds. A beautiful thought. Haynes, of course, will be spitting blood, thinking Revenge; but what's he gonna do, have me beaten up, have one of the gorillas he knocks around with beat me up? Somehow I

56

doubt he'll do that. He's stupid, but he's not *that* stupid. He has me beaten up, he knows I'll shoot my mouth off – about what happened in his office today; he knows me well enough to know I'd do that. Haynes the Arsehole Bandit. He'd rather lose his last arm than have a name like that hung on him.

From Haynes my thoughts go to money ... and time. Eight months. That's all I've got. Eight months to raise a thousand pounds (the cost, I figure, of Jimmy's and my trip to Arizona). No, that's wrong. I don't even have eight months. I try to remember when it was the eye specialist broke the news to the old lady. Five weeks ago. A Monday. Jesus, what a day that was. I can see the old lady now. Tears streaming down her face. I had to force the words out of her. *Retinitis Pigmentosa. Incurable. Eight months of sight.* I flipped. Like I said, I howled like a dog, banged my head against walls. The old lady called a doctor. I was sedated for two days.

That, as I say, was five weeks ago. Which means I've got – what? Twenty-seven weeks. Twenty-seven weeks to find a thousand pounds.

A piece of cake.

If I had a job.

I take a mouthful of dog piss, swallow, and when I've finished grimacing, see Wally. He's coming through the door, his face and the jeans and T he's wearing spotted and streaked with yellow. He looks sort of dazed. It's how he always looks.

I wait till he's seated opposite me with a cup of pig piss in front of him, then nod at his T. "What's that shit on you?" I ask.

Wally fills his mouth with pig piss, swallows, and

says, "Clay. I've got a job on a building site and we're, like, draining the soil – getting it ready for, like, you know, the foundations."

"When'd you start?"

"What?"

"The job, stupid."

Wally smiles. He's happy, I can tell. Wally's been looking for a job since leaving school (who hasn't?), so now he's found one he's happy.

"Today," he says.

"Where'd you get to on Saturday?"

"Watched the match – England, Spain."

"Where was Stan?" I ask. Then, quickly, "Don't tell me – watching the match."

Wally takes another swallow of pig piss (the way he's knocking it back you'd think it was liquid paradise). "Why aren't you at the showroom?" he asks.

"I quit."

"Why'd you do that?"

I explain, and Wally's eyes light up and a silly, kid's grin comes on his face. Whenever Wally is shocked by something, his eyes light up and a silly, kid's grin comes on his face. Wally is like a kid. He thinks I'm zero cool. I think he sees me as some kind of hero or something. Ridiculous, I know.

Still grinning, he says, "You let Haynes screw you?"

"Yeah," I say. I smile.

"Fuck off," Wally says.

"Truth," I say.

"Fuck off," Wally says again, and then, in a sort of whiney, kid's voice, "Come on, Si, why'd you quit?"

There's no way he's gonna believe me, so I say, "I

finally had it with Haynes", and leave it at that. After a pause I ask, "How's Stan?"

"OK," Wally replies.

"He still thinking of joining the army?"

"Yeah," says Wally, and in the same breath, "He wants to get a mountain bike. I'm thinking about getting one, too."

"Very beautiful," I say.

We return to the subject of Wally's job and he tells me his pay is four-forty an hour, time-and-a-half Saturdays. He starts work at eight and finishes at five. He gets a thirty-minute lunch break, which he's on now.

"How you finding it?" I ask. "The job?"

"OK," Wally says. Wally'd find Devil's Island OK. He picks a piece of clay from his chin and says, "Why? You interested?"

I shrug. It's not the career opportunity I'm looking for, but beggars, as they say, can't be choosers.

"Have a word with the foreman," Wally suggests.

* * *

The foreman is about six-foot-three and has a lavender nose, watery eyes, and hair you could pick locks with. He's wearing a not-bad grey jacket, a collar and tie, and navy trousers tucked into heavy-duty Wellingtons. "I'm looking for work," I tell him. "Anything going?" My voice is cheery.

The foreman looks down lavender at me for a few seconds, then looks off. Still looking off, he says, "Be here tomorrow. Eight o'clock."

Easy as that.

Leaving the site, I see Wally wrestling with a tube the size of a tree, and there's yellow goop hitting him from all directions. "Farewell, young prince," I call, but he doesn't hear me. A guy pads past me looking like he's just escaped from a bag of cement.

* * *

From the site I go directly to a travel agent's (there's this travel agent's on Albion Street), a picture of the Grand Canyon in my head.

As soon as I'm through the door a fem in a red blazer comes up and says, "Good afternoon. May I be of help?" She's slim and dark and pixie-looking. Not bad. She's not exactly two-packs-of-three-please, but she's not bad.

"I want to price a return trip to the Grand Canyon in Arizona," I say. The place is stifling, and there's a strong nail-polishy smell in the air.

"Certainly," the fem says. "Won't you take a seat?"

She leads me to a desk that has a computer terminal on it (what else is new?) and I sit in a steel-framed chair with padded arm-rests. The fem sits across from me in an upholstered swivel.

"We don't have many enquiries for the Grand Canyon," the fem says, smiling.

"I'm poetically attracted to it," I hear myself say, and the fem gives me a funny look.

"When were you thinking of going?" she asks.

"October time," I tell her.

"I'll see what we have," the fem says. She moves her chair closer to the desk and starts pressing keys on the terminal's keyboard. I sit back in my chair and look around me. Glossy brochures everywhere, and on the walls in fiery space-age colours holiday posters, one showing a guy having a big time surfing. (Surfing is something I wouldn't mind trying. I think I'd be pretty good at it.) Just to hear my voice, I say: "What's that smell? Nail polish?"

"Nail polish?" the fem says. She's still pressing keys.

"The smell in here. Or it could be peardrops. Somebody been eating peardrops?"

The fem doesn't answer. Instead she tells me of a holiday package: Six nights, three-star hotel: £490.

I'm not interested. One night, yes. Six, no. Six'd be too many. What I want, I've decided, is to book into a hotel – say late evening – and at sunrise the next day be standing with Jimmy on top of the Grand Canyon. Just the two of us. Nobody else in sight. Spend an hour up there, then leave and get the plane home. No hanging around the place for a week, seeing the Canyon over and over. It's my belief that if you see something over and over, you become – what's the word? – indifferent – you become indifferent to it. Imagine becoming indifferent to something as incredible, as *awesome*, as the Grand Canyon. It wouldn't be right. Ideally – and this has just occurred to me – a helicopter would drop us – Jimmy and me – on the ridge, and an hour later return and take us to the airport. That way there'd be no distractions, nothing to take our minds off what we'd just seen. We'd have our overnight bags with us and we'd board the plane for England. We'd arrive in England with the Canyon fresh in our heads.

"I don't wanna week's stay," I say, "I wanna fly back the day after arrival."

The fem takes this in her stride. "I see," she says. She presses a few more keys, checks out the screen above the keyboard, and says, "There's an Economy Class flight at £694."

"That's record money," I say. I do some arithmetic. Two tickets: £1,388. "How come I'd be paying more for a one-night stay than I would for a week's stay?"

"Well," the fem says, and then proceeds to give me a long explanation, which I won't repeat on account it'd bore you rigid.

I put another question: "What're the chances of hiring a helicopter when I get there?"

The fem looks at me like I've just told her I'm Marco the Magnificent.

"I'm not kidding," I say.

"I'm afraid I don't have that information available," the fem says. "It's something I'd have to look into. You'd maybe able to hire one at the airport."

I get the fem to write down the figures she's given me, and leave, but not before I've told her, "Thanks for your help," and flipped her a nice smile.

Two minutes later insanity seizes hold of me and I return to the agency and ask the price of a First Class ticket.

Straight off the bat, the fem says, "Two thousand four hundred pounds."

"Is that so?" I say.

That's all I say.

CHAPTER 7

I'm wearing washed out chinos, a had-it V-neck over a had-it shirt, and a pair of banged-up Doc Martens – the crummiest threads I could find. Even so, compared with the guy coming towards me I look Savile Row. This guy should be in a field scaring crows.

I'll be working, the foreman has told me, with Henry. Who Henry is and where I'll find him, the foreman didn't say. ("Henry?" I said. "Henry," the foreman said. "And get yourself a hard-hat. Safety regulations." That was it.)

"Are you Henry?" I ask the scarecrow guy.

Without looking at me and without slackening his pace he shakes his head no.

"Where can I find him?"

Nothing.

That's a thing I love – being ignored by the person I'm speaking to. I really love that.

"Hi," a voice behind me says.

It's Wally. His hair is sticking out in all directions and his face is swollen with sleep. Stuck to a corner of his mouth is a piece of what looks like cornflake.

"Ah – Wally!" I say. "Just the man. Where can I find Henry? And I need a hard-hat."

Wally digs grunge from an eye, and when he's given it some scrutiny and wiped it off on his jeans (he's not Mr Sophisticated, Wally), takes me to a long, mud-stained trailer that stands on hard-core in a corner of the site.

Inside, seated on a wooden bench, pulling on gumboots, are six crappily-dressed guys with unshaved faces and sullen expressions.

Jesus, the stink! Feet, farts and Old Holborn. No talk, just boots being pulled on. It's like something out of a chain-gang movie.

Wally takes a yellow hard-hat off a peg in the wall, hands it to me, and then joins the *Blue Peter* team on the bench. He sorts himself out a pair of boots from a pile on the floor and tries one on. It's too big, so he scoops up a few sheets of newspaper that're lying around, makes a ball of them and stuffs it into the toe. Seated amongst all these guys with their whiskery chins he looks about twelve. I find it a pretty heartbreaking sight.

To nobody in particular, I say, "There a Henry here?" and a wiry little guy with a thin, lined face looks up and says, "I'll be wid yer in a minute." I've got my hard-hat and I've found Henry. All I need now is fresh air: the stink in the trailer is getting to me. If I don't get out of here quick, I'm gonna have a little bout of vomiting. "I'll be outside," I tell Henry. To Wally, I say, "Hook up with you later."

Outside I look around me, and a small voice in my head says, "Okay, this is it. Here's where you'll be working for the next Christ-knows-how-long. How d'you like it? Happy with what you see – all that dust and nothingness?" And then Henry is saying, "This way", and's off at a gallop across piles of scaffolding and reinforcing materials and other bone-breaking stuff I can't put a name to. He's like a mountain goat.

Eventually we come to a heap of rubble, and Henry

leads me down a flight of incredibly steep concrete steps to the left of it. Now I'm in semi-darkness and instead of tripping over scaffolding I'm tripping over masonry. There's the smell of damp and rot in the air and I figure we're in some kind of basement or cellar. Wherever we are, Henry knows it like the back of his hand, because in no time at all he's handing me a shovel. "As I get the wall down, move the bricks to the wall behind you," he says.

I glance behind me and make out a wall. "I think I can manage that, Henry," I say.

Henry moves off, and a second or two later an engine starts up – and a few seconds after that there's the sound of a drill hitting brick. The noise! I think my eardrums are gonna burst.

It doesn't get better. As Henry murders the wall, so all this grit flies from it; I can feel it hitting my face. Pretty soon I'm chewing on it. 'This is not happening,' I tell myself. 'I'm not here. In a minute I'll wake up.' I think of pinching myself.

Instead, I make with the shovel.

Do I make with the shovel! Henry's going through the wall like it's nothing. Bricks are dropping like rain. For every six I move, twenty fill their place. They're piling up. They're knee high. The way Henry is cutting out those bricks you'd think they were made of gold and at the end of the day we're gonna crate them up and take them home.

I heave bricks for about two-and-a-half hours and then heave a sigh of relief. Why I heave a sigh of relief is because Henry has lighted a cigarette – it's time for a breather. I can tell you, I need one: my back is breaking and my arms feel as if I've been swinging through trees; my throat is so dust-filled I can hardly swallow. When I sit on a pile of bricks – what else? – I think I'm never gonna get up again. "You been doing this work long, Henry?" I croak. All I can see of him is his outline and the glow of his cigarette when he draws on it.

"Long enough," Henry says. "Since I left school."

"How d'you like it?"

"It's a job," Henry says. "It pays the rent."

"You got a family, Henry?"

"Oh, yes – wife and tree kids." His voice has a beautiful musicalness to it.

"How old're the kids?"

"The youngest's two, then I've a girl twelve and a boy fourteen."

"Will you *always* do this work, d'you think?"

"I expect so," says Henry. "It's all I know, you see."

I judge Henry to be in his mid thirties and I get a picture of him at sixty still cutting out bricks. That's if he makes it to sixty. "Don't they give out masks here?" I ask. "Like, to keep the dust out of your lungs?"

"Oh, yes," Henry says, "there's a mask if you want one; but I can't work wid the bloody tings. Ask the gov'nor, he'll give you a mask."

Henry finishes his cigarette and we resume work. We work like maniacs until a siren sounds for lunch.

Up in the daylight I run a hand over my face and feel a thick coating of dust. "Not the cleanest of jobs, Henry," I say.

"Dis the first time you've done this work?" Henry asks.

"Yes," I answer.

"The first day's always the worst," Henry says.

"I don't think I'll sleep better tonight for knowing that, Henry," I reply.

I ask Henry where he's taking his break, and he says, "The trailer – I'll have a sandwich in the trailer."

The trailer! Jesus!

I go to where Wally's working and find him waiting for me. "Let's get a drink," I say. "I've got a thirst like a sump."

In Toni's I order a can of Fanta. Wally gets involved with pig piss.

When we're seated, I say, "I tell you, man, I don't know if I can handle this." I remove my hard-hat and place it on the floor. My scalp itches, and when I scratch it I get grit under my nails. The stuff's taken me over.

"What, the job?" Wally asks.

I give him a long look. "Oh, you're sharp, Walter," I say. Then, "Yeah, the job."

Wally grins. "You'll get used to it," he says.

"I wouldn't bet on it," I say. Toni passes, saying, "I hope you stamp your feet before you come in. I got *enough* fuckin' cleanin' to do."

I ignore this and say to Wally, "You think building work is something you'll stick with?"

Wally shrugs, and I see him ten years from now eating a sandwich in a stinking trailer, maybe sitting alongside Henry.

"Maybe Stan's got the right idea," he says. "Join the army."

"Yeah," I say, "and dodge bullets in Afghanistan or somewhere."

I'm quiet after that.

We both are.

Back at the site I find Henry hard at work – and feel guilty. That's the trouble with people who don't take their full break: they make those of us who do feel guilty. Henry must want this job very badly, I decide. I take hold of my shovel, load it with bricks, and let fly.

My swing must've been wrong, because the bricks, instead of sailing over my shoulder like they're supposed to, zip off to the left and nearly take out the person who's suddenly appeared at the bottom of the steps.

"Sorry," I say, and get a reply that doesn't sound like tut, tut. It's the foreman and he wants Henry *up top*. "*Now*, Henry," he says

Henry doesn't say a word. He very carefully lays down his drill (the way he lays down that drill you'd think it was a priceless work of art, the Venus de Milo or something) and after he's cleared his throat and spat a ton of dust, gets a cigarette going. He takes a pull on it, then starts towards the steps.

"Seeyah, Henry," I say. I feel really sorry for him. People like Henry: they don't stand a chance.

"Seeyuz," Henry says, and climbs the steps. I grip my shovel and slide it under bricks.

I'm still sliding it under bricks when the siren sounds four hours later (you've no idea how good that siren sounds. Music made in heaven).

I collect my day's pay from the site office, hang my hard-hat in the trailer, and take off for a pub – my tongue leading the way.

The nearest pub is on Albion Street, but when I get to

it what do I find? (Wait till you hear this, beautiful and touching this.) I find a notice taped to the door, saying, "Sorry, no site workers."

I go home feeling like I'm a leper or something.

Work? Who needs it?

CHAPTER 8

"I've quit," I say.

I'm in the kitchen talking to the old lady, who's just asked me why I'm not at work.

"All that dust and noise ... I just couldn't take it any more."

The old lady looks up from the pillowcase she's ironing and fixes me with a stare. "Good," she says eventually. She softens her eyes. "It wasn't *you*, Simon."

I run a hand over a just-ironed bed-sheet that rests on the table next to a blue plastic laundry basket. "It wasn't – isn't – *any*one," I say.

The old lady goes back to the pillowcase. "So what will you do now?"

I shuffle my feet. "I don't know."

Not looking at me, the old lady says, "*Something* will come along." She finishes ironing the pillow-case and places it on top of the bed-sheet. She reaches across to the laundry basket, dips a hand into it, and pulls out a silk square. She gives me an up from under look. "*You'll* see," she adds.

I don't say anything. My eyes are on the silk square and I'm smiling to myself. Why I'm smiling to myself is because the silk square has reminded me of Sarah Jane's and my talk with Mrs Hollis.

CHAPTER 9

So here I am at Sarah Jane's. It's eight-thirty in the morning and I'm standing with my back to the counter while Mrs Hollis and her two assistants look me over, Mrs Hollis with her brow furrowed: she's trying to come to a decision on what I should wear for my first appearance – my debut, if you like – as a model. Being big on colour, I've suggested – for starters – a canary-yellow number patterned with, like, baked beans, but Mrs Hollis isn't keen. She'd rather I wore something "less vibrant". Her assistants, Janice and Helen, would like to see me in red leather ("Red leather!" Mrs Hollis said. "He'll look like a tart"). Janice is the fem who served me with Jimmy's coat and dress and is, as I may've said, slim, blonde, and aged about 25. Very tasty. Helen is a lot older – around 48 – and has dark fluffy hair, a two-handsful arse, and a round, pouchy face. Mrs Hollis is about 60 and is heavy furniture. Big hips, pillowy tits, and legs like bollards. Her hair is red and scraped back, and she has watery eyes; her nose is bottle-shaped. Nobody'll be coming through *her* window with a box of Milk Tray.

"How about the blue organdie?" Helen suggests.

"Too Barbara Cartland," Janice says.

Helen gets the blue organdie, anyway, and holds it against me. "Yes," she says, "I see what you mean."

"I don't want him in anything fussy," Mrs Hollis puts in. "He hasn't the face for it. Let's have a look at the black cocktail."

Out comes the "black cocktail" and there's a long silence while they make up their minds.

"I must say, I *do* like it," Mrs Hollis says finally. She's scratching her chin, which is a bit hairy.

"Very chic," Janice says, and lays a big smile on me. I get the feeling Janice is hot for me. I get the feeling Janice is a very hot ticket. Definitely back row action.

"It needs something at the waist," Helen says. "A twist of chiffon."

Janice makes a face at this, so Helen says, "I *am* entitled to an opinion, Janice."

Mrs Hollis says, "Look, why don't we start him off in the fuchsia overshirt and pleated trousers, then at four, four-thirty we'll put him in the black cocktail. In between times: the cerise two-piece with the rounded lapels, and," she closes her eyes for a few seconds, "and the hounds-tooth bolero. Perhaps the charcoal executive as well." She looks at Helen, then at Janice. "Yes?"

Janice opens her mouth to say something, but before she can get a word out Mrs Hollis says, "Yes – we'll do that." She takes a deep happy breath and when she's let it out and looked at us like we're idiots and she's Albert Einstein, says, "Now, I simply *must* get that card in the window." She's stoked up, no question.

The card she simply *has* to get in the window has big letters printed on it in black felt tip that say:

HERE TODAY – SIMON!

That's all – HERE TODAY – SIMON!

Smart. Simon could be *any*one. Simon a pop singer? Simon a movie star? Simon a Hollywood hairdresser? People are gonna wanna find out.

The card was Helen's idea. "It'll act as a magnet,"

she said. That's what she said – it'll act as a magnet. "You think so?" I said, and flipped her a wink. Which made her blush. I like Helen a lot.

While Mrs Hollis is fucking about in the window, Janice busies herself making a space in the middle of the floor. It's there, it's been decided, that I'll get the treatment. Like, it's there my face'll be made up.

I give Janice a hand, and, as I do, I see her keep cutting looks at me, which tells me I'm reacting on her emotional system. After a while, she says, "Won't you feel embarrassed wearing a dress?"

I handle this cool. "Embarrassed?" I say. "Why should I feel embarrassed?"

Janice reddens a little and says, "I don't know. It's just that – "

"I'm not queer, if that's what you're thinking."

"Oh no, I didn't mean to – "

"I've had more girls than Mrs Hollis's had hot flushes."

Janice loves that: she giggles. I get the impression that Mrs Hollis is not one of Janice's favourite people. Whenever Mrs Hollis says something, Janice rolls her eyes.

"I'm doing this strictly for money," I add.

"Oh – right," Janice says.

I notice she's wearing a wedding ring, but nevertheless ask, "You married?"

Janice moves a rail of leather accessories to one side and in a kind of guilty voice, says, "Yes."

"What's he do, your husband?"

"He's in the building trade."

For a second I see a big pile of bricks and hear the sound of Henry's drill. "What's he work at?"

"I don't know, exactly," Janice says.

This rocks me. I mean, how can a wife not know how her old man makes his money? Is Janice Mrs Average? I wonder. "Howd's he look when he gets home?" I ask.

"All right," Janice says.

In that case, I tell myself, he's definitely not shovelling bricks in a filthy cellar with a drill going in his ear.

"Right," Mrs Hollis says. She's back from the window and rubbing her hands together like she's a mad surgeon waiting for the next patient to be wheeled in. "Table and chair please, Janice."

Janice rolls her eyes, then gets a small tubular-framed table and chair from somewhere and sets them down in the space we've made.

"Now, Simon ..." Mrs Hollis says, and grips my arm (her grip would strangle an elephant). "If you will sit here ..."

I sit in the tubular-framed chair.

"Good," Mrs Holllis says, and gives me a big smile. "I'll just get my make-up case and we can get started."

She goes off, skips off, practically, and Janice says, "Nervous?"

"Nervous?" I say. "You kidding?" (Me being cool again.) I lay a wink on her.

Janice laughs. "You're mad," she says, which tells me she wants me badly.

Mrs Hollis returns with a blue leatherette case the size of a cake tin and places it on the table. Her eyes are glazed and she's grinning like she knows something nobody else does. It wouldn't surprise me if she was to

74

start whistling a tune – *Happy Days Are Here Again*.

She unzips the case and takes out a bottle with a mushroom-shaped top. She unscrews the top, hands it to Janice (who rolls her eyes), and very carefully upends the bottle onto her fingers. "Tilt your head back," she says.

I tilt my head back.

Her fingers feel good. Very soothing. "What's that you're putting on me?" I ask.

"Foundation cream," Mrs Hollis says.

Foundation makes me think of foundations, and I picture Wally on the building site, goop hitting him from all directions. My heart goes out to him.

"You're going to look wonderful," Mrs Hollis says.

"What, better than I do now?"

Mrs Hollis gives me a schoolteacher look. "Don't be conceited," she says.

I fix my eyes on one of Mrs Hollis's tits and watch it vibrate as she applies the cream.

The cream, or rather the applying of it, reminds me of my fourth meeting with Mrs Fisher – my fourth Friday meeting, that is. On that occasion Mrs Fisher covered our bodies with Mr Fisher's shaving foam. Gillette. There's not one Friday meeting with Mrs Fisher I don't remember.

"You've got a great figure, Mrs Hollis," I say. "A great set."

"Don't be naughty," Mrs Hollis says, and at this point the door opens and the first customer comes in.

She's tall-ish, thirty-ish, and has a high-rise hairdo. Nice legs. She wanders around the Teens 'n' Twenties section for a while (*who'd's she think she's kidding?*), then comes and stands next to Mrs Hollis, who shoots her a look.

"This is Simon," Mrs Hollis says. "Simon will be modelling for us today."

"Simon?" the woman says.

"Hi," I say.

The woman gives me a washy smile and touches her hair. She touches it like it might bite or sting her to death or something. Pretty soon a woman with a kid joins her. The kid is wearing a Mary Poppins dress and looks about forty.

The kid glares at me for a few seconds, then, in a smacked-arse voice, says, "It's a *man*", and tugs at her old lady's sleeve to leave.

"Stop it," her old lady tells her. "Wait!" And the thought crosses my mind: she must *hate* waking up to that kid's face every morning.

I stick my tongue out at the kid, and the kid does the same to me.

* * *

Mrs Hollis's fingers don't stop – a dab of something here, a smear of something somewhere else. She's inspired, engrossed, you can tell she is. She's so engrossed that I doubt she realises the shop is filling. People are pressing in on all sides. They're straining their necks to get a look at me. HERE TODAY – SIMON! I'm the big picture everyone wants to see – the big picture with cramp in its leg: I shift in my chair.

"Keep still," Mrs Hollis says (she's doing something to my eyes).

"I've got cramp," I say. I sound about ten.

"Voila!" Mrs Hollis says suddenly and takes a step back. It's Van Gogh just painted his sunflowers.

She turns and addresses the punters: "Ladies and gentlemen (there's a beard or two on the premises), Simon will now leave us for a few minutes," she motions at me to stand, "to get changed; so while we wait for him to return why don't you take the opportunity to look round the floor and see if there's anything that catches your eye? You'll find our garments and accessories both stylish and reasonably-priced. Thank you." She summons Janice, and I hear her tell her, "Help Simon get dressed." In a lower voice, she says, "Take your time. Give them a chance to inspect the goods."

No flies on Mrs Hollis.

Janice takes hold of my arm and we go to a room at the back of the shop, but not before we've stopped at a mirror and I've told my reflection, "Don't go away, Honeylips, I'll be right back."

In the room, laid out on a straight-backed chair, is the first of the outfits I'll be wearing: a black singlet, a purplish-red top, black silky trousers, and a shoulder-length blonde wig. No shoes.

"What about shoes?" I ask.

"Mrs Hollis thinks you'll look better *without* shoes," Janice says. "Sexier."

"Sexier?"

"Haven't you noticed ...? Women in stockinged feet look sexy."

"I can't say that I have," I say.

"Men!" Janice says.

I change the conversation: "Tell me about your old man – your husband."

"What d'you want to know?"

"What's he like?"

"Tall," Janice says, "brown eyes, not bad-looking. A bit boring."

"Why's he boring?"

"All he talks about is football."

"I've got a couple of pals he should meet," I say. Then, "You go out much?"

"Not much," says Janice. "We're saving up to get our own place."

"What d'you do when you do – go out?"

"Have a drink, a meal."

"What d'you drink?"

"Campari and soda mostly. White wine."

"What's your old man drink?" (Not what you'd call a riveting conversation.)

"Beer."

"You ever been drunk, like really slaughtered?"

"Once."

"Only once?"

"We were on holiday in Greece and I was drinking this stuff called Ouzo. I passed out in the bar. Steve had to call a taxi to take me back to the hotel."

"That your old man's name – Steve?"

"Yes."

"Where'd you meet him?"

"In a pub."

"You like being married?"

"It's all right."

"You've got terrific eyes, Janice. Steve ever tell you

you've got terrific eyes?"

"Come on," Janice says, "let's get you changed."

I take hold of the cotton sweatshirt I'm wearing and pull it off. "I bet Steve never tells you you've got terrific eyes."

Janice doesn't answer. She's looking at my smooth-as-silk chest. "You've got terrific hair, too." I say. As a matter of fact her hair's pretty crummy – brittle-looking – but she *has* got terrific eyes. Very blue and widely spaced.

I unbuckle my jeans and wait for Janice's look of astonishment when she sees I'm not wearing shorts. I'm a little aroused, so what she'll see'll be worth seeing.

"Simon! Oh, my God!" Janice covers her eyes and turns away.

"Sorry," I say, "but shorts are not part of my wardrobe."

"Well, you should have told me," Janice says.

"What's the problem? It's only flesh."

"Yes," Janice says, "flesh I'd rather not see, thank you very much."

I slip off my loafers and step out of my jeans.

Janice faces me again and for a fraction of a second her eyes go to my dick.

"I'm sorry," I say, "it's just that I never wear shorts."

"It's all right," Janice says. "Next time I'll know what to expect." She holds out her hand. "Hand me the singlet."

I hand her the singlet, and she slips it over my head, and I put my arms through the holes.

"Now the top."

I hand her the top, and she holds it open, and I turn

and put my arms into the sleeves, and for a moment the feeling comes over me that I'm a kid again and that it's not Janice who's dressing me, it's the old lady. I'm standing on a chair and she's talking to me as she fixes my shirt, telling me what a good time we're gonna have when we get to wherever it is we're going. We were always going places. Me, Jimmy, and the old lady.

Janice starts to button the top, and on impulse I put my hands on her waist and draw her to me (I have to admit: self-control is not one of my strong points).

Janice doesn't resist. She acts like it's not happening.

"Ah, Janice," I whisper.

"No," she whispers back.

I kiss her neck.

"No," she says again. Still she doesn't resist.

I kiss the corner of her mouth.

"Please ... " she says.

I raise the skirt of the atomic-yellow two-piece she's wearing.

"Oh ... " she goes. She puts her arms around my neck and presses against me.

"When was the last time you had it?" I whisper.

"This mor – " And that's as far as she gets. That's as far as *either* of us get: Mrs Hollis is knocking on the door calling, "Are you ready, Simon?"

I tell you, we're out of that room in one minute flat, Janice looking hot and overwhelmed.

Mrs Hollis, when she sees me, beams. "Ladies and gentlemen," she calls. "Simon!" She raises her arm in a pre-arranged signal to Helen – and a split second later music – *Wild Thing* – is coming from a speaker above the door. And a split second after that I'm strutting across the floor along a specially made path that runs the width of the shop. When I say 'strutting', I mean I'm walking the way those models you see on TV walk: I take short, bouncy steps and swing my shoulders – like, I really flaunt myself.

The punters love it: big, eager smiles. I catch sight of Janice. Her eyes are so full of excitement that I half expect her to jump up and down. This is something she'll never forget, I tell myself. As an old lady with all the spirit knocked out of her and nobody to believe in, she'll remember a happy day in July when a horny young guy strutted his stuff and made her heart beat fast.

* * *

In all, I made twenty-nine changes. There were five outfits to wear/model and I gave six performances – like, I wore each outfit six times. Twenty-nine changes. Work it out.

And then there were what I would call the peep shows. Mrs Hollis said it was important that the customers see me as a guy – to keep them from thinking they'd been conned. In women's clothes and with my face made up I look so like a fem, Mrs Hollis said, that if they, the customers, didn't see me as a guy, that's what they'd think – that I was a "she" pretending to be a "he" pretending to be a "she".

So what Mrs Hollis did: at the end of each performance she sat me in a chair, stripped me to the waist ("Look, no tits" kind of thing), removed the wig I was wearing and wiped the make-up from my face.

Then she stood to one side, threw out an arm, and, in a Master of Ceremonies voice (you've got to hand it to that woman), said, "Ladies ... I give you Simon!" Then, once the tittering and murmuring had stopped, she hit me with fresh make-up.

Five times that happened. Five times!

But getting back to the actual modelling: I didn't realise it could be so tiring. I tell you, it totally wiped me out. All that walking ... I was glad when it was time to go home. The same went for Janice and Helen. They'd never known Sarah Jane's to be so busy, they said. The only person, it seemed to me, who *wasn't* glad when it was time to go home was Mrs Hollis. Mrs Hollis, it seemed to me, would've liked to've gone another six rounds. And who could blame her? The tills hadn't stop going.

CHAPTER 10

It's a week later and I'm having a drink with Janice. We're in Frisby's Wine Bar, which is across the street from Centrepoint's front entrance. Janice is drinking dry white and I'm drinking Pils. We've just come from Sarah Jane's, where not too long ago – get this – I was being photographed. Truth. Like, a little after three o'clock a guy with a camera showed up, asking could he take some pictures of me. He explained he was from *The Echo* (the local rag). I wondered who'd tipped him off – until I saw Mrs Hollis smiling to herself.

The pictures the guy wanted were Before and After shots: me in my street threads, me in a Sarah Jane's outfit; me wearing make up, me clean faced. That kind of thing. He must've fired off about fifteen miles of film. "Super!" he kept saying. Before leaving, he took a group shot: Me, Mrs Hollis, Helen and Janice, Janice with her arm round my waist – tightly round my waist. Janice can't keep her hands off me. She's entirely infatuated with me. No shit. A fact. The weird thing is, though, she won't allow me to get sweaty with her until I'm schlocked out in wig and tights. Then it's anything goes. Then it's put it where you want it.

Anyway, this drink we're having: it was Janice's idea. "Fancy a drink?" she said. This was at 5.30, knocking off time. She was at the door, waiting for me. She's emotionally fixated on me, no discussion.

"Why not," I said. I didn't really want a drink, but it

would've been shitty of me to've refused. I don't like to hurt people's feelings; it's a big thing with me. At Janice's suggestion we came to Frisby's.

Except for the prices, it's not too bad a place: taped piano music (Errol Garner, sounds like) that you can hear without cocking your head, no gunky candles in bottles, and tables that are bigger than cow pats. Janice chose one in a corner – where there's not much light.

"I feel whacked," she says. She takes a sip of wine.

I swallow some Pils. "It's been a heavy day," I say.

"We need more staff," Janice says. "On *Saturdays* we do – now that *you're* here. I can't serve *and* be a dresser: it's too much. And it's not fair on Helen. She's run off her feet."

"Speak to Mrs Hollis about it," I suggest.

"I have," Janice replies.

"What she say?"

"She says she can't afford to – take on more staff."

"That's what they *all* say," I say. I switch to another channel. "Won't Steve be wondering where you are?"

"Probably," Janice says. She says "probably" like she's saying, "So what the fuck if he is?", and I think, If I was interested in getting seriously involved with Janice, what I'd say now is, "You and Steve get on OK?" so that Janice could come back with, "Not really", which is what she would do, I know she would. However, I'm *not* interested in getting seriously involved with Janice (I'm not interested in getting seriously involved with *any* fem; I value my freedom too much), so I keep my mouth shut.

Errol Garner gives way to a guitar solo and I drink off my Pils and say, "How about another?"

"*I'll* get these," Janice says and goes to the bar. When she returns, she says, "You doing anything on Thursday?"

Uh-oh, here it comes.

"Nothing special," I reply.

"Only I've got a half day off. P'raps we could meet. You could come to my place."

"What about Steve?"

Dumb question.

"Well, he won't be there, will he?"

Of course he won't be there, just Janice waiting to tear my pants off. Which brings me nicely to something I've been meaning to say. It's this:

I sometimes wish – you probably won't believe this, but it's true – I sometimes wish I was a little ordinary-looking. Not ordinary-looking exactly, *different*-looking. I mean, if I was different-looking, if I had the face of … of a Spanish guitarist, say, maybe the fems wouldn't crowd me so much, I'd maybe have a little more time to myself, a little more energy. I tell you, fems tire you out. If you're good-looking they do.

Okay, to continue:

Janice can see I'm not exactly straining at the leash, and says, "We could put on some music, and I've got a bottle of Bacardi left over from Christmas. We could have it with Coke."

"And ice?"

"Ice if you want it."

"And a slice?"

Janice sighs. "Yes," she says.

"You're on," I say.

As I said, I don't like to hurt people's feelings.

CHAPTER 11

A pause here to let you know of two Jimmy-related decisions I've made.

First, I'm gonna take him to a few places in London: Westminster Abbey; St Paul's Cathedral; the Tower ... Places like that, places worth remembering, worth making a mental photograph of. That doesn't mean I won't be taking him to Arizona; I will. It's just that I want him to see a few *other* places. Another place I want him to see is the National Gallery – not the Gallery itself, but what's inside it.

Second, I'm gonna get him a guide dog. I don't want him tapping his way around with a white stick. I couldn't bear it. It would break my heart, people. It would break my fucking heart.

CHAPTER 12

Janice lives on Brooklands Estate, a large council development which Prince Charles, speaking on a TV programme about architecture (this was about 16 months ago, a few weeks after Brooklands was officially opened), described as excremental, or execrable. Something like that.

Now, I know Prince Charles talks to the birds – or is it plants he talks to? I forget – but what he said about Brooklands Estate was one thousand per cent sane. I mean, you should see this place. Row upon row of grey houses; here and there a three-storey block of flats – grey like the houses. Grey stucco. Everywhere you look: grey stucco. Nothing to break the monotony. No trees or grassy verges; nothing like that. Just row upon row of these drab-as-shit houses. A sign should be hung at the entrance to Brooklands Estate:

YOU'D BE BETTER OFF LIVING IN A
TENT THAN LIVE HERE

Janice lives at No 7a Laburnum Walk (Laburnum Walk! Not a tree in sight), which is a maisonette. Grey stucco. I ring the bell, and, after a wait of about one hundredth of a second, the door opens and Janice is saying, "Hi, come in."

She's wearing a yellow tank top that shows her nipples, a lot of eyeliner, and ripped designer jeans. I'm wearing a white T, washed out blue jeans, and navy loafers with a white rubber sole. Very nice loafers.

I give her my quick little-boy smile that makes people crazy for me and say, "You sure it's okay?"

"Of course," Janice says. Her face is flushed and she's looking at me like she's been waiting for me all her life.

We go up a narrow staircase and into a smallish living-room done in green. Everything's green. Green drapes, grey-green walls, green L-shaped seating unit, green lampshades, green carpet. All the room needs are a few trailing vines and Tarzan. Standing in the middle of the room is a tile-topped coffee table, on top of which are a bottle of Bacardi and two club glasses.

"Sit down," Janice says. She's smiling. "Get comfortable while I put some music on."

She goes to an expensive-looking stereo system that stands against a wall, and pretty soon we're hearing Aretha Franklin's *Answer My Prayer* – a favourite number of mine. In my book, Aretha's one of the best. Aretha. Marvin. Bruce. The best.

"Would you like a drink?" Janice asks.

"You know me," I say.

Janice goes to the table, picks up the bottle of Bacardi and pours two large ones. "I'll get some Coke and ice," she says, and crosses to louvered swing doors (green) that have to lead to the kitchen.

I sit on the seating unit and wait.

A minute later Janice is back with a small ice bucket and two cans of Coke, which she places on the table. She flashes me a 100-kilowatt smile. "Help yourself," she says. "I don't have any lemon, I'm afraid."

"Why not?" I ask.

"What?" Janice says.

"Just kidding," I say.

I go to the table and fix my drink: four cubes of ice (I'm big on ice) and a small amount of Coke, about two thimblefuls of Coke. I carry my drink back to the seating unit and sit down again. Janice, minus a drink, comes and sits beside me.

She's wearing perfume that smells like custard, or Instant Whip, so to make conversation I mention this – like, I tell her she smells of custard. "Nice."

This puts a sparkle in Janice's beautiful blue eyes, and she giggles; and a split second later she's all over me like a dog with a pork chop. "Let me put this drink down," I say. But Janice, it seems, doesn't hear me; her mind, it seems, is taken up with getting my T-shirt off. It's off. Soon *everything's* off. Aretha Franklin's not halfway through *Answer My Prayer* and already we're stark naked.

"Let's dance," Janice says. She gets to her feet, pulls me to mine, and wriggles into me.

Now, I don't know if you've ever danced naked with someone, but if you haven't, you should try it. If you're a guy, try it with your dick tucked under your partner's crotch – male or female, whatever your speed is – it's terrific. It's so terrific that when *Answer My Prayer* comes to an end and Janice says, "Let's go into the bedroom," I say, "Why don't we dance some more?"

"Come into the bedroom first," Janice says. She moves me to a door next to the stereo system and opens it. The bedroom –

And on the bed – wait for it – a red wig and a pair of green fishnet tights. They're for me of course. Janice wants me in drag. I recognize the wig as one I've worn at Sarah Jane's.

I give what must look like a grimace, because Janice touches my face and says, "Please wear them for me, Simon. *Please.*"

"We can have just as much fun with*out* that stuff," I say.

"Please," Janice says again.

I smile. I'm finding the situation amusing now. "If that's what you want," I say.

"Oh, God," Janice says, "you're such a terrific guy." She pulls me into the bedroom. "Sit on the bed," she says, "I wanna make up your face."

"Hey, come on!" I say.

"Please, Simon." Janice drags my head down and gives me a long kiss (plenty of tongue). Then she goes to a dressing table and returns with a handful of cosmetics.

While she's making up my face, I play around with her fanny, and wonder what would happen if Steve was to walk in. Something not too glorious is my guess.

Her fanny is leaking love juice, so I collect some on my fingers and circle her nipples with it. Her nipples are very hard. "You do this with Steve?" I ask. "Like, make up his face and stuff?"

Janice stops what she's doing to moan, and rotate her hips. "No," she says. She thrusts out her fanny and I take more juice and smooth it over her belly. "He wouldn't – " She's panting. "He wouldn't like it."

She finishes with my face and picks up the wig. She's so worked up her hands are shaking.

She fits the wig on me and says, "Now the tights."

She gets the tights over my feet and pulls them up to my knees. "Stand," she says. I stand, and she pulls the tights up to my waist. They're very tight tights. I don't have balls any more, I have a pancake. I'd like to take a look in a mirror, see what's been done to my face, but Janice doesn't give me the opportunity: she wraps herself around me and starts grinding away with her crotch.

"Let's get on the bed," I say.

"No," Janice says, "let's do it standing up – against a wall."

"It'd be more comfortable on the bed," I suggest.

"Please," Janice says.

"It's your house," I say.

Against a wall, after we've kissed for a while, when we're both in serious heat, Janice whispers, "Give me a Corleone fuck."

This throws me. "A Corleone fuck? What's that?"

"Haven't you seen *The Godfather*?"

I twig. I've remembered the scene where Sonny Corleone and his sister's best friend make out in a bedroom, the friend with her back to the door and her legs around Sonny's thighs. "I catch your drift," I say. "Let me get these tights off and I'll see what I can do."

"No," Janice says, "keep them on.

She goes away, and I think, 'This is weird; how'm I gonna give her the Corleone treatment wearing tights?'

Janice has the answer: she returns with a pair of nail scissors, cuts a hole in the tights' crotch, and pulls my balls and dick through. "Now ..." she says. She lets the scissors fall to the floor, and I lift her on to me.

I have three more pops with Janice (it's Olympic sex with Janice), then start out for home. It's a beautiful day, the sky a big shout of blue, and looking around me I see everything in sharp focus: a blade of grass (I'm off the estate now), a hairline crack in a paving stone, a ladybird on a car's windscreen. It's as if I'm gifted with extra-terrestrial vision. Also, some of things I'm seeing, even though I've grown up with them, appear completely foreign to me; it's as if I'm seeing them for the first time. For instance, there's a house I must've passed a thousand times, but until now hadn't noticed that its roof is four-sided and that it has green shutters at the windows. Really weird – my seeing things as if for the first time, I mean. Maybe it's the same with *people*. Like, you could live with a person, a woman, say, for thirty years, then one day look at her and notice something about her – something beautiful maybe, like a quietness in her eyes – that you hadn't noticed before – something that makes her new and interesting, a stranger, even.

I bet it happens. I bet it happens all the time.

When I get home I find Jimmy and the old lady seated at the table in the kitchen, the old lady wearing a blue polyester overall with "The Willows" embroidered in orange on the breast pocket. The Willows is a privately-owned nursing home, where the old lady works as a care assistant. She's worked there now for three years. Prior to working at The Willows, she worked in a restaurant waiting on tables, a job she hated. "Don't ever take a job as a waiter," she once told me. "The work is demeaning."

"I won't," I told her.

And I won't take a job as a care assistant, either. Not at The Willows I won't. Jesus, the things the old lady has to do there! Most of the time she's up to her armpits in shit; like, the Willows' residents keep shitting themselves ("messing themselves" is how the old lady puts it (apart from the occasional "bloody" the old lady doesn't swear, something I respect her for), and the old lady has to clean them up. When she's not cleaning them up she's creaming their bedsores or changing their piss-soaked ("urine-soaked" is the word the old lady uses) bed-sheets, hauling them out of chairs and taking them to the toilet – that's if they haven't already shit themselves – spoon-feeding them and wiping drool from their faces. Cutting their toenails.

Not exactly a job to put a spring in your step.

I pull out a chair and sit down. Terrific – the three of us seated round the kitchen table. It's not often we do this – like, sit together in the kitchen; our usual place for sitting together is the living-room; but sitting together in the living-room is not, as far as I'm concerned, the same as sitting together in the kitchen. When I say 'not the same', I mean the intimacy-levels are different: High in the kitchen, Medium in the living-room. At one time, when Jimmy and me were kids, this sitting together in the kitchen was part of our weekly routine. Every Saturday morning the old lady would go the baker's and fetch back half a dozen freshly baked crusty rolls. Then the three of us – Jimmy and me in our pyjamas – mine a bit pissy-smelling – would sit round the kitchen table piling butter onto the rolls and dunking them in steaming hot tea. I tell you, it was pure magic. Any mother who wants her kids to have something beautiful to look back on in old age should sit with them in the kitchen on Saturday mornings and feed them freshly-baked rolls and hot tea.

"Remember those rolls you used to get?" I say.

The old lady's face lights up and she says, "Oh, Simon, weren't they delicious?" She says this like she's surprised I remembered them. "Remember how you and Jimmy would wait for me in your pyjamas?"

"Right," I say, and glance at Jimmy, who's looking a lot of brotherliness at me. "Crumbs everywhere," he says.

"And butter floating in the tea," the old lady adds. And then it's do-you-remember time. Do you remember when Simon came home with a broken collar-bone after falling off Mr Carter's wall? And the night you and Jimmy stayed up your tree (the plane tree that grows outside the house two up from ours. *Our* tree – Jimmy's and mine) and I had the whole street looking for you? And the time Aunt Dolly got drunk on my homemade wine? And the day we went to the boating lake (this is Jimmy to the old lady) and you lost your purse and we had to walk the four miles home? And how about that time (me to Jimmy) you rode your bike into old man Baker's new Ford and he smacked you in the mouth?

What's *not* recalled – not out loud, anyway – is the day the old lady found the condom I'd worn when screwing Stella Finch who lives across the street. I'd put it in my shirt pocket, with the intention of dropping it down a drain, but I forgot about it, and when I took off my shirt to wash the smell of Stella's perfume from me, it must've fallen out. The old lady went for a leak, and there it was. "I think there's something of yours on the bathroom floor," she said to me when she came out.

I went back into the bathroom, took a look, and haemorrhaged. I can't tell you how embarrassed I was. Total embarrassment. You know what I did? (And this is something that will haunt me for the rest of my life). I left it, the condom, on the floor, got back to the old lady, and said, "It's not mine, it must be Jimmy's."

How could I have done such a shitty thing?

"Oh, by the way," the old lady says suddenly, "I've got something to show you." She pulls a folded newspaper from a bag at her feet and opens it out. It's the local rag – and on the front page is a picture of me in a cocktail dress. My hands are on my hips and I'm looking at the camera like I'm telling it to kiss my arse. Very haughty-looking. Across the top of the picture, which is three columns wide, is the headline, *Oh Boy, What A Knockout*! And beneath it a line in heavy type, saying, *Simon Does It In Style – Page 3.*

Page three you wouldn't believe – nothing but me. Me in jeans and T-shirt, me swinging along in silk top and pants, me having my face made up. (The group shot the cameraman took doesn't appear, which won't please Mrs Hollis.) Above the pictures is the headline, *Simon – Dressed To Thrill*, and beneath it a five-paragraph story. Why there are only five paragraphs is because the pictures are so big that's all there's room for.

The old lady gives me time to read the story, then says, "Explain, please." I can see she's trying hard not to smile.

I pass the paper to Jimmy, and then say to the old lady, "I look pretty cool, don't you think?"

The old lady can't help herself: she smiles. "You look absolutely stunning," she says.

I fake a hurt expression. "That's not fair," I say. "When Jimmy wore *his* dress, you told him he looked absolutely fabulous."

There's a small pause. Then, still smiling, looking at me with loving eyes, the old lady says, "Now, tell me: what's with this modelling?"

I make my face look serious. "I needed the money," I say.

That's the only explanation I give; and the old lady doesn't press me.

I change the subject: "What we got to eat tonight?"

The old lady gives me a sort of defiant look. "Curry," she says.

"Industrial strength?" I ask, and we all laugh our heads off; and, as we do, this feeling comes over me, this feeling that life can never get better than this.

CHAPTER 13

I'm looking at Helen with my mouth open. It fell open a second ago when she said, "Oh, of course, you don't know – she's been sacked" – the 'she' referred to being Janice. I'd looked around for her, and, not seeing her, had asked, "What, no Janice this morning?" I thought she might be sick or something. "You're kidding," I say now.

Helen shakes her head no. "Mrs Hollis caught her sneaking back a wig she'd borrowed and sacked her on the spot."

I raise my eyebrows. "What, she sacked her for borrowing a wig!"

"I will not have staff taking articles off the premises without my permission, Simon."

It's Mrs Hollis. She's come up behind us. Her stomach is going in and out. "As far as I'm concerned it is tantamount to theft."

I give this some thought, then say, "That's stronging it a bit, isn't it, Mrs H?" I picture a pissed-off Janice sitting at home staring at grey-green walls.

Mrs Hollis puffs herself up. "*You* may think so, Simon," she says, "but *I* don't."

I look at Helen, who looks at the floor. No support from Helen.

"And Simon," Mrs Hollis goes on – she closes her eyes – "please don't call me 'Mrs H.'"

There's some heavy silence until I say, "So who's

gonna help me get dressed?" My mind is still on Janice. I'll miss her. Janice was OK.

Mrs Hollis says, "For the time being you will have to manage on your own."

"Some of those outfits are tricky," I say. "You need five arms and a fish-hook to get into some of those outfits."

"Well," Mrs Hollis says, "if you find yourself in difficulties, give me or Helen a call – but do remember, we're going to be extremely busy."

Later, making up my face, Mrs Hollis says, "By the way, Simon, how would you like to work Fridays as well as Saturdays?"

"I'd like three days better," I say.

Mrs Hollis makes a sucking noise with her teeth. "I'm afraid not," she says. "Up until Friday the mall is very quiet; there would be no point in your being here a third day."

"Friday and Saturday is fine by me," I say.

"You're a good boy, Simon," Mrs Hollis says.

"You got any kids, Mrs Hollis?" I ask.

"No," says Mrs Hollis.

"I've got a kid of two," I say.

* * *

It's weird – you keep something to yourself for two years and suddenly you're dishing it to someone you hardly know. The reason I never told anyone, not even Jimmy, I had a kid is I didn't want it to get back to Mr Fisher. I still don't. It gets back to Mr Fisher, he might start asking himself questions. Such as: *Why was that*

Sixsmith kid always hanging around outside my shop? What happened to my low sperm count (Mrs Fisher told me Mr Fisher has a low sperm count), *it got high all of a sudden? That being the case, why isn't there another bagel in the oven?* Questions of that sort. And before you know it the man's talking blood tests. And before you know something else lives are being ruined.

So why, if I don't want the kid deal getting back to Mr Fisher, have I blabbed it to Mrs Hollis, who for all *I* know is a world-class gossip and a member of the same Chamber of Commerce lodge as Mr Fisher? Why have I done that?

I don't know why. All I know is, as soon as those words 'I've got a kid of two' leave my mouth I realise there's something I have to do, something that requires the co-operation of Mrs Fisher.

CHAPTER 14

Fisher's has one customer – a grey-haired number in carpet slippers and rolled down stockings. Mrs Fisher is serving her. Mr Fisher – and here my luck's in – is nowhere in sight. It could be he's resting: he's been putting in a lot of hours recently, I've noticed – to compete, I wouldn't mind betting, with the Patel shop that's opened across the street.

Seeing me, Mrs Fisher's face lights up. She's wearing a blue polka-dotted dress with small bows at the front, and long, white earrings. Her lips are painted bright red and her hair is swept up and tied in a knot. She looks beautiful. I count myself very lucky to have been involved with such a beautiful woman.

"Thanks, dear," the customer says, and makes for the door, tearing the wrapping from a packet of twenty. She can't wait to light up.

As soon as she's gone I shoot a look past Mrs Fisher's shoulder to the room behind her. "Is it okay to talk?" I ask.

In a soft voice, Mrs Fisher says, "It's all right, Mr Fisher's at the synagogue."

I wonder what Mr Fisher's doing at the synagogue, but don't ask; I figure it's none of my business. Maybe he's praying for the Patel shop to burn down.

"I want to know if you'll do something for me," I say. "Can we talk without somebody coming in?"

Mrs Fisher looks at me with tender eyes for a long

time, then goes to the door and turns the OPEN sign around to CLOSED. Not moving from the door, she says, "Benjamin looks very much like you. He gets more like you every day."

"Lucky kid," I say, but not in a smartarse way – like, I say the words gently and with a gentle smile. "Where is he?" I ask.

"Upstairs, sleeping," Mrs Fisher says.

"He has your hair," I say. "He's gonna look a million when he gets older." I pause. "It's Benjamin I wanna talk to you about."

Mrs Fisher comes away from the door and stands behind the counter. "Would you like a 7-Up?" she asks. She smiles asking this.

I return the smile and shake my head no. We're both thinking the same thing, and for an instant I recall her hot breath and her wild heartbeat. "I want my brother Jimmy to know about Benjamin," I say. "He's losing his sight and I want him to see the kid and know that he's mine – ours. I wondered how you'd feel about that. Nobody else will know. You can trust Jimmy."

"Jimmy's losing his sight?" Mrs Fisher says. Her voice is like sad music. Her mouth trembles, and a second later her eyes fill. "Oh, Simon, I'm so sorry," she says.

"It's just that I'd like him to see Benjamin – you know, close up. Have him know he's ours. Play with him and stuff. I was wondering if we could meet somewhere. The park. Tomorrow. Would that be possible?"

With two fat tears sliding down her face, Mrs Fisher says, "Yes, of course it would."

"Ten o'clock at the gates," I say.

"I'll be there," Mrs Fisher says.

"With Benjamin?"

"With Benjamin."

I'd swim through burning oil for Mrs Fisher.

CHAPTER 15

"We should have brought a ball," Jimmy says.

At a slow pace and with the sun hot on our backs we're moving along Ferndale Avenue. From Ferndale Avenue we'll move into Oakdale Road and from Oakdale Road into Clairmont Terrace. At the end of Clairmont Terrace is Ranleigh Avenue and at the end of Ranleigh Avenue Ranleigh Park, our ultimate destination.

Because it's Sunday and a little after nine a.m., the streets are pretty quiet, but soon the vacs'll start up. Around here, Sunday is house-cleaning day. Come ten o'clock, every house'll have a vac plugged into it. Front door open, vac on Max. You'd think you were at a race-track – Brands Hatch or somewhere.

"A ball?" I say. And then I catch on. He's thinking back to when we were kids. (As kids, we'd take a ball to the park and practise penalty-taking, tackling. Shit like that. We were always kicking a ball around.) "Oh, right," I say. And after a small pause, "Remember the guys with the bikes?" Like Jimmy, I'm recalling our days at the park. We were always being pestered by guys with bikes, these old guys with beat-up bikes. "Like a ride, son?" they'd say, patting the saddle. We'd stare at them. "Nah," we'd say. Ten minutes later: "Like a ride, son?" Once when I was roaming the park on my own, instead of saying Nah, I said, OK. The guy had me in a clump of bushes in five minutes flat.

Jimmy smiles, but doesn't say anything. A car drifts by banging out music:

Who's gonna drive you ho-o-o-o-o-me to-n-I-I-I-I-ght?

The Cars' *Drive*. A really nice number. I play it a lot.

Midway along Ranleigh is a run-down corner shop – Jackson's – and when we come to it I step inside for a bag of Dolly Mixture: a gift for Benjamin. It's the first thing I've ever bought him and I make a note to buy him something on a regular basis: I want him to get to know me, to think of me as his friend, as someone he can trust. I want him to get to know Jimmy, too. I do some simple arithmetic: Benjamin is two, Jimmy is 18, and I'm 17. Come Benjamin's twentieth birthday, Jimmy'll be 36 and I'll be 35. Not too big an age gap. We could be really close. Go around together. Take holidays together. Maybe share a flat.

By the time we hit the park we're business partners.

Mrs Fisher is at the gates, squatting in front of Benjamin's pushchair, doing something to his face – wiping it or something. She has her back is to us, so she doesn't see us approach. She's wearing a yellow and white summer dress that looks brand new and white wedge-heeled canvas shoes that show her heels. I notice the sheen of her hair (it hangs in loose waves to her shoulders today) and the shapeliness of her hips. "Hi," I say.

Mrs Fisher swivels round and looks up at me with big black eyes. "Oh ... hello," she says. She stands. "Hello, Jimmy."

The way she says "Hello, Jimmy" – like, with a note of embarrassment in her voice – makes me think that she thinks I may've told him the reason for our being here. I haven't. ("Fancy a walk, bro?" I said. "Where to?" Jimmy asked. "How about the park?" I said. "Okay," Jimmy said. That's all that was said.)

Jimmy says hello back (this is after he's darted me a What's-going-on-here? look) and squats in front of Benjamin, who's staring at me like I'm the man from Planet X. "What's his name?" Jimmy asks.

"Benjamin," Mrs Fisher says.

"Hi, Benjamin," Jimmy says, and touches the kid's cheek with the backs of his fingers. Simple stuff, but nice. I wouldn't mind touching the kid's cheek myself, but it wouldn't be a cool thing to do. "Let's walk," I say.

In the park, Mrs Fisher says, "I haven't been here in years." There's nobody in sight and it's very quiet, a few birds chirping. I'm on one side of Mrs Fisher and Jimmy's on the other. We could be a young family out for a Sunday morning stroll.

"Me neither," I say. I look around. "It hasn't changed much."

"I wonder if the bandstand's still here?" Mrs Fisher says. "There was a bandstand near some swings and a roundabout."

"And a sand-pit," Jimmy puts in. "We used to call it the flea-pit."

"Oh, yes, the sand-pit ... " Mrs Fisher says.

"Why don't we sit down for a while," I suggest. I want to get what I have to say over with.

Far away in the neighbourhood a dog starts to bark.

Jimmy and me throw ourselves on the grass, and Mrs Fisher frees Benjamin from his pushchair.

Looking at Benjamin, seeing him tottering around with his arms outstretched, I feel a big charge of affection circuit through me.

"You won't remember this," Mrs Fisher says, "but every Saturday night in the summer there would be a band playing and people dancing under coloured lights strung from the trees."

I picture Mrs Fisher dancing under coloured lights and wish I'd been around to partner her.

"They had dancing here?" I say. "I didn't know that." I feel cheated somehow.

A sadness creeps into Mrs Fisher's voice as she says, "Every Saturday night. It was wonderful." She joins Jimmy and me on the grass and we sit without speaking. All around us is the sweet smell of summer.

Eventually, turning to Jimmy, I say, "I've got something to tell you, bro", and I see Mrs Fisher glance at Jimmy and a small worried look come into her eyes. A shiver of excitement runs down my spine knowing that any second now Jimmy is gonna learn the truth about Benjamin. It's like I'm about to present him with a magical gift.

"What's that?" Jimmy asks.

I clear my throat. "What would you say if I was to tell you Benjamin is my kid?"

Jimmy doesn't straight off answer; he looks at Mrs Fisher for a few seconds. Then he looks back at me. He smiles. "I'd say that that makes me an uncle," he says.

That's Jimmy for you.

CHAPTER 16

When I started work at Sarah Jane's I was practically broke. Now, six weeks later, six weeks of hard saving later, I can boast £450: my plans for Jimmy are looking good. And knowing this, knowing that I'm getting there, so to speak, I feel very up. I walk with a light step and say Hi to people I've never seen before. I smile a lot. I was smiling half an hour ago when I entered the Benefit Office. Once a fortnight I come to the Benefit Office and sign on. What happens when you sign on – and I hope to shit you never have to – is you stand in line with a lot of sad-faced people, people with a hopeless look in their eyes, and when you reach the signing-on point, hand your identity card to a fem, who, as soon as she's finished telling some other fem about this terrific guy she met at a disco last night, goes to an index box that sits on a table with five or six others, searches through it, and after a while returns with a bunch of papers – your records. Attached to, or rather, sticking out of your records is a white docket, which the fem gives you to sign and date. You sign and date it: you're signed on. All you do then is wait for your money to come through. And when it does, try to live on it.

OK, I'm at the Benefit Office and I've reached the signing-on point; the fem has my identity card. Pretty soon she'll find my records and pretty soon after that I'll be beating it out of here. I'm dying to beat it out of here. I'm hot and sticky and there's a sweaty-feet smell in the air. It's so bad, the smell, it's taking a terrific effort on my part not to throw up.

The fem finds my records, reads a note that's pinned to them, and then, instead of handing me a docket to sign, tells me to go to the Enquiries desk (there's an Enquiries desk to the left of the signing-on point, with a guy sitting at it). This is iffy, I think.

"The Enquiries desk?" I say.

"Yes," the fem says.

"What do I want with Enquiries?"

"If you will go to the Enquiries desk, please," the fem says. She says this very politely, with a smile. The people who work in this benefit office are always very polite. This is because they know that if they're *not* very polite they're liable to get a smack in the mouth, or worse, get cut with a knife. I've seen it happen. I tell you, some very tricky numbers visit this benefit office. A couple of months ago a guy walked in waving a gun. Shot the place up. It was in all the papers.

Mr Enquiries has a long narrow face, a yellowish complexion and nicotine-stained fingers bitten at the nail. His hair is camel-coloured and tied in a ponytail held with a rubber band. His expression seems to say, "Don't give me a hard time, please."

"Sit down," he says. And when I'm seated, "Do you know your insurance number?"

I do.

He feeds my insurance number into a computer terminal (there's a computer terminal on his desk) and calls up something on the screen.

"What's this all about?" I ask.

The guy doesn't answer. He reads what's on the

screen, clears it, and gets to his feet. "I won't keep you a moment," he says, and goes off.

A minute later he's back with a big bald-headed guy with veiny cheeks and a kiss-my-arse moustache. I feel a chill.

"Mr Sixsmith?" the big guy asks.

"Yes," I say.

"Mr Sixsmith, I'm afraid your benefit has been suspended."

I'm getting hold of some misery here. "Oh, is that right?" I say. "Why's that?"

The guy glances at a piece of paper he's holding. "Well," he says, "it seems you've been working in paid employment." He makes me feel like I've been cutting up babies.

"Who says so?" I ask. And all at once I flash what's happened. Somebody at the Benefit Office, a clerk or somebody, has seen those pictures of me in the local rag, recognized me as a claimant (remember, I've got a face you don't forget), and's shot his mouth off, gone running to his boss and shot his mouth off. *Take a look at this, Mr Jones* (he's waving a copy of *The Echo*). *I think we've got a case here.*

Like I said, there's always someone ready to fuck you over.

"I'm afraid we're not at liberty to divulge that information," the big guy says.

He pauses.

"Until our – the DSS's – investigations are complete you won't be entitled to benefit. You'll be receiving a letter to that effect in due course."

"So do I get any money *this* week?" My scalp is beginning to sweat.

"I'm afraid not."

"So how'm I supposed to live?"

"That's something you'll have to take up with the DSS. Do you know where their offices are? Or you could telephone them. I'll write down the number for you." Helpful. Oh, he's helpful all right. He's remembering the guy with the gun, no doubt.

I get to my feet. "Don't trouble yourself," I say, and make for the door. I'm all fluttery inside.

At the door, I turn. The big guy is looking at me.

"This is not something I'm likely to forget," I tell him. Scare the shit out of him.

The big guy just stands there looking kind of helpless. I can't help but feel sorry for him. I pull open the door and exit.

Out on the street I stand still and think. Jesus fucking Christ, I think, no Benefit money. What am I gonna do now? I'm kind of dazed. I feel as if I've been mugged or something. Okay, the Benefit money wasn't much (£39 a week, as I said), but it helped, it allowed me to save what I get from Sarah Jane's. Like, I gave thirty pounds to the old lady, kept nine for myself (nine!), and the Sarah Jane's money I put away. That's how I was working things. *Was*. Past tense. I want to quit, switch off. I want to throw back my head and shout so everyone can hear, Enough!

But do I? I don't. I don't even sit down somewhere and feel terrible. No, what I do is I think of work and of replacing my lost £39. I'm on Sutton Street, which parallels Albion Street and which, like Albion Street, is heavy with shops and stores. A little way up is a bathroom centre. Maybe they need a salesperson. Or an apprentice pipe-fitter. Somebody to make the tea.

They don't.

Two doors along from the bathroom centre is a hardware store. I try my luck here.

"Sorry," I'm told.

I try my luck at other places. *Do I try my luck at other places!* Men's outfitters, delicatessens, super-marts, mini-marts, furniture and carpet stores, an halal butcher's ...

At every place of business, I try my luck – without success.

I don't give up. I head for Manor High Street, which is the district's biggest shopping area. All the big-name stores are there: Habitat, Next, Marks & Spencer ... you name it.

I try my luck on Manor High Street. Up one side, down the other.

A waste of time.

I return to the Benefit Office and look on the Vacancies board. There's one vacancy ... for a polyurethane sprayer. That's it; I call it a day. A person can only take so much.

By the time I get home I'm practically in a coma. I stagger up the steps of the house and wave to the old lady, who's inside the house, cleaning the front downstairs windows. It's the old lady's day off and instead of taking it easy she's cleaning windows. After she's cleaned the windows she'll probably do a little quarrying, I tell myself.

Inside the house, I haul up the stairs to my room. I need rest. Apart from a £500,000 yacht, that's all I need.

I throw myself on my bed and close my eyes. *After she's cleaned the windows she'll probably do a little quarrying.*

The words are on 'replay' in my head. *Cleaned the windows ... Window cleaning ...* Window cleaning! Bingo! I'm back in business.

CHAPTER 17

It's nine a.m. the following day, and I'm leaving the house feeling relaxed and confident. With one hand I'm carrying a bucket of soapy water and with the other a set of lightweight ladders I liberated from the shed at the bottom of our garden (you should see this shed – it looks as if a sumo wrestler's been dropped on it). From the rear pocket of my jeans hang a bunch of cleaning rags. Sexy.

I take the route I took with Jimmy to the park – along Ferndale Avenue into Oakdale Road. For no special reason, I've decided I'll work Oakdale first. What I *haven't* decided yet is how much I'm gonna charge for my services. I ponder the question now: *Twelve pounds a house? No, too much. Eight? Not enough. How about ten? Sounds reasonable enough. With luck, I'll make – what? £150? – and, who knows, get laid by a beautiful blonde in a negligee.* It happens – window cleaners getting laid by beautiful blondes in negligees, I mean. Oh yes. You hear about it all the time. Some of those window cleaners: they don't so much *clean* windows as help steam them up.

The first house I call at, the door is opened by a small egg-shaped number who, when it comes to looks, has just got the edge over Homer Simpson.

"Good morning, madam," I say. "I wonder – "

"No thank you," the woman says, "I already have someone."

I try her neighbour.

She, too, has someone.

The next three doors I knock at stay closed. This is not such a glorious start, but I'm not disheartened. As you may have gathered, I'm not a person to be easily defeated.

I try a house with paint peeling off the window frames.

The door is opened by an old dear in a tartan dressing gown, who, although she doesn't want her windows cleaned, *does* want her hedge trimmed.

"I'm your man," I tell her. I scope the hedge. It's about two hundred feet high. "Somebody's been asleep here," I say.

"Cut it right back," the old dear says, and hands me a pair of beat-up shears. She must carry them around with her.

I get to work.

Clip! The shears are blunt. Clip! I feel the bones in my arms jar; the hedge has pokers for stems. A poker hedge. Clip! One of the shears' handles comes loose and I lose purchase. These are historic shears I'm using, no question. I clip on. Some of the stems are so thick they take six cuts before they fall. Intelligence tells me it'd be quicker to break them off with my hands. I get inside the hedge and start breaking and snapping. Snap! A stem catches me in the eye. What's a stem in the eye? I keep breaking and snapping. I hear a sound. It's sort of tinkly. It's the sound falling soot makes. A *sooty* poker hedge. And what's this…? I look closer. Jesus, a nest of caterpillars! I draw back quick (I've a natural fear of caterpillars) – and – *Shit!* – snag my T-shirt. I check out my T-shirt and notice there's blood on it. The blood is from my hands and arms. I'm getting torn to pieces.

After about an hour-an-a-half I take a break. The sun is powering down and there's a strong smell of drains in the air. From across the street, through an open window, comes the sound of Bob Marley. I'm sweaty and itching and something is crawling up my leg. I slap at my leg with my hand, and, as I do, the old dear reappears and says Christallfuckingmighty – or words to that effect.

She's right: the hedge doesn't look too clever. It wouldn't make *House and Garden*. It'd make *World War II*, but not *House and Garden*. I flash the old dear a thousand-pound smile. "I'm getting there," I say.

The old dear looks at me and says, "It's crooked." She means the hedge. She has a saliva problem, I notice.

"That's 'cos I'm not finished with it yet," I explain.

"It's very crooked," the old dear says. Her eyes have a sort of tragic look, so I say, "Hey, lighten up, it'll be okay. I'll straighten it out for you."

The old dear looks at the ground. "Oh dear," she says. She stoops down, and ten minutes later comes up with a leaf. One leaf. "The mess!" she says.

I flash her another smile, a tight one this time. "We won't let it get to us, though, will we?" I say, and return to the hedge. There's still a lot of it to come down.

I work very quickly. I want out of this. I've realised I've made a terrible mistake. I shouldn't be here. I'm a window cleaner, I should be cleaning windows – and getting laid by beautiful blondes in negligees. And another thing: how much is the old dear gonna pay me?

I'm thinking this and other stuff – like, 'There goes my other eye' – when I hear kids on the street. The schools have turned out for lunch. It's twelve, twelve-thirty. I've been working for three hours!

OK, cut to like fifteen years later and I'm knocking on the old dear's door, the hedge – my work on it – finished. I'm black all over and there's a million tiny caterpillars hanging by threads from my hair. Still, I feel pretty good; like, I feel I've done a pretty good job. Considering I've had nothing but my bare hands to work with, I've done a *very* good job. I must have taken at least five feet off that hedge. There's sun on the house where before there was only shadow. I've brought sun into the old dear's life.

"Oh dear," the old dear says. She's at the door, clocking the hedge. She takes a step forward – carefully. It's like she's stepping onto an ice floe or something. "Oh dear," she says again.

I'm gonged, entirely gonged. I mean, I've worked my balls off, and all she can say is, *Oh dear*. When I speak, my voice has an emotional note: "It was the best I could do. Those shears of yours wouldn't cut through mousse."

"Mousse?" the old dear says.

"Right – mousse," I say.

"I'll get you a broom," the old dear says.

She'll get me a broom. She expects me to clean up. She thinks I'm an Adventure Scout or something. "Hey, look," I say. "I don't have a lot of time", but the old dear turns her back on me and totters off. A minute later she's handing me a broom and telling me to sweep the "clippings" into a pile.

"Look, lady," I say, "this is not my work – like, I'm a window cleaner. I shouldn't be here."

"When you've got them into a pile, take them through the house to the back of the garden and put them next to the incinerator."

I start sweeping.

I'm still sweeping when the old dear's clock strikes two. I hear the clock because I'm now sweeping *inside* the house (I've had a few mishaps with the "clippings" and I'm on my knees in the kitchen, with a brush and dustpan).

"There's one *there* you've missed," the old dear says. She's pointing to a twig the size of a matchstick.

I sweep the twig into the pan and get to my feet. The old dear has her purse in her hand. Pay time. 'You've some large ones coming here, Sixsmith,' I tell myself. I place the pan and brush on the window-ledge and wait.

The old dear opens her purse and takes out a fifty pence piece.

I stare at it, then at her. She's got to be kidding.

She's not. "Thank you," she says, and offers me the coin.

I look in her purse and see two coppers. I look at the old dear. "You're a riot; you know that, don't you?" I say. I take the coin and return it to the purse. "It'll pay for the soap and water I wanna use."

As I leave the house, after I've cleaned myself up, I hear the old dear from the sink:

"The mess!"

I door-to-door it along Oakdale, then move into Clairmont. It's now two-thirty or thereabouts and I haven't cleaned one window. I can't help but feel pissed off. I feel like suing someone. A baby caterpillar is abseiling down my face. If I had a gun I'd shoot it.

No joy on Clairmont; so I move into Ranleigh, which is a very long road.

Nothing on Ranleigh ... just one weird experience: A door I knocked at, a woman with long whacked-out hair opened it and said, "Please go away. PLEASE GO AWAY!" It was as if she knew me and couldn't stand the sight of me. "It's okay, I'm going," I said, and backed off. "GO AWAY!" the woman screamed. "GO AWAY!" She was deranged, no question. I gave her a nice smile. "Try to get some rest," I told her.

You have to feel sorry for people like that.

From Ranleigh I progress to Caistor Avenue. Even though the sky is light, it's getting seriously late. Through windows with gathered-back curtains I see TV screens flickering and families seated around tables, having their evening meal. I'm very thirsty. The ladders are a hundred times heavier than they were when I started out, and the bucket feels like it's filled with cement. My head is starting to ache and I'm sweating like a dog. 'I can't handle this,' I tell myself. It's too much for a soul to bear.' But then I tell myself, 'Give it one more shot.'

The door is opened by an old guy with two balls of phlegm for eyes and a nose like a dead thumb. He's wearing a moth-eaten cardigan over a stained pyjama top, and trousers you wouldn't let a diseased animal sleep on. His hair, which is lead-coloured, looks as if it might have mice living in it. It's like he's in some state of decay. I give him my spiel and wait for him to say no.

"Come in," he says.

Come in?

I lay down my ladders, and, holding my bucket, step inside the house.

"Close the door behind you."

I do as he says, and follow him into a horror-hole that I take to be the kitchen. I tell you, the place is unbelievable. Dishes are piled in the sink, and a small table that stands opposite a beat-up, grease-covered oven is so loaded with crap it'd take a week to clear. Pots, pans, cereal packets, bottles, jars, cans – a mountain of garbage. The one window in the room has so much crap on it it's impossible to see through. This, I figure, is the reason for my being here: El Filtho wants a little light on his garbage. I nod at the window and make a joke: "Gimme a serious hammer and chisel and I'll have that cleaned for you in no time."

"Do you ever wear leather?" the guy asks.

"What?"

"Leather. Do you like leather?"

"It doesn't exactly wipe me out."

"I like to see boys in leather."

I look at him cool. "Okay," I say, "what is it you want, and how much are you willing to pay for it?" I put down my bucket. There's no way this guy wants his windows cleaned.

"I've got a leather jacket upstairs ... Would you put it on?"

"Just put it on?"

"I'll go and get it." He leaves the horror-hole and returns a few minutes later holding a leather flying jacket with a lambswool collar. There are tears in the jacket's sleeves, and the lambswool is yellow with age. John Wayne could've worn it in one of those crappy war films he made. "Put it on," the guy says.

I give him a spiky smile and put on the jacket. "Okay, where's the plane and what time's take-off?"

"Drop your jeans and turn around."

"First, how much? And second, what happens when I drop my jeans?"

"Nothing. I won't touch you. Just lift your shirt."

"How much?"

"Five."

"Ten."

"All right."

"We're talking pounds here?"

"Yes."

"And no touching?"

"No. Yes. I mean, no touching."

"Lemme see the money."

The guy pockets a hand and pulls out two tens and a five.

"You can touch for twenty," I say.

"No," the guy says.

I drop my jeans and show him what he can have for twenty.

He's not interested. "Turn around," he says.

I recall my experience with Haynes, and think, 'Nobody's gonna put that kind of shit over on me again.'

"Money first," I say.

The guy hands me a ten, and I turn around and raise my shirt.

A second later, a second after I've told myself, 'This

is one for the collection, Sixsmith,' I hear a zip pulled, and a couple of minutes after that heavy breathing. Then a little gasp.

Two minutes, that's all it takes. Ten pounds. I remove the jacket, pull up my jeans, and exit the horror hole, my career as a window cleaner over before it's begun.

CHAPTER 18

The telephone rings. I lift the receiver. "Hello."

"Si?"

"Yeah."

"It's Wally."

"Hi."

"Si?"

"What?"

"Stan's gone and joined the army."

"Yeah?"

"For ten years." (Giggling.)

"What's so funny?"

"I dunno." (More giggling.)

"Call me back when you've had your shock therapy."

"He's having a Going Away drink."

"Stan?"

"Yeah."

"When?"

"Saturday."

"Where?"

"The Castle."

"What time?"

"Half seven." (Background noise.) "I've gotta go."

"Why?"

"*Win, Lose or Draw* is on." (*Win, Lose or Draw* is a TV sports quiz for kids. Wally never misses it. He's no mental giant, Wally.)

"What time did you – " Click.
He's hung up in my ear.
Fuck you very much, Wally.

CHAPTER 19

OK, flash-forward to Saturday and I'm seated at a table in The Castle, which, in case you're not familiar with East London, is a tall red-bricked Free House that stands on the corners of Albion and Queen's streets. Apart from its cellar, which is supposed to be haunted by a fourteen-year-old kitchen maid, and its ceiling, which has a huge watermark shaped like a giant shark smoking a pipe, what's interesting about The Castle is that three years ago a girl and the guy she was running with were murdered here. I'm not shitting you. The girl was Indian, and the guy Irish. I didn't know them to talk to, but I'd often seen them on the street together. The girl was really beautiful: hair down to her waist, and high cheekbones. The guy was slim, with curly red hair and shining blue eyes. A very happy-go-lucky person, he seemed. Always smiling. You couldn't help but like him. Sean, I think his name was.

Anyway, according to newspaper reports and stuff I got from people in the know, Sean was warned by the girl's two brothers to stay away from her (something to do with her being a Muslim and him a Christian), but he wouldn't; so one night they went looking for him – and found him with the girl in The Castle, the girl fucked up on port and lemon. The brothers hacked them to death with machetes. A real bloodbath. Wall-to-wall blood. One of the girl's fingers was found in an ice bucket. No shit. A fact. Everyone around here was in shock over it, over what'd happened. The old lady, when she heard what'd happened, broke down. Like me, she'd seen the girl and the guy on the street together and thought them an incredibly nice couple. "Religion," she said. "Bloody religion." (The old lady's not too big on religion. She's big on human rights, but not religion. If there's one religion that *really* pisses her off it's the Catholic religion. This is because of its opposition to birth control. The old lady is very big on birth control. Abortions, contraceptives. Stuff like that. I admire the old lady a lot. For the views she holds. I wouldn't mind seeing the old lady in charge of the country. I mean that.)

Anyway, back to The Castle: The bar I'm in (the saloon bar) is square-shaped, high-ceilinged and has round pillars painted to give a marble effect. Red and blue carpet tiles, unvarnished chairs and tables, a juke, two slots, a cigarette machine, and, on a shelf above a piano that looks like it fell out of a 'plane, a busted TV set. You wouldn't find Ivana Trump drinking here.

From where I'm sitting I can see Mr Satch. He's standing at the bar drinking scotch, his regular tipple – scotch with a small amount of water. Mr Satch is a neighbour of ours and has this terrible beetroot-coloured birthmark that covers the left side of his face, ear included. It's the worst birthmark I've ever seen. A guy I know from school – Alfred Parmenter – has a birthmark, but compared with Mr Satch's his is nothing – a little hairy patch on his temple. Nothing. Mr Satch's is sort of frightening and is probably the reason for his never looking happy. Who *would* look happy with that kind of disfigurement? Nobody. If *I* had a disfigurement like that, it'd be Goodbye world, goodbye Mick Jagger. That's the truth; I couldn't live with it.

Mr Satch is about fifty and has a son who's an officer in the Merchant Navy and who, whenever he's home on leave, drives an old Bentley. A really terrific-looking car. Green, with a rubber side-horn and spoked wheels. A collector's car, I guess you'd call it. The son is called Michael, and, like his old man, never speaks to anyone. I forgot to mention: Mr Satch never speaks to anyone. He looks right through you, even though you're his neighbour. Where *Mrs* Satch is, nobody knows. It's a kind of mystery family. I once saw Mr Satch take a woman into his house, but I don't think it was Mrs Satch. The woman was quite a looker: tall, with exciting golden-red hair. Very well-dressed. Mr Satch always looks scruffy (his clothes kind of curl at the edges), but you somehow get the impression he's well-heeled and's used to giving orders. I once followed him onto a bus (this was when I was a kid), and as he started up the stairs, the conductor (until about four years ago the buses around here still had two-man crews) asked him, "Take it up, guv?" (meaning the ticket), and Mr Satch, in a really gruff voice, told him, "Come up and get it" (meaning the fare), and continued climbing the stairs.

That's Mr Satch for you.

While my thoughts are on Mr Satch and his terrible disfigurement, The Castle's frosted-glass door opens and Wally and Stan walk in. They're followed by Stan's old man and lady, Mr and Mrs Thomson, two terrific people who treat Stan like he's a six-year-old. The way they treat Stan you'd think he was made of bone china. Stan's old man is an engineer with British Gas, and his old lady a school cook. Both have neat faces and both are very small. How they came to have a kid as tall as Stan is a mystery. "I must be a throwback," Stan once told me. "Throwback is right," I replied.

I get to my feet, and Stan sees me and comes over, Wally and Mr and Mrs Thomson trailing behind. Stan is wearing a day-glo yellow jacket over a turquoise shirt, and Wally a day-glo orange jacket over a pink T. Both are wearing plum-coloured jeans. They look like a circus act. Me? I'm wearing a navy crew-neck, white jeans and my main-course orange-leather moccasins. Very French Riviera.

After hellos've been said and I've pulled out a chair for Mrs Thomson to sit on ("Oh, what a gentleman you are, Simon!"), Mr Thomson gets drinks, and pretty soon the five of us are talking away and laughing at one another's jokes the way old friends should, words and laughter all fitting together as easily as a kid's jigsaw. In my opinion, there's nothing as good as being with friends in a pub. You just can't beat it.

After a while there's a break in the conversation, so to fix it I say to Stan, "So you're Mister Military now?"

Stan, who unconsciously is spilling beer down the front of his jacket, grins. "Yeah," he says.

You have to push Stan.

I push him and he tells me he's joined the junior section of the Tank Regiment (the Tank Regiment!) and will join the adult section as soon as he's completed a year's training, which will be carried out at Nuneaton. He leaves for Nuneaton on Monday. Once he's completed his training he'll get his first posting. He'd like an overseas posting, but won't be too disintegrated if he doesn't get one. He wouldn't mind a posting to Malaya (Malaya!), but isn't sure if we have troops out there. His pay will be £70 a week and he'll get four free travel warrants a year.

While he's telling me all this, I cut looks at his old man and lady and I can tell from their expressions that their hearts are breaking. Stan's their only kid; they don't want to lose him. Not yet. They want him with *them* so they can take care of him, make sure he sticks to a high-fibre diet, uses T-Gel shampoo (Stan suffers from constipation and dandruff), remind him of the dangers of sex and drugs. That's what they want. But Stan's joined the army. There was no work going, so he joined the army.

"What about the mountain bike Wally told me you were gonna get – that out the window now?"

Stan gives a naughty-kid smile and shrugs, and for a split second I see him in a tin helmet taking fire in Bosnia or some other screwed up country our dickhead politicians've decided we've got to have a presence in.

Mrs Thomson pulls a tiny handkerchief from her sleeve and dabs her eyes with it. She's choked up. She's seeing what I saw.

Mr Thomson touches her arm. "Don't upset yourself, dear," he says. He looks embarrassed.

"Come on, Mum, cheer up," says Stan.

I switch the conversation to Wally. "You still with the tube?" I ask.

Wally grins at me like he doesn't have a brain in his head. "No," he says, "we're laying foundations now."

I ask after Henry, and Wally tells me he's off sick with an injured back. The injury happened at home, so he doesn't get sick pay. His wife's expecting another kid. Every Friday the guys at the site put their hands in their pocket to make sure the family don't go short. "Give him my best when you next see him," I say.

"And what are *you* doing these days, Simon?" Mrs Thomson asks brightly. She's making an effort. She's trying hard for Stan's sake.

Before I can answer, Wally explodes into his beer, which tells me he's seen the local rag, those pictures of me. I look at him and share the joke.

"I'm in ladies' fashions," I say eventually.

This gets everybody's interest, and in no time at all I'm giving a highly entertaining account of my work at Sarah Jane's. Everybody cracks a rib laughing,

"Oh, Simon," Mrs Thomson says when I'm finished. "What an exciting job! All those frocks to wear! How lucky you are!"

This rocks me. *All those frocks to wear? How lucky I am? She can't be serious.*

She is. How I know she is is because Mr Thomson is looking at her like he's saying, "Get a grip, dear." I give a small, fake cough – *ahem*. "Well, Mrs T," I say, "it beats *working* for a living", and then, noticing that our drinks are getting low, I get to my feet and go to the bar for fresh ones.

And – uh-oh – see Harry Haynes.

He's standing way off to my right, talking to two guys built like bottle banks; shoulders you wouldn't believe.

Haynes's radar system must be working, because a second after I've clocked him he stops talking, turns his head like it's on Slow and fixes me with a stare that'd curl a leaf.

This of course doesn't flap me. It's meant to, but it doesn't. I'm not a person that flaps easy. I give him my cold-killer smile, get the drinks, and return to the party.

Mrs Thomson is on one of her talking jags. Mrs Thomson's got this nervous thing that makes her want to yak all the time. Once she gets started she can't stop. It wouldn't be so bad if the stuff she came out with was worth listening to, but mostly it's crap – like how it took her two days to wash and dry a duvet. Stuff like that. And she goes from one subject to the next, the way a kid does. Listening to Mrs Thomson, you get the impression of a plane in a crash dive.

Her subject tonight – or rather her *first* subject tonight – is her living-room. She wants it redecorated, new wallpaper put up. First she wants the wallpaper blue, then she wants it peach. Of course, the colour of the wallpaper will have to match the colour of the carpet they're gonna get. "We must get a new carpet, Simon. The one we've got is a disgrace." She thinks she would like a green carpet, which means that blue wallpaper would be out – blue wouldn't go with green. Nor would peach. No, the wallpaper, if they get a green carpet, will have to be beige, or maybe not beige, maybe white would be better. Yes, white – with just a hint of green. What she *really* would like is a new three-piece suite: something in chintz. Or leather. No, not leather, leather's too cold and it cracks. She's seen a nice three-piece in brown corduroy, but corduroy attracts dust, and if there's one thing she can't abide it's dust. Oh, and that reminds her, she must get a new feather duster.

On and on: she doesn't stop. She's a terrific person, but once she's on Talk you wanna throttle her. She needs help. The woman definitely needs a year or two with a world-class shrink.

While she's yakking on like this, I cut a look at Haynes, and see him in a huddle with his two gorillas, Haynes every so often pinning me with his eyes. Which leads me to believe he's cooking something up – something that has *me* as its main ingredient. But I don't panic; I wait for an opportunity to handle it cool. How I'll handle it cool, I'll laugh. This'll tell Haynes he's not getting to me. As soon as Mrs Thomson stops yakking, I'll crack a few hilarious jokes, and everyone in our party, including me, will break up laughing. I'll be handling it cool.

But Mrs Thomson *doesn't* stop yakking. She's on Go with the wind behind her. Yak, yak, yak. I keep hoping I'll hear her say something funny, something that'll give me a laugh, but I don't. You don't get a laugh from knowing that a dining-room table is on sale at Collier's for seventy-five-ninety-nine, or that runner beans have no taste to them this year. If you do, there's something seriously wrong with you. I get a few, 'Well-how-about-that' smiles, but that's all; nothing that tells Haynes and his gorillas they're not getting to me.

We listen to Mrs Thomson's crap for maybe forty minutes, then I step in with this: "Going back to wallpaper, Mrs Thomson, you might appreciate this joke I heard about a Jewish decorator."

"Oh, how I'd like to move house, Simon," Mrs Thomson says.

I might as well've been talking to an Egyptian mummy.

More than anything Mrs Thomson would like to

move house. Get away from the dirt and noise and pollution. The pollution! We're all gonna die from it. Did we see that article in the newspaper the other day about car fumes and the damage they do to our health? Move out, that's the only solution to pollution. Cornwall. She'd love to live in Cornwall. No, not Cornwall, Devon; Devon is where she'd love to live. Devon is where her parents came from. Her parents were wonderful people who never laid a finger on her. If they had, she'd have left home and gone into nursing. Looked after children. She loves children. Baby children. Some of those poor children ... Do we know how many children's hospitals closed last month? Nine. Nine! How are sick children gonna get treated if there're no hospitals for them? She looks at Stan's kid's face and burst into tears. It's over. I go for a leak.

And – catch this – heartbreaking this – finish up in hospital.

* * *

What happened is, while I was aiming at the bowl and thinking that maybe Mrs Thomson should be in a little white room with bars at the window, I felt a terrific blow in the small of my back. It was as if I'd been hit by a wrecking ball, absolutely as if I'd been hit by a wrecking ball. The pain was intense – like, I was overcome with it. I fell to the floor, but before I could crawl into a corner and die or something (with my dick hanging out and piss staining my jeans) I was hauled to my feet and pinned against a wall. There was a hand – courtesy of British Steel, it felt like – around my throat which, when I was able to focus my eyes, I could see belonged to one of Haynes's gorillas. Close up he looked like something out of *Man Through The Ages* – one of the back issues; a really awesome sight: thick lips, big fleshy nose with veins standing out on it, and tiny yellow eyes. His hair was cut skin close. "If you're trying to get my attention, you've got it," I told him. Bam! I took one just below the heart. Then another. That wasn't enough – Mr Aaahhrrggh went to work on my face – a quick one to my mouth followed by two choreographed headbutts.

The stars I saw were mega-sized.

When I came to, I was flat on my back on a trolley and Wally and Stan were looking down at me with anxious eyes. They didn't say anything, just looked at me.

"Where am I?" I asked. I felt like I'd been starched and pressed.

"In hospital," Wally said, and grinned one of his idiot grins. "How d'you feel?" Stan asked. There I was at death's door and Stan was asking me how I felt. "Oh, wonderful, just wonderful," I replied, and closed my eyes: his jacket was blinding.

* * *

So here I am in hospital – and not liking it; I want out of here quick (hospitals are not places I can easily cope with). I call the Ward Sister to my bed and inform her I'm leaving.

The Ward Sister looks at me like I'm a drug fiend. "Stay where you are until a doctor sees you," she says.

An hour later a doctor with a manic haircut sees me and allows me to leave.

* * *

Incidentally, the joke about the Jewish decorator, the one I was gonna tell Mrs Thomson: you might like to hear it.

A Jewish decorator on a step ladder, hanging wallpaper, loses his balance and falls. Bam! He hits the floor and breaks every bone in his body.

The woman whose house he's decorating runs to him and kneels at his side. "Oh, my poor man," she says, "are you all right?"

The Jewish decorator closes his eyes and shrugs. "I'm making a living," he says.

That joke was told to me by Mrs Fisher.

CHAPTER 20

My injuries are: two cracked ribs, two hamburger-sized shiners and a mouth out here. The old lady, when she sees me, flips. Jimmy, when he sees me, shakes his head in disbelief. Mrs Hollis sort of shrinks back. "Oh, Simon," she says, "you can't work looking like *that*."

"Pile on the make-up," I say, "I need the money."

"Simon," Mrs Hollis says, "this is a boutique, not a freak show."

Helen comes up and stares at me. Her mouth is open. She puts a hand to it. "Oh, Simon ... "she says.

I let a week go by, then get back to Mrs Hollis, who looks at me with tragic eyes. "I'm sorry, Simon," she says, "but I'm going to have to let you go. I can no longer afford to keep you on."

She blames rising interest rates. Suddenly people have stopped spending. At this time of the year her sales should be way up, but they're not, they're at an all-time low. She thinks she may have to lay off Helen and take on a school-leaver (cheap labour). It doesn't matter that I'm a crowd-puller. "Why attract people into the shop if they're not going to buy anything? They'd just dirty the place up." No, she's awfully sorry, but she'll have to let me go.

Fine, terrific. No unemployment benefit, nobody wanting their windows cleaned, and I've lost my job at Sarah Jane's. Life is taking a giant shit on me, no question.

But I soldier on. I call on Toni the Greek and hit him with a proposition: *he* makes up sandwiches and *I* hawk them around offices: Toni's Sandwich Service.

"Offices?" Toni says. "What fuckin' offices? You losin' you fuckin' marbles, Simon."

Still I soldier on. I tramp the streets, asking people if they want their car washed.

They don't.

I travel five miles to a soap factory – and see a notice outside: No vacancies.

I call at a dog track, hoping to be taken on as a kennel hand (that's how desperate I am, I'm even prepared to shovel dog shit).

No luck at the dog track.

I pay daily visits to the Job Centre. There are ten people for every job.

I become – what's the word? – dispirited – I become very dispirited. I sit around the house all day, or roam the streets. I'm roaming the streets now. 'Forget the Arizona trip, Sixsmith,' I tell myself, 'it's not gonna happen.' Oh, I'm dispirited all right.

I turn a corner and come to a newsagent's.

Outside the newsagent's, fixed to an *Evening Standard* billboard, is a poster: Scandal of London's Rent Boys.

* * *

The story, in part, is about the rise in the number of young prostitutes. More and more kids, boys especially, the *Standard* reports, are taking up prostitution.

Now, you'd think that the person who wrote the story would want to know *why* more and more kids are taking up prostitution; but he doesn't. The fact that there's no work for them and they're turning to prostitution in order to eat, to provide shelter for themselves, to live a little, buy a nice pair of jeans, a nice pair of trainers (my reading of the situation and a pretty accurate one it is too, I bet), doesn't interest him. He couldn't give a squat about that. All he's concerned about is the effect these kids are having on – wait for it – the property market. True. Like, the kids are tricking in the front gardens of private properties, and this, the writer says, is making the properties difficult, if not impossible, to sell. Like, who wants a house whose front garden is a screwing zone?

That's the main thrust of the story. No sympathy for the kids. The kids don't matter. Only property matters.

However, all that's beside the point. What counts is the story's given me the green light. I'm once more on Go. Or I will be as soon as my face heals. It's coming along. The bruising around my eyes is fading and my mouth no longer resembles two rolls of oilcloth. Give me a week – make that ten days – and I'll be my old hot-shit self again; I'll be ready for the Meat Rack.

So, the question now is: how to kill time until my looks, my movie-star looks return?

Easy. How I'll kill time is I'll take Jimmy to some – if not *all* – of those places in London I mentioned. Starting tomorrow, that's what I'll do.

CHAPTER 21

Our first port of call, so to speak, is the National Gallery, recently extended, as you may've read, at a cost to the taxpayer of six million pounds. I'm not complaining: more National Gallery means more art – and we can all do with more art, right? Art is important I think – it helps keep us sane. More art, fewer missiles, is my motto.

On the subject of art: I don't know about you, but personally – and this'll sound weird coming from someone who's only once been inside a church (for the funeral service of a good neighbour of ours: Mrs Cutts, who died of cervical cancer) – I go for religious pictures. And in my opinion there was no finer painter of religious pictures than Caravaggio. I once saw his *The Death of the Virgin Mary* – no shit – and I tell you, it stopped my mind – like, it just took me over; I was up there with the guys in the robes (there are all these guys in robes in the picture). I was transported, as they say.

I'm also big on landscapes and my main man for landscapes is Canaletto. In my book, Canaletto is the best. I mean, some of those views of Venice he painted … You can almost breathe the air. You look at a Canaletto and you want to take a deep breath. In my opinion – I'm wearing that phrase out – the painters of today, as compared with Caravaggio and Canaletto, are amateurs. Take Hockney, for example. As far as I'm concerned, Hockney's pictures are about as interesting as a satellite dish. The only modern-day painter I've got time for is Bacon. OK, his stuff may look a little Hannibal the Cannibal but at least it says something. To *me* it does. It tells me there's a lot of grief in the world. Bacon is one person I would like to've met, had a conversation with; I imagine he had plenty of interesting things to say about Life, and about Art. From what I've heard about his sex life, he probably would've liked to've met me!

How I know about paintings: at the school I went to, kids reckoned by our art teacher – a guy called Blakely – to be good at drawing were taken on trips to galleries. I was one of Blakely's star pupils, so I always got to go on these trips. Kids reckoned by Blakely to be lousy at drawing were out of it, which, in my opinion, wasn't right. I mean, just because you're not good at something doesn't mean you don't have an interest in it, or can't appreciate it, does it?

Try telling that to Blakely

Sudden thought: Did Bacon's pals call him Streaky?

We cruise the gallery for two hours, and then, after we've refreshed ourselves with a nice cup of tea in the gallery's cafeteria, discussed some of the paintings we've seen (some of those paintings ... They make you feel – I dunno – humble), we take the Underground to Westminster. I want Jimmy, as I've said, to see Westminster Abbey. *I* want to see Westminster Abbey.

Something I've just remembered: As we were leaving the gallery – you won't believe this – as we were leaving the gallery a not-bad-looking guy of about forty wearing a business suit and striped tie and carrying a furled umbrella stepped up to me and quickly and not looking at me handed me a folded piece of paper. Then he darted off. Real undercover stuff. I expected to hear spy-movie music. I waited until the guy was out of sight, then unfolded the paper and read what was on it. This is what I read: *If you or your friend would care for a drink one evening, please ring* (here a number was given) *between 7 and 8.30 and ask for Matthew.*

That actually happened.

I didn't keep the paper; I showed it to Jimmy (he found it pretty funny), and then, marvelling at the guy's nerve, threw it away.

At the Abbey we wait in a queue for twenty minutes, then step inside. And – wow! – I'm entirely sledged. I mean, what a piece of architecture! It's as if two giant spiders had been at work – one spinning stone, the other wood. Really intricate architecture. And the size of the place! Looking around and up, I feel ant-sized.

I turn to Jimmy to say, "It makes Tesco look a bit thin, bro," but he's not with me. We've not been in the place two minutes and already I've lost him.

You lose someone you make a search.

I wander around, eyes on Scan, and after what seems a long time find myself in what I take to be a private chapel. It's very small and has a small stone altar and lectern and a dozen or so fragile-looking chairs, each fitted with a thin red-velvet cushion trimmed with gold cord. I can straight-off see that Jimmy's not on the premises, but I don't immediately leave: I approach the altar, shoot a look over my shoulder to make sure nobody's come through the door, then close my eyes and say a prayer:

Please don't let Jimmy go blind. Please don't take his sight away. I'm begging you, don't do that.

It's the first prayer I've said since I was a kid. When I was a kid I prayed every night. I had this fear of something bad happening to the old lady, specifically that she'd get hit by a car while out shopping; so every night I prayed to Him to keep her safe. Then one day I got home from school and there she was sitting in a chair with her head bandaged. She'd been hit by a bus. It sounds like a terrible joke, I know, but it actually happened. A bus mounted a pavement and – bam! – hit the old lady, sort of side-swiped her and knocked her off her feet. Fortunately, she wasn't badly hurt – a gashed head. But after that I stopped praying. What's the fucking point? I thought.

OK, I continue my search for Jimmy and at last spot him. He's standing by a railed-off tomb or something, talking with a tall silver-haired guy in a purple cassock; a really important-looking guy.

I don't interrupt them; I stand a short distance off and watch them. And see something that makes me think I'm going down with insanity. What I see is, I see tears come into the guy's eyes and a second later see Jimmy touch the guy's arm, as if to comfort him; this important-looking guy.

After about five minutes the guy goes off, so I go up to Jimmy and say, "Who was that?"

"I don't know," Jimmy says.

"What'd he want?"

Jimmy shrugs. "He wanted to know my name and where I lived; who my father was."

"That it?"

"He said he thought he knew me. He asked if he

could do anything for me, if he could be of help in any way."

"Help? How help?"

"I don't know."

"What did *you* say?"

"I said I didn't need any help."

"It looked to me like he was crying."

"Yes, he was," says Jimmy.

That's Jimmy's reply. I tell you, some wild thoughts go through my head – too wild to mention.

I change the conversation: "So how bad is this place?"

Jimmy looks around him, looks at me. He grins. "Dynosupreme," he says, and we both have a good laugh.

Sometime later, maybe an hour later, we leave the Abbey and soon afterwards are on the river heading for the Tower of London. And for my money, this, so far, is the best part of the day. Sitting out on deck under an all-blue sky and with a hot breeze in my face, I feel terrifically content, terrifically complete. If ever I came into a pile of money, I tell myself, what I'd do is, I'd buy a boat and sail around the world with Jimmy, visit some of those beautiful faraway countries I've seen on TV. India, Japan, countries like that. Sri Lanka. Then it dawns on me: Jimmy wouldn't be able to *see* any of those beautiful faraway countries, and giant claws sink into my heart.

We get to the Tower, and, after we've inspected the dungeons and the Weapons Room, go up a winding stairway to a balcony that looks on to St John's Chapel – the place where Lady Jane Grey prayed the night before she was beheaded.

It's the most beautiful place I've ever seen. It's kind of perfect. Still and white and perfect – the sort of place where, if you believed in miracles, you might expect to experience one. I glance at Jimmy and see a look in his eyes that makes me think he's been taking something. And then I twig: the place has blissed him out.

We look all over the Tower (me paying particular attention to the giant codpiece on a suit of armour worn by Henry VIII, and smiling when I hear a little kid with a bright, hopeful face and a dazzling stream of yellow hair point to it and say to her father, "Is that his horse, daddy?"), and when we leave, we're in a peaceful, happy state.

* * *

We round things off with a meal at The New Friends, a Chinese restaurant in Docklands. (Docklands, in case you're interested, is about a 15-minutes drive from the Tower.)

The meal we have – fried lobster balls, noodles, egg fried rice, lychee in syrup – is delicious, something to remember, and when it comes time to settle the bill I tell the waitress as much. The waitress is Chinese and really beautiful. Moon-coloured skin and dark drowning eyes. Really beautiful. Every time she catches my eye, or I catch hers, she giggles. Which tells me she's hot for me. I get her to call a cab – giggle, giggle – and we – Jimmy and me – ride home to the sound of Andrew Lloyd-Webber music played on a tape deck.

When we get home, there's a dynamite surprise waiting for us: the old lady tells us she's gonna get married.

Some day, eh?

CHAPTER 22

The old lady's story:

The old lady is the youngest of two daughters (the eldest being Aunt Dolly) born to Mr and Mrs Goodhew, who lived in Brighton in Sussex, and who, a few days before the old lady's 10th birthday and a few days after Aunt Dolly's 17th, were killed in a road accident. They were driving to Portsmouth to visit friends when a petrol tanker overturned and crushed their car. They died instantly.

Orphaned, Aunt Dolly and the old lady (the old lady's first name is Patricia, by the way) went to live with their godmother, a Mrs Montague, in the house we're living in now.

According to the old lady, Mrs Montague was a spinster and a bit eccentric: she always wore a fur coat – even in the hottest weather – and a black wide-brimmed felt hat featuring a long blue feather. She was also a charity worker, and it was through her charity work that the old lady met her first husband, Jimmy's father; but that – the old lady's meeting with her first husband – came after Aunt Dolly's marriage to Uncle Henry.

Aunt Dolly married at the age of 26 and she and Uncle Henry went to live with Uncle Henry's parents. They could, had they wanted to, have lived with Mrs Montague, but Aunt Dolly couldn't get away from Mrs Montague quick enough. This was because of Mrs Montague's name-calling. Mrs Montague, the old lady told me, used to refer to Aunt Dolly as Moaning Minnie or Misery Guts. "What's wrong with Moaning Minnie today?" she would ask, or "Look out, here comes Misery Guts". Once, when Mrs Montague said, "Look out, here comes Misery Guts", Aunt Dolly lost her temper. She snatched Mrs Montague's hat off the hat-stand, threw it on the floor and jumped on it, which caused Mrs Montague to slap Aunt Dolly's face. Aunt Dolly's answer to that was to call Mrs Montague a fat cow (apparently, Mrs Montague was pretty fat).

The charity organisation Mrs Montague was involved with provided aid for the world's starving, and each Sunday five or six of its members, Mrs Montague included, would gather in the front room of Mrs Montague's house and discuss fund-raising, say a few prayers, etcetera. At one of these gatherings was a handsome young black guy named Joshua – Joshua Murphy.

"He was so handsome," the old lady told me, "every time I looked at him my heart stopped."

A year later, a year after Joshua first stopped the old lady's heart, they were married. And six months after that, Jimmy was born. Then, as they say, tragedy struck: a few days after the birth of Jimmy, Joshua contracted meningitis. He died soon afterwards. As did Mrs Montague, Mrs Montague dying of a brain haemorrhage.

I guess the old lady must've been something of a sex fiend, because no sooner was Joshua dead than she was involved with my father, or rather my father-to-be. She'd picked him up in the street. Literally. He'd tripped and fallen, and the old lady helped him to his feet. In no time at all – a matter of weeks – they were living together. They lived together for seven months, then tied the knot. Twenty-four hours after tying the knot the old lady was on her way to hospital ... for the birth of her second son: me. (I was a premature baby, conceived, like Jimmy, outside of what the church calls wedlock.)

I once asked the old lady who – whom – she had loved the most, Jimmy's father or mine. "I adored them both," she said. Which was a pretty good answer.

My father died when I was a month old – of leukaemia. He was 25. Jimmy's father died at the age of 28. Mrs Montague died at the age of 67 and left her house and its debts to the old lady. The old lady still has Mrs Montague's hat with the feather in it. She wouldn't part with it for the world, she says. My father's name was John. Even though I didn't know him, I miss him a lot.

CHAPTER 23

Now, I always thought that if ever the old lady tied the knot again, she'd tie it with a William Hurt or a Michael Johnson, someone with a lot going for him, career-wise as well as appearance-wise (remember, the old lady is still very high in the looks league: she could have any guy she wanted), so I'm a little surprised that her intended is a dental mechanic who looks like Woody Allen. Don't get me wrong: Dave Melford is an extremely nice person. Anyone who goes around fixing old people's teeth free of charge, as Dave does, *has* to be nice. That's how the old lady got to know him – through his fixing of old people's teeth. One day he called at The Willows and he and the old lady got talking – over a set of dentures. That was six months ago. They've been seeing each other, on and off, ever since. Not long after their first meeting, the old lady invited Dave to the house – to meet, as she put it, "my two handsome sons."

It went OK, the meeting. Dave was really good company. Not loud or smart-alecky or anything. I liked him a lot. We got on really well together. I told him he looked like one of my all-time favourite people – Woody Allen – and he said he knew he did; he'd had that said to him before. His friends at work called him Woody and kids came up to him on the street and asked, "How's Mia?" On a train once, a woman looked at him and started laughing. She couldn't stop, he said. He'd never, he said, felt so embarrassed.

He blushed telling me that.

Who needs William Hurt?

According to the old lady, Dave is 45 and's never been married. His parents are dead, so he lives alone. He lives not too far from where *we* live, in a block of council flats; a really shitty, disgusting place, running alive with cockroaches. It also has a lot of asbestos, and this, if you'll excuse the pun, bugs the tenants more than the cockroaches do. The tenants keep asking the council to replace it with a non-dangerous material, but the council says no, it would like to, but it doesn't have the money. Why it doesn't have the money is because the Government has rate-capped it for overspending. We've got what the Tory rags call a loony-left council. As far as the Tory rags are concerned, any council that does something for minority groups has to be made up of loony leftists. Our council, until it was rate-capped, was always doing things for pensioners and underprivileged kids – throwing parties for them and taking them on trips to the coast and stuff. It also did a lot for one-parent families and battered wives: a really caring sort of council. It once planned to hold a Gay Week so that a friendship could be – what was the word? – forged – so that a friendship could be forged between the community's straights and non-straights (there was a lot of queer-bashing going on at the time), but one of the red-tops got to hear about it and did a knocking piece, the headline for which was *Loonies' Meet-The-Poofters Plan*. This put the cat among the pigeons, so to speak, and following a big row in the council chamber the Gay Week was called off.

Loonies' Meet-The-Poofters Plan, I ask you.

The old lady, when she heard what the red-top had done, threw a mental. "That bloody paper," she said. "What kind of people work for it?"

Anyway, Dave: As I said, he's a really nice guy, and when the old lady announces she's gonna marry him, I say, "Hey, that's great!" and mean it. The old lady *needs* someone. Okay, she's got Jimmy and me, but she needs someone who can give her what *we* can't, if you catch my drift. I only hope Dave is up to it. He doesn't look as if he is, but you never can tell. One thing's certain, he's not the type to hand the old lady a bad time – unlike the creep she got mixed up with last year. Why she allowed herself to get mixed up with this creep is something I'll never understand. As soon as I saw him I thought, "Trouble." And he was. In the end I had to take drastic action to get rid of him. Here's the story: One day I answered a knock on the door and found myself looking at a tall bony-faced guy with dark, greased-back hair and sideburns down to his jawbone. He was wearing a white satin shirt and tie and a powder-blue jacket that reached his knees. His trousers were black drainpipes and his shoes navy suede with inch-thick crepe soles. My first thought after thinking, "Trouble" was, "Where's his guitar?"

He asked to see the old lady, and when I told her she wasn't in, he said, "Tell her Steve called."

"Steve who?" I asked.

"*She'll* know," he said.

"Steve Sheelno. – Okay," I said. The reason I gave such a smartarse reply is I didn't like his tone. It was sort of hostile. Also, I didn't like hearing the old lady referred to as "she". I still don't. It gets my goat, as the expression goes.

Smartarse, I could see the guy was thinking, and for a second I thought he was gonna punch me out. Instead, he turned his back on me and ran down the steps.

"Oh, no!" the old lady said when I told her who'd called. Then it all came out. The guy was pestering her. She'd dated him a couple of times (I couldn't believe this; I thought she had taste), dumped him, and now he was pestering her, waiting for her outside the old people's home. That kind of thing. I somehow got the impression he'd threatened her.

The next day he was back, and this time I told him to piss off. "Piss off, Elvis," I said, "my mother doesn't wanna see you", and then quick as lightning slammed the door in his face.

He was back the next day. And the next. We couldn't get rid of him. We called the police, but they didn't do shit (what else is new?).

OK, I thought, if the police won't do anything, *I* will; I went to see a guy I know, who owed me. This guy is a very tough article, and looks it. Very tall – around six four – with wall-to-wall shoulders and a pockmarked face you better not stare at. Jack Fields is his name, though he's known locally as Knuckles, Knucks to his pals. Knucks is never without two small blocks of wood which he carries in his jacket side pockets and which he uses as grips when he punches someone out. You see Knucks reach into his jacket pockets you know somebody's gonna get seriously hurt. "Timber!" the guys yell when they see Knucks reach into his pockets.

Knucks owed me because I'd fixed him up with Rosina Collins, a really nice-looking girl whose father's a tic-tac man at the dog tracks. Rosina is not too bright in the head.

Anyway, I told Knucks about Elvis and he said to leave it with him. He'd handle it, he said.

The following day: bang, bang, bang on the door. Elvis.

I peeked out the window and saw Knucks standing across the street.

Bang, bang, bang. The guy wouldn't let up; he was murdering the door.

I saw Knucks' hands go into his pockets, and a voice in my head yelled "Timber!" Then Knucks made his move.

You know how some people when they walk, bounce? Well, that's how Knucks walks – as if he's really happy about something. He bounced over to the house, and a few seconds later the banging stopped and a *new* sound took over – the sound of someone going through a meat grinder.

After that, Elvis was history.

Anyway, Dave and the old lady: I'm really happy for them.

* * *

The rest of the week is taken up with more sightseeing: St Paul's, St James's Park, The Planetarium, The Natural History Museum, London Zoo, Keats's house (Jimmy's nuts about Keats), Kew Gardens, The Tate Gallery .... We crowd it in.

CHAPTER 24

According to the article in the *Standard*, one of London's "growth areas" for teenage prostitution is Leicester Square, but looking to my left and right as I exit the station I can see only middle-agers and oldies. Not a teenager in sight. It's 3p.m., Sunday and really hot. We're having this freak weather – something to do with the disappearance of the ozone layer over the North Pole. According to the radio, it's hotter in London than it is in Madrid; people are passing out on the streets. All around me now are people with clammy-looking faces and sweat patches under their arms. Me, I'm cool – *cool* cool – for the simple reason I'm wearing a cut-off sleeveless T – this to show my biceps and my cute as shit, send-you-over-the-edge stomach. I'd like you to see my stomach. Firm – wow! – and flat as a knife; terrifically neat belly button (Mrs Fisher once licked strawberry yogurt from it). Stencilled across the T's front and back are the words – get this – WHO WANTS SOME YA -YA? It's my most daring piece of clothing. Very sexy. A real jeans creamer, as they say.

My intention at this moment is to find a rent-boy and have him put me in the picture; like, fill me in on what it is I have to do to score with the johns. Do I walk up and down waving my arse, or what? I need to know. There are other things I need to know, but I'll get to those later.

So – where do I find a rent-boy? It ought to be easy: the *Standard* mentioned a greasy spoon where they congregate; but I've forgotten the name of it. Which means I'll have to rely on instinct.

* * *

Instinct takes me to an amusement arcade that has Leisuredrome spelt out in coloured lights above the entrance.

There must be two hundred slots in the place and most of them are being played; the noise is intense. There's a smell in the air that I can't identify. Whatever it is, it doesn't make me wanna take a deep breath and go *Aaaah ...*

I find myself a *Lucky 7* and feed it a thick one.

There are slots on either side of me. The one on my immediate left is being played by a kid of about thirteen wearing a red school cap and blazer, and the one on my immediate right by a guy who's about my age – possibly a little younger – wearing a greasy-looking black shirt with the sleeves rolled up, red and black sweatsuit pants, and white, dirt-ingrained trainers. He has reddish-brown, sticky-looking hair and a lot of zits.

I play my slot a few times, then say to the zits guy, "How you doin' there?"

Not looking at me, concentrating on his game, he says, "Not so good." His voice has a slightly pissed-off note.

"You play these things much?"

"Every day." He presses his Hold button.

"What, here at the Leisuredrome?"

"Yeah." He hits his Start button.

"You must know a lot of what goes on around here then?"

Now he takes his first look at me, his eyes going to my T and staying there for a few seconds. His eyes have a washed-out look and one of his zits has a yellow head to it. His face is heart-shaped and snub-nosed. Without the zits it'd be a pretty nice face.

I lay a smile like sparkling water on him (I know my smiles because I practise them in a mirror at home) and say, "Is it OK if I ask you a personal question?"

This gets me a shrug. Mr Talkative he's not.

Hoping I won't embarrass him, I ask, "Are you trade?"

He stares at me. "What d'you mean?" He's playing the innocent, I can tell.

"Like, are you selling it?" I nod at his lower region.

He feeds money into his slot, but doesn't play it – he waits till he's said, "Why d'you wanna know?"

"I'm interested in getting some action. Like, I'm looking for, you know, someone who knows the score."

I pause.

"My name's Simon, by the way – Si. What's yours?"

Nothing.

I'm not put off by this. "How about we talk somewhere?"

More nothing. This is hard work.

I make my eyes look pleading. "C'mon – whaddaya say? I really need your help. I need to get some money together."

The guy remains silent. He's looking at me, weighing me up.

"OK," he says at last, "but first let me finish here."

"Take your time," I tell him.

Behind us somewhere, a tinny computerised voice

says, "Welcome to the B-I-I-I-G game."

The guy plays out his credits, and after he's said, "Seeyuh, Titch" to the kid in the cap and blazer and's got a, "Seeyuh, Pebbles" back, we leave.

We walk quickly, without speaking, down back-streets and alleyways, and stop when we come to a run-down greasy spoon that has Roll-In Cafe printed in sloping red capitals on buckled white fascia. It's the greasy spoon (I've remembered now) mentioned in the *Standard*.

"Fancy a coffee?" the guy asks.

I crack him a big smile. "I'm not hostile to that suggestion," I say.

* * *

The Roll-In is long and narrow and furnished with four-seater formica-topped tables that run in two lines to a counter the width of the room. The walls are half tiled in white, and, except for a tin Bovril sign, bare. The lighting is white strip. Three of the tables are occupied by guys whose ages, I'd say, range from seventeen to twenty-three – the Roll-In's only customers. My eye is caught by two auburn-haired guys in flower-patterned shirts and make-up. Apart from the make-up, there's something about their faces that strikes me as odd, but what that something is doesn't register with me. A slim guy with cropped ginger hair and wearing camouflage fatigues is holding a mobilephone to his ear. As we pass, a couple of guys in T's look up and say, "Hi, Pebbles", and a voice says, "Check out the top."

At the counter we order coffee from a sweaty-looking

woman with long black hair, hollow cheeks, and dark-ringed eyes. Looking at her, I'm reminded of Anna Magnani, star – one of the stars – Burt Lancaster was the other – of *The Rose Tattoo*, an old movie I watched with Jimmy and the old lady on our black and white menu-sized TV last summer. (TV is not something I'm big on: all those crappy soaps and sitcoms: *Neighbours*, etc. Total shit.)

Our coffee comes up, and as I pay for it (with the last of my money – a £5 note I've dug from my jeans) I hear someone behind me say, "Anyone for ya-ya?"

I turn – not with any bad feelings in me – to find out who the joker is, and see one of the made-up guys staring at me and smiling.

I smile back. "You've had *enough* ya-ya for one day, I bet," I say, and he and the guys he's with laugh, which gives me a good feeling inside.

I collect and trouser my change, and after Pebbles has taken a heaped spoonful of sugar from a white china bowl on the counter and stirred it into his coffee, I go with him to a table near the door.

We sit facing each other.

The coffee's not bad, a little sour but a lot better than Toni the Greek's. Pebbles doesn't touch his; he fixes me with his washed-out eyes and says, "So what is it you wanna know?"

I try to avoid looking at his zits and say, "How I go about things. Like, where do I hang out? What do I do to pull the johns? Where do I take a john once I've pulled him? How much do I charge? That kind of thing." (The 'other things' I mentioned.)

"Well," Pebbles says, "before you do *anything*, you've gotta get the OK from the General." He cuts a look over

156

my shoulder. "He's the guy behind you in the fatigues. Don't look now." He pauses. "The General's in charge of things around here. If he likes the look of you, you're in." He takes a sip of coffee. "The General's OK. There shouldn't be any problems. You pay him what he asks, and you'll be okay."

This last bit doesn't strike a beautiful chord in my head. "I pay him what he asks?"

"The General takes a slice of everybody's earnings. Normally it's twenty per cent. With you it could be he'll want twenty-five. If you work one of the *top* places, he'll want twenty-five."

I shrug. Twenty-five per cent: I'm comfortable with that. "Tell me about the *top* places."

"Clubs ... Hotel-bars ... Places like that."

A thrill of excitement goes through me when he says this. Clubs, hotel-bars ... I've never been in a club or hotel-bar in my life.

"So what do I do, have a word with him?"

"Wait here," Pebbles says. He gets up and goes to the table where the guy in camouflage is sitting – the General's table. 'This is serious shit, Sixsmith,' I tell myself.

A couple of minutes go by, then Pebbles returns looking a little flushed, a little excited. "Be here at eight," he says. "The General will see you then." He sits down again, and I look him in the eyes and say, "Hey, thanks a lot. I really appreciate what you've done."

"Forget it," Pebbles says. He seems embarrassed. He sips his coffee, looking at me over the rim. I get the feeling he wants to talk, so I say, "Tell me about yourself."

He's sixteen, he tells me, and before coming to London he lived with his mother and two younger brothers on a council estate in Hastings. His mother has a drink problem and was always beating up on him. She once threw him down the stairs of their house, breaking his arm. Another time she split his head with a bottle. He came to London to get away from her. His father's doing time for drug-dealing.

He arrived in London eight months ago. He was broke, so he slept rough – in doorways and on benches in railway stations. During the day he walked the streets looking for work. Soon he was begging. He'd sit on a pavement, holding a piece of cardboard with *Please Help Me* written on it. Not many people did.

One day he was approached by two guys in track suits. They were about thirty. One of them asked him if he wanted a job. The other gave him coffee from a flask. They seemed well-educated. They took him to a house in Battersea and raped him.

A few weeks later he was approached by a guy in army fatigues – the General.

"He was really good to me," Pebbles says. "He bought me a meal, and afterwards, after I'd agreed his terms, gave me money and found me a pad in Notting Hill."

The terms were that he joined the General's army, worked the arcades, and paid the General twenty per cent of everything he made. In return he was promised protection from other operators and sick pay should he become ill. (What, with AIDS? I wonder.)

"So how's business?" I ask.

"Not so hot," Pebbles says. "Things have gone quiet

all of a sudden. Up until recently I was clearing a hundred, a hundred-and-fifty a day. Now I'm lucky if I clear sixty."

"That bad, eh?" I say. Then, after I've swallowed some coffee, "How many guys the General have in his army?"

"Seventy," Pebbles says, "or he did have until a couple of months ago when one of the team went missing."

"Went missing?"

"We heard there're some snuff freaks cruising the area. We think he may've got caught up with them."

"Snuff as in dead?" I ask.

"Right," Pebbles says.

He says this like it's nothing.

"Where'd he trade, the guy?"

"The Leisuredrome," Pebbles says. He glances at the cheapo watch he's wearing. "Anyway, I've gotta shove. I wanna freshen up. If you want, you can use my pad till it's time for your meet with the General. Or maybe you'd rather stay here?"

"I'm with you," I say.

* * *

Pebbles' pad is one room in a wide-fronted, white painted terraced house a few minutes walk from Notting Hill Station. There are, so Pebbles has told me, three other people living in the house, but Pebbles never sees them. The owner doesn't live there and the only time Pebbles sees him is once a month when he calls for the rent.

The room is OK. Large. Very clean. Very neat. A single bed, a small dark table, a waist-high glass-fronted bookcase (desolate-looking on account of it doesn't have any books in it), a chest of drawers, an armchair done in fake tapestry, two straight-backed chairs, and a heavy-duty wardrobe. The carpet is seaweed-green and there's an apple-green bedside rug. On the chest of drawers are a cheap-looking record player and a stack of LPs in their sleeves. The walls are papered oatmeal and hung with a pink oval mirror, a group of fox-hunting pictures, a china dog's face, and, out-of-keeping with this stuff, a chromium-framed poster of Laurel and Hardy – Hardy looking at Laurel like he's just dropped one.

"Sit down," Pebbles says. "Relax." There's a light in his eyes that wasn't there before; his voice is different too – less flat-sounding. He seems happy all of a sudden. I get the feeling he's glad to have company.

To please him, I say, "Nice pad. Really nice." I sit in the armchair, looking around. "Cosy."

"*I* like it," Pebbles says. He goes to the chest of drawers, opens a drawer and takes out a hand towel and a washbag. "I won't be a minute," he says, and makes to leave.

I catch him at the door and say, "I've been meaning to ask: what's with this Pebbles stuff?"

Pebbles looks at the floor, then up again. "It's a name the guys gave me. On account of my pimples." He pauses. "Pebbles – you know, like in pebble-dash."

I sense the pain he feels, and, after I've told myself I should have my mouth sewn up, say, "What're you called when you're not Pebbles?"

"Alan," Pebbles says.

"Okay," I say, "I'll call you Alan. Al."

Pebbles' eyes get a worried look. "I'd rather you didn't," he says. "Not in front of the guys, anyway. They'd rag shit out of me."

"Whatever you say," I say, then, in a caring voice, "You know, there's stuff you can get – cream and stuff – that clears up zits in no time."

Pebbles gives a hopeless kind of smile and leaves the room.

While he's away I take a look at his records and see names like George Michael and Jason Donovan. The Pet Shop Boys. Names like that. Kids' stuff, really.

I return to the armchair and sit down again. I can't get over how neat the room is. It's as if no one ever entered it. It's the room of someone who's lived in a shit-hole.

Pebbles is back in five minutes, dabbing his face with the towel, his hair wet-combed. He dabs his face very carefully and when it's dry folds the towel into a precise square and places it on the bed, his washbag on top. His zits look very red, angry. One – a big one on his chin – must be troubling him, because he's touching it, brushing it with his finger.

"You'll make it worse," I say.

Pebbles stares at me. "What?" he says. Then, "Oh … yeah," and drops his hand.

He goes to the chest of drawers, reaches into the drawer that'd held his washbag and towel, and takes out a mustard-coloured T. I sit still in the armchair trying to think of something to say. Finally I say, "Would you mind if I ask what tricks you turn?"

Without embarrassment, Pebbles says, "Hand and

blow jobs mainly. Some anal." He goes to the bed, lays the T on it, and takes off the shirt he's wearing. He lays the shirt on the bed, picks up the T and pulls it on, tucking it into his sweatsuit pants. He tucks it in any-old-how – the way a kid would.

"What are your asking prices?" I ask.

Pebbles sits on the bed. "Blow jobs ten, hand jobs five, anal twenty."

This seems a little bargain-basement, so I say, "Aren't you under selling yourself?"

Pebbles smoothes the surface of the bed with his hand, and not looking at me, looking at the bed, says, "I'm *rough* trade." He tries to sound cool saying this, but doesn't quite swing it.

"You'll be asking a lot more," he adds.

I prick up my ears at this. "I will? How much?"

"Depends on how the General scores you. The General marks up the prices."

For an instant I see myself with a price-tag round my neck. "The General trick?" I ask.

"He did once, not any more."

After a short silence, I say, "How about the johns – they ever give you a bad time?"

"Sometimes," Pebbles says. "Usually, though, you can spot a bad john a mile off. Thirty to forty. Gold chains. Had a drink. A lot of mouth." A picture of Haynes comes into my head and I say, "I know the type. How about you – you had any bad times?"

"A few, not many. I had a really bad one once."

"Yeah?"

"Yeah. A guy drove me to a car park and after I'd given him what he wanted – like a blow-job – he beat me up."

"Jesus. Why'd he do that?"

"I don't know."

He looks away at nothing for a second.

"The General reckons the guy had some kind of hang-up – like, he hated himself for what he had me do to him and took his hate out on me." He lowers his voice saying, "I finished up in hospital with a fractured jaw and a detached retina." In a brighter voice, he says, "I got sick pay, though."

I don't say anything – not even *Big fucking deal*: I'm picturing poor Pebbles having the daylights knocked out of him by some guy who's fucked up in the head about sex.

There's a five-second silence, then Pebbles says, "Look, I've got to split", and gets to his feet; and thinking that he may've changed his mind about my having the use of his pad, I get to mine.

"It's okay," Pebbles says, "*you* don't have to go. But when you do, make sure the door is shut. The catch doesn't work unless you pull it hard."

"Okay," I say. "Thanks. I'll hook up with you later, maybe."

Pebbles says, "I'll be in the Roll-In about eight-thirty."

He goes to the door and opens it.

"I'm always in the Roll-In four-thirty to five, eight-thirty to nine. It's where some of the guys meet up. We meet up there every day at those times."

"I'll be there," I tell him.

He makes a try at a smile. "Seeyuh," he says.

* * *

Alone, I twiddle my thumbs for a while, then get to

thinking about Pebbles. I see him sitting in this room listening to his George Michael records – volume on low so as not to disturb the other residents – and staring at the china dog's face on the wall, maybe not seeing the dog's face but the face of one of the ugly johns he's blown that day, or his old lady's after she's had a skinful. And it occurs to me: for a lot of people, life is a pile of shit.

* * *

I leave Pebbles' pad at around seven, have a beer, and get to the Roll-In dead on eight.

The General is at his table, drinking something from a cup. With him are two guys – a wide-shouldered black guy, and a guy who looks as if he's been tripping on quarter-pounders most of his life. I approach them, and when I get up close, the General, who's had his eyes on me ever since I came through the door, says, "You're Simon – right? He has an oval face, a small turned-up nose, a curly mouth, and very green eyes. Good-looking in a minor way. He's in camouflage still.

"Right," I answer.

"Pebbles told me about you. Take a pew."

I pull out the chair that's next to the fat guy and sit down. The air is hot, with smoke hanging in it, and there's the smell of bacon being fried. From a turned-down radio comes country-and-western music. (Country-and-western music is not something that makes the blood run fast in my veins.) The General digs out a cigarette from a pack on the table, sticks it in his mouth, flips the top of a brass Zippo, lights up, and

164

when he's taken a deep drag and blown out smoke, looks into my face. He looks into it for a long time. Then, just when I'm beginning to feel uncomfortable, just when I'm beginning to think, 'I don't like this', he starts making introductions.

I've cracked it. I'm in.

The black guy is Stick, and the fat guy Tits. I can see how Tits got his name, but 'Stick' puzzles me. Tits is baby-faced – button nose and mouth – and's wearing a white T you could billet a troop of scouts in. Stick has heavy lips, a broad but not ugly nose, beautiful dark brown eyes like a cow's, and strong cheekbones. He's wearing a pale green string top (string tops are definitely in) and a white tennis cap set square on his head. Around his neck is a thin – so thin you can hardly see it – gold chain. He's very big, but not in the way Tits is. This guy is all muscle and sinew. I put his age at eighteen. The General, I'd say, is about twenty-eight. Tits is about Stick's age, maybe a little older.

"Like something to drink?" the General asks.

"No thanks," I say, "I've just had a beer."

The General places a hand on Stick's shoulder, and looking first at Tits then at Stick, says, "If you don't mind, fellas, I'd like a private word with Simon", and straightaway they get to their feet and move away. I follow them with my eyes and notice that Stick is wearing white jeans hacked off at mid thigh. Tits's leg gear is a pair of shellsuit pants – in which a *second* troop of scouts could be billeted.

"Well, Simon," the General says – he clears his throat – "Pebbles tells me you're looking for work."

I make my eyes look bright. "Right," I say.

"How old are you?"

"Seventeen."

"You look older."

I give a nice smile. "It's the frantic life I lead."

The General lets this go and says, "When can you start?"

I shrug. "Whenever you want me to."

"How about Tuesday?"

"Fine."

"Good." A pause. "Did Pebbles mention anything about how we operate?"

"He told me a few things. Nothing specific."

Nothing specific. Cool.

"Okay, well here's the deal: You will work six days a week, eleven hours a day, and I will take twenty-five per cent of everything you make."

Twenty-five per cent! I think. Brilliant. He wants me for the Premier League. I see myself in some dark nightclub, sipping champagne.

"If you want to work seven days a week, you can. Most of the guys work six. If you work seven, the take from the extra day is all yours. I don't take a cut from it. OK?"

I nod. He has a tiny scar on the bridge of his nose, I notice.

"You will start work at one and finish at midnight. That's if nothing comes up."

"What could – come up?"

"An all-night stand. If a trick wants an all-night stand, there will be no saying, 'Sorry, my shift ends at twelve'; I'll expect you to trick. This is not the Civil Service."

I smile at this.

"What you get in return for the twenty-five per cent you hand me is protection and clients: I will do my best to see that no harm comes to you, and provide you with well-heeled clients. Also, I will make sure no other trick moves in on your territory."

He leans forward, taps ash into a tin ashtray.

"Now – tariff. The tariff is as follows: hand-jobs thirty, blow-jobs fifty, anal one hundred. Should your trick happen to be an Arab or a Japanese, these prices will increase by one hundred per cent."

He glances at the tip of his cigarette.

"All-night stands are three hundred, twos-on-one -" He breaks off. "You know what a two-on-one is?"

I have an idea, but shake my head no.

"A two-on-one is when two males, or a male and a female, trick with a third party – *you*, for instance. The charge for a two-on-one – short time – is two hundred and fifty. An all-nighter will cost a grand."

I wonder how I'm gonna remember all this; I wish I had a pen and paper with me so I could take notes.

"At this point," the General goes on, "I want to make one thing clear: Because of the AIDS virus, you will not be expected to engage in *anal* sex. If a trick offers you two hundred, *five* hundred for anal sex and you say no, I will understand. Most of the guys in my charge *do* engage in anal sex – it's where the money is – but never without protection. They always carry skins." He looks at me hard. "Never have anal sex without protection. That's very important."

He continues looking at me hard, so I say, "You're reaching me."

"A lot of tricks," he continues, "carry their own skins, but under no circumstances will you allow them to use them on you."

Before I can ask, "Why's that?" the General says, "There are guys with AIDS who want *everyone* to have it, so what they do, they turn their skins into tea-strainers."

I do what you do when you can't believe what you've heard: I shake my head.

"Now – places of work. We have four main fields of operation: amusement arcades, main-line stations, hotels, and clubs. You will work hotels – specifically The Connaught Hotel and The Massingham Hotel, both of which have a residents' bar and a *non*-residents' bar. The non-residents' bars you will work in the afternoons and the residents' bars in the evenings."

He takes a pull on his cigarette.

"At start of work you will approach the desk and give your name to the person manning it. In return, you'll be given a key to a dressing-room. The dressing-room is where you will trick." He gives me a studying look. "Is everything clear so far?"

"Crystal."

"Dress. Jeans and – " He looks at my T. " – and T-shirts are out. You will wear a loosely-woven Harris Tweed jacket – light blue in colour – grey strides, ox-blood loungers, navy crew-neck, and a white shirt, the collar of the shirt to be worn outside – *outside* – the neck of the crew-neck. Make you look boyish."

He gives me a long look.

"You'll need money." He dips into a pocket of his fatigues, pulls out a giant roll of notes, counts off ten twenties and hands them to me.

Two hundred pounds. Just like that.

"The money will be repaid when you start earning." His cigarette has gone out, so he makes with the Zippo again. "I'd like you to start work on Tuesday. Be here at one and I'll introduce you to a guy who'll take you along to the hotels."

"Fine," I say.

"One other thing," the General says. "If ever I find you've been wrong-dealing me, I'll cut your balls off."

"That won't happen," I say.

"I believe you," the General says. "You got a roof for the night?"

I give him a yes.

The General nods. "Should you want to get in touch with me – night or day – call me on this number." He dips into another pocket of his fatigues, pulls out a card, and hands it to me. On the card, written in ink, is a number with a lot of eights in it. "Don't lose it," he says. He runs a hand over his cropped hair. "Now, do you have any questions?" It's almost an order.

"Yes," I say, "how do I go about pulling the johns?"

The General sits back in his chair. "Good question," he says. Then, after a pause, "What you *don't* do is walk up to a john in a bar and say, 'Hi, looking for a good time?' Do that and somebody is liable to make trouble – not a member of staff – the staff, the ones that count, have been taken care of – a customer or guest. These are respectable hotels you'll be working in. Remember that."

"I will," I say.

"OK, here's the routine: After you've collected your key from the desk – let's say it's early afternoon and you're working the Massingham – after you've collected your key from the desk you go to the non-residents' bar and order a drink. While you're waiting for your drink to arrive, take a look around you, see if there're any unaccompanied johns present. If there are, choose one you sense might want to trick; you sometimes can tell a trick just by looking at his face."

This surprises me. "You can?"

"Take my word for it," the General says quickly. Not stopping, he says, "When your drink comes up, take it to a table that's directly in the john's line of vision, and sit facing him. It's important he gets an unrestricted view of your groin area. If necessary, move your chair so that he does. Sit with your legs unfolded and a hand resting on your thigh – very casual, very butch. Remember, you're not a hip queer."

I'm not *any* kind of queer, I feel like saying, but don't; it's not important.

"From time to time turn your head, let the john see your profile. Run a hand through your hair. Let him see what nice hands you've got. After five or six minutes, start throwing looks at him. Let him see you're interested in him. If he's interested in *you*, he'll throw looks back. If he's not, he'll bury his head in a newspaper, or sit facing another way. We'll make it that he *is* interested in you: he throws looks back. You've got eye contact."

He goes on, "Let this eye contact continue for a while, then give him some body work. Run a hand over your thigh a few times, then move it to your crotch and start finger-stroking your balls. Nothing gross; nothing the whole bar can see; you're not looking for community impact. Let the whole bar see what you're doing, and you'll scare the john off. The balls routine is for the john's eyes only."

This last bit, the balls bit, has flipped my mind back to the come-on I gave Haynes, and I think, You're talking to a professional here, General.

"You keep the balls-play up for ten or fifteen minutes, then get to your feet, take your jacket off, and hang it on the back of your chair. Now the john can see your neat little arse."

The General fixes me with a look.

"I take it it *is* neat?" he says.

"Double neat," I say. "Like two hard boiled eggs."

The General gives me a sweet and natural-looking smile.

"Okay," he says, "you show the john your neat little arse, and, just to make sure he doesn't forget it, you go to the bar and order another drink, or, if you don't want another drink, cigarettes – anything." I see myself ordering a large vodka and tonic. Plenty of ice.

"While you're waiting for your drink, flex and unflex your arse muscles. Give the john plenty of arse. Place a foot on the bar rail and lean your elbows on the counter. This will give you a tight trouser fit. Also, while you're at the bar, lay a smile on the john."

The General takes a big pull on his cigarette. Through smoke he says, "Back at your table give the john more balls-play. Let him see some tongue. Keep exchanging looks between him and your crotch like you're saying, 'Want some?' You're softening, or rather you're hardening him up for your next move. You'll know when to make it when you see him shift in his chair – like, when you see him unfold or spread his legs. Him shifting in his chair is a sign he's getting horny; his Johnson is thickening and needs more space.

"When you see him shift in his chair, here's what you do: you get to your feet and make a pretence of looking for the toilet. I say 'make a pretence' because you know where it is – it's out the bar, along the corridor. The make-believe is for the john's benefit: you want him to know you're going to the toilet."

The General sits up straight and uses his index finger to scratch the bridge of his nose.

"So where is it, the toilet? You can't see it. You ask at the bar and get directions. The barman will give you directions – with arm movements: he has my instructions. Through the door and turn right. Plenty of arm movements. The john, unless he's a complete idiot, has to know exactly what it is you want. You go to the door and as you pull it open, you throw the john a look. You've invited him to follow."

After a little pause, the General says, "Don't expect him to follow straight off; he'll take his time. It's what's known as bar-room behaviourism – a guy doesn't follow another guy into the toilet: people might get the wrong idea. Be prepared for a four or five minute wait. While you're waiting, play with yourself. Give the john something to get excited about when he comes through the door. Most guys your age go around with a permanent hard-on, so I doubt self-arousal'll be necessary."

"I have to keep it strapped down," I say.

The General likes that: his eyes twinkle. "OK, you're in the toilet, standing at the bowl with your dick out, and eventually the john comes in and stands – what? –

two, three bowls away. What you do now is you start sliding looks at him – first at his face, then at what he's holding. You let him get a look at what *you're* holding – a *good* look. You show it to him, in fact. Point it at him. Wave it a little. Pretty soon he'll want it in his hand. He'll reach out for it." There's a two second silence before the General continues, "When he reaches out for it, pop it back in, zip up, and tell him to meet you outside the hotel. Outside the hotel, in the entrance, is where you'll proposition him, acquaint him with your terms. He either accepts them or he doesn't. No haggling. If he accepts, take him to the dressing room, get his money, and give him what he wants. I'm having a coffee, want one?"

The General goes to the counter and returns with two coffees. When he's seated, and after he's mashed his cigarette in the tin ash-tray, he says, "One thing I forgot to mention: always get the john's money before you trick. Cash before delivery – remember that."

Oh, I'll remember that, all right.

"You bet," I say, and then, "What about cops? How do I know that the john I'm waving my dick at's not a cop plained up?"

"Forget the cops," the General says.

He looks away at nothing for a second, then says, "The cops won't bother you."

He doesn't enlarge on this and I don't ask him to. Maybe the cops, like the hotel staff, have been taken care of.

"What if someone's in the toilet?"

"No sweat – you wait until he leaves. One of the ace things about hotel toilets is they're never busy. Most hotel-users drink shorts, which means they're not taking a piss every five minutes. You'll have all the privacy you need."

After we've sipped some coffee, the General says, "Not all your tricks will be johns. There'll be janes, too." He raises his eyebrows. "You think you can handle that: tricking with a jane? Some of the guys find tricking with a jane difficult – like, they can't get an erection."

"No prob," I say.

"Good," the General says. He scratches his nose again, then says, "With janes, of course, the approach is different. There's no playing around with your balls. With janes it's all eye contact. You sit and you look. Not stare, *look*. It's okay to show some arse – in fact it's a good idea to show some arse – but no balls-play. If you feel you're getting somewhere, give the jane a smile. That's all you do. You don't go near her. She'll come to you. Janes are not as diffident as johns. They'll come and sit at your table. You take it from there. Buy the jane a drink, get talking. After a few drinks she'll be coming on strong. Janes don't fuck about. They want sex, they go for it."

These last words bring Mrs Fisher into my head. *Will you do something for me, Simon?*

"If the jane's staying at the hotel, she'll invite you to her room. Ninety per cent of the unaccompanied janes you see in the bar'll be staying at the hotel – you'll rarely find one who's not.

"When the jane hands you the invitation, that's when you let her know it's gonna cost. You do not go with her to her room and tell her there. Do that and she'll go total – she'll feel she's been made to look ridiculous."

He looks off past my shoulder for a moment, then says, "It's amazing how many janes, when you start talking money, don't take offence. In fact, most of them find it cute. They've never had to pay for it before. It's a new experience. It gives them a buzz. By paying for it they feel they can really let their hair down. You're theirs, kind of thing; they can do whatever they like with you – have things done to them they've always wanted to have done. They want an arse fuck, why not? – it's *their* money, they're gonna enjoy themselves. The johns are not like that. The johns don't enjoy themselves. A quick hand or blowjob and away. You'll never see a *smile* on a john's face."

The General lights up again and, when he's waved away a wisp of smoke, says, "You'll get most of your jane trade in the evening. The afternoons they spend having their hair done, or shopping."

"What's the, uh, tariff for janes?" I ask.

"Short time one fifty, an all-nighter five hundred."

I swallow some coffee and the General does the same.

"You said you'd be providing me with clients."

The General wipes coffee from his mouth with his fingers. "You'll receive ten to fifteen clients a week. I'll let you know when to expect one. They'll approach you in the bar and address you by name. No money will be handed over – the clients pay *me*. You'll get your cut at the end of each week. Clients are big money, so be extra nice to them – we want them to come back. Anything else you'd like to know?"

I think quick. "Yes," I say. "How did Stick get his name?"

"Short for Sweetstick. He's got a dork like a peppermill. Anything else?"

"Nothing I can think of."

"In that case I'll introduce you to some of the guys. You'll be seeing a lot of them, so you may as well know their names." He stands up. "That's another thing – you get work breaks. Yours will be from four-thirty to five, and eight-thirty to nine. You'll need them, sitting around in hotels all day. All the guys get breaks. Most of those working this turf meet up here. They're all nice guys. You'll like them."

I hadn't noticed, but the place is beginning to fill. All the chairs at four tables are occupied, and there're a couple of down-and-out-looking types sitting alone, staring into space. There's a lot of noise – most of it coming from one table.

It's to this table the General takes me. Seated at it are Pebbles, the two guys in make-up, and the kid Pebbles spoke to in the arcade – the kid in the schoolcap and blazer: Titch. Looking at the guys in make-up, I suddenly flash what it is about their faces that threw me when I first saw them: they're identical. Their names, so the General informs me, are Twin Pat and Twin Paul. Both are now wearing – get this – black Lurex ski pants, silver flip-flops and cut-off tank tops made of pink see-through plastic; their auburn hair has had green tips and streaks added to it. Both giggle like fuck when I ask, "How do I tell you apart?"

"I'm the one with the gorgeous arse," Twin Pat says, and he and his twin giggle again.

Very, very gay. Both of them.

Titch surprises me. Like, when I first saw him I

thought he was about thirteen, but seeing him now – maybe it's because I'm seeing the whole of his face and not just his profile – he looks a lot older – like nine or ten years older. And he's smoking a cheroot. He's a midget. Gay twins and a midget .... This is a fucking circus I've joined, I can't help thinking.

We move to the next table.

Seated at it are Stick and Tits (Tits snarfing down a three-tier bacon sandwich with fat dripping from it) and two youngish, average-looking guys in white T's that have JACKIE WILSON LIVES stencilled on them in black (Jackie Wilson's *Higher and Higher* is one of my all-time favourite numbers.)

The General introduces me to the Wilson fans, and after they've nodded hello, Stick says, "Glad to have you on the team, man," and I straightaway get a good feeling about us. I straightaway feel that we're, like, destined to be close.

The guys at the next two tables are repeats, practically, of the Wilson duo: average-looking, youngish, and wearing T's. When I'm introduced to them, each gives me a nice smile and says, Hi. A really nice bunch of guys, they seem. "Where you from, Simon?" one of them asks, and no sooner am I asked this than the door bangs open and in breezes a young aristocratic-looking dude wearing a white suit and a salmon-coloured silk cravat. He has wheat-coloured hair parted on the side and a face that's pure Hollywood – an incredibly good-looking guy.

"General!" he bawls. "The client you sent me was a shit-chute, and as you know, as I've told you on numerous occasions, I can no longer accommodate shit-chutes, certainly not haemorrhoidal shit-chutes, as this one was. Why did you send him to me – WHY?" His voice is Prince Charles … straight from the top drawer.

I half expect the General to give an order: "Place this man under arrest" (I mean, generals are not spoken to like that), but he doesn't, he's smiling. "Calm down, College," he says, "it was a mistake." Then, "Let me buy you a coffee."

"Fuck coffee," College says, "I want to know why you sent me a shit-chute."

Here Twin Pat calls out, "If you can't lick 'em, College darling, join 'em", and everyone breaks up laughing.

"Come on, have a coffee," the General says. He takes hold of College's arm and, with a jerk of the head that tells me I should follow, leads him away.

The General gets coffees, and when we're seated, says to College, "This is Simon. Simon will be working the hotels with you."

College, who up until now hasn't looked at me, says, "Then you have my deepest sympathy, Simon,"and gives me the most terrific smile. This dazzling, movie-star smile.

I smile back at him and watch him as he fixes a cigarette into an ebony holder. I'm sort of in awe of him, of his looks and accent and everything.

"Actually," he goes on, "it's rather fun, or it would be if the General here," he turns to face the General, "wouldn't keep sending me shit-chutes. It really (it comes our rarely) is very naughty of you, General. This is the second shit-chute you've sent me in three weeks."

He goes on, "I wouldn't have minded so much, but I had the most wonderful fuck lined up – a *Japanese* fuck,

General. Double dosh and all that." He leans forward and looks into the General's eyes. In a teasing voice and raising his eyebrows, he says, "*Double dosh*, General? Yes?"

The General grins but doesn't say anything.

College sits up straight again. "Instead I find myself with this monstrous old cunt with haemorrhoids." He lights his cigarette with a lighter that didn't come from Ratner's, blows out a thin stream of smoke, and says, "This rarely (really) has to be my last shit-chute, General. I simply cannot cope with them any more." He turns to me and, as if he's known me for years, says, "They're quite ruining my taste buds, Simon. Everything I eat tastes vaguely excremental. Madeira cake... everything."

I laugh out loud at this.

Through a big smile, the General says, "It was a mistake, College. He should have gone to Savoy Harry. I must've got the names mixed up. Put it down to pressure of work." He flips me a wink to let me know he's kidding, and I wonder who Savoy Harry is. I get a picture of a guy wearing a monocle and carrying a silver-topped cane.

"Did you *fuck* get the names mixed up," College says. "You knew perfectly *well* what you were doing – admit it."

Still smiling, the General says, "Okay, I admit it. It's just that Savoy Harry was fully booked and the john is a regular. I didn't want to disappoint him."

"That's all very well," College says, "but the same thing happened the week before last."

"That really *was* a mistake," the General says.

"Well," College says, "if you send me another, and I

sincerely hope you don't, please give me advance warning so that I may fortify myself with brandy. My god, haemorrhoids!"

He turns back to me and says, "Anyway, Simon, I'm overjoyed to know that you'll be working with me. It's not before time I had some assistance; my hampton's quite worn out, poor luv."

I can't help myself, I giggle. "Glad to be of help," I say.

To the General, College says, "I've never known it to be so busy, General. What's the reason d'you suppose – confidence in the Stock Market?"

I expect the General to laugh at this, but he doesn't. He says, "Beats me. The rough trade's fallen off and the hotel and club trade's picked up. It doesn't make sense."

College switches channels: "So when do you commence battle, Simon old chap?" he asks.

Simon old chap. I like that. "Tuesday," I answer.

"Splendid," College says. He swallows some coffee, gets to his feet and says to me, "Well, I *must* get back. Just popped in to let the General here know what a cad I think he is."

I give him a big smile. "Nice to've met you," I say.

"My pleasure entirely," College says, and gives a little bow, this little bow.

"I'd like you to call in on Tuesday – say one o'clock – and show Simon the ropes," the General says.

"Delighted," College says. He moves off, and when he gets to the door, calls, "Remember, General, no more shit-chutes."

"You know you love them," one of the twins calls.

"Bollocks," College calls back cheerily.

"*And* those," the twin replies; but College is gone, leaving behind him a big silence.

I lean back in my chair. "Jesus," I say, "what a character!"

The General smiles, shakes his head like he's agreeing with me, and after lighting a cigarette and drawing on it hard so that his eyes crease, acquaints me with College's form: He's the only son of one of England's richest landowners, and until the age of eighteen, when he inherited eight million pounds from his grandfather (an international banker), lived with his parents on their five thousand acre estate in Gloucestershire. His current address is a mews house in Chelsea, which he shares with his sister Poppy. Aged twenty-six, he has four convictions for speeding, two for dangerous driving and three for gross indecency, the last act of gross indecency having been committed – listen to this – in the men's toilet of the Royal Opera House during a performance of Madam Butterfly. He has a light aircraft, which he likes to fly upside down, a flame red Ferrari Testarossa, a flame red Bentley Turbo, six racehorses, and twenty white suits. His friends include actors, writers, and most of the porters at Billingsgate Fish Market, where you'll often find him drinking at six in the morning, in a pub there.

The General came across him in a pub in Hackney. His back was to a wall, and a guy, a black guy, was shouting in his face. It seemed he'd just told the guy he would love to blow him, and the guy had taken exception to this. He had earlier, so the General discovered, propositioned the guy's drinking partner, a white guy with a face like – this is the General's description – like a bowl of Ready Brek, whose reply had been to drench College with Guinness.

The end-up was, the General and College took a liking to one another and, over a drink, College, among other things, told the General he had a "hopeless passion for cocks". He made this statement, the General says, like he was talking about Walnut Whips. "I've dedicated my life to cocks and their arousal," he told the General. Naturally, when the General heard this, he invited College to join his stable, and College was practically overcome with gratitude.

All this happened 18 months ago and College has been with the General ever since.

"I've never known a guy with such a sexual appetite," the General says. "He's into sex like British Airways is into planes. He can't get enough of it. He'll try anything."

There's a silence between us, and I can tell from the General's expression he's thinking about College. I am, too – about how I can't wait to see him again.

Eventually the General says, "College is one of the nicest, most generous people you'll ever meet. The money he makes from tricking he gives to a charity – Homes for the Abandoned Elderly."

He moves his chair back and gets to his feet. "Okay, boys and girls," he calls, "it's showtime. Let me see you stretch those jeans." To me, he says, "See you on Tuesday, Simon." And, not really wanting to, I leave the Roll-In and head for home.

* * *

I arrived home two hours ago, dog tired but terrifically happy; like, I was kind of saturated with happiness. I felt I'd achieved something – not just for myself but for Jimmy too. And now, lying naked on my bed with lilac-coloured moonlight coming in the half open window and a soft breeze feathering and exciting my body, I conjure up all the people I've met this day – Stick and Pebbles, the gay twins Pat and Paul, Titch, Tits, the General, and, of course, College. And still seeing these people and thinking that life is good, I slide down into sleep.

CHAPTER 25

Finding a jacket that conformed to the General's specifications – Harris tweed, pale blue, etcetera – was more difficult than I'd imagined. I finally got lucky at Dunn's on Sutton Street. It was in a mid-summer sale, priced £55; a single vent number with pocket flaps and leather-covered, football-looking buttons. Nice buttons. The rest of the stuff – the crew-neck and stuff – I got from Denny's, a small shop on Albion Street whose owner, Denny Abrahams, once played saxophone in a dance band. Even though he's pushing eighty, Denny wears tight fitting pants, Italian silk shirts and pointed patent shoes. Whenever I see Denny a little voice in my head says, "You don't have to be young to look sharp."

The stuff I got at Denny's came to £120.90.

* * *

"Not bad," the General says. He's looking me up and down. "Turn around."

I turn around.

"Not bad," the General repeats. Apart from a bag lady with long grey hairs growing from her chin and all her buttons done up, we're the Roll-In's only customers. The radio is on and a DJ is reading a letter from one of his listeners. A guy named John has died in a road accident, and the letter writer, the dead guy's girlfriend, blames herself for his death. A few minutes before the accident she'd picked a fight with him and told him she never wanted to see him again. The guy walked off and – bam! – was hit by a car. Something like that. This is what this particular DJ does – like, he gets people to write to him about all the terrible things that've happened in their lives, then reads their letters over the air. Talk about cashing in on people's misery.

"There's change," I say. I go to put my hand in my pocket, but the General says, "Hold on to it, you'll need it for drinks."

"How'd you know I wouldn't run off with the money?" I ask.

"I had you followed," the General says. "If you hadn't put in an appearance today, I'd've been knocking on your door with the business end of a baseball bat."

There's nothing you can say to that, so I get a couple of coffees, and over them, while we wait for College to show (my scalp tingles with pleasure at the thought of seeing College again), the General, at my request, fills me in on some of his team members.

Titch is aged twenty-four and dresses the way he does to pull the paedos. To help with his schoolboy look, he carries a satchel – in which he keeps a butcher's knife. This he pulls on johns who give him trouble. One john who gave him trouble was left with a slashed throat; another with half a nose. Every year Titch takes his mother – herself a midget – to the Cannes Film Festival, where they hope to be spotted by a film director. Two years ago they were and were offered parts as baby werewolves in a horror movie. Unfortunately, the movie never got made. One of Titch's ambitions is to blow Arnold Schwarzenegger while wearing nipple clamps.

The twins Pat and Paul are heavily into drag and both have won Best Outfit prizes at the Kinky Gerlinky monthly drag queen show. Their parents are divorced, and when the twins take a break they stay with their mother, a writer of children's books. They're crazy about their mother, and she's crazy about them. At her home in Oxford she has photographs of the twins covering two walls. Aged eighteen, the twins will be travelling to Holland next year for sex-change operations. "I can't wait to be fucked from the front," Twin Paul tells everyone.

Tits is Jewish and was disowned by his parents following an incident in a public lavatory. Caught short one night, Tits's father stepped into a public lavatory – and found himself witnessing a sex scene – starring Tits and a dark-skinned guy in a turban. He (Tits's father) beat Tits up and afterwards wouldn't speak to him. Nor would Tits's mother, a member of AALP – Action Against Lax Parenting (on learning of the lavatory deal she tore up her membership card). Tits took the silence for two months, and then left home. Before leaving, he wrote his parents a note: "Dear Mum and Dad, You'll be interested to know that the guy fucking me was an Arab. I do love to be fucked by Arabs. And get this, dad: I don't charge."

Stick comes from a broken home. His father, a Jamaican, took off when Stick was twelve, leaving Stick and his three sisters with their Trinidadian mother, who kept the girls, but put Stick in an institution, where he spent the next four years being sexually abused by staff there. One of Stick's big disappointments in life is that he's not able to make it with women, his experiences at the institution having turned him into a homo – a whites-only homo (Stick's partners have to be white – the colour of his abusers). Once a week Stick visits his mother and gives her money. His all-time favourite person is Whoopi Goldberg. Stick is nineteen.

The General starts to tell me about Pebbles, but I interrupt, saying, "I know Pebbles' case. What about yours?"

The General smiles. "Inquisitive," he says.

"Just interested," I say.

The General shrugs. Then he tells me his story.

His father was a bully and a drunk and when he wasn't beating on his kids was screwing them. He started screwing the General shortly after the General's ninth birthday. "One night my bedroom door opened and the next thing I knew he was in bed with me, tearing at my pyjamas. After he'd screwed me, he said, 'You tell anyone what happened and I'll knock you all round this room.' From then on it was part of my life."

The General's two teenaged sisters were screwed every Sunday morning when they brought the old man his breakfast. On Sundays the old man had his breakfast in bed, and the sisters had to bring it to him. He'd screw one while the other watched, and then, after he'd eaten, screw the one who'd been watching.

Did his mother know what was going on?

"Yeah, but she was too scared to say anything. We all were. We lived in fear of the old man's fists."

They stopped living in fear of the old man's fists on his death, twelve years ago, from suffocation. The General and his sisters suffocated him to death. They waited for him to come home from the pub, and when he was in bed snoring his head off, smothered him with a pillow. At the time, the General was fifteen and his sisters eighteen and nineteen. All three were sent for trial accused of manslaughter, but after hearing the evidence the judge allowed them to go free.

"Not long after the case, I left home and started picking up johns," the General says, "(a) to get some money, and (b) to get my nuts off. Like Stick, I'd been sexually disorientated – I could only make it with men – until I met Julie. Julie's the woman I'm living with."

I don't say anything. I'm picturing a nine-year-old kid alone in bed in the dead of night waiting for the door to open and his beery old man – his old man for Christ's sake! – to come in and stick his scuzzy dick into him, force it into him. Imagine that happening to you. Not once – once is bad enough – but night after night.

"I'm sorry," I say finally. "If I'd had any idea ... "

"It's okay," the General says. He looks down at his coffee. "It's good to talk things out." He looks up again. "Therapeutic." He takes a pack of cigarettes from his fatigues (he's in camouflage still), lights up, and after he's blown a not-bad smoke-ring, says, "So what's your tale of woe? Trouble at home?"

"No," I say, "things are okay at home."

"Why trick, then?"

"I need the money."

That doesn't seem enough, not after what I've just heard, so I tell the General about Jimmy and the Arizona trip, concluding with, "I'd also like to get him a guide dog."

"There's a waiting list for guide dogs," the General says.

"There is?" I say, "I didn't know that." My voice sounds dead. I'm seeing that nine-year-old kid again.

"What do you intend doing after Arizona – get back into tricking?"

"I don't know. That's something I'll have to think about."

There's a little silence before the General says, "You know, once you're into tricking it's very difficult to get out of – like, it's a very easy way of making money."

"I can imagine it would be – difficult to get out of, I mean."

"What you *don't* want to do is stay with it too long. Stay with it too long and you won't want any other way of life. You'll finish up a queen: lavender hair and a poodle in your lap. Make a pile and get out." He gives me a cool stare. "How old are you, seventeen?"

I nod, and he says, "In five years, if you stay off drugs – there's a heavy drugs scene going on around here – you could have enough in your pot to start up a business, retire, even. If you go on the drugs kick you'll end up with nothing."

I look him straight in the eye. "I severely doubt I'll do that," I say, and at this instant College shows.

But not the College of yesterday. His appearance has changed. His eyes are red-rimmed and his face has a sagged, greasy look to it that makes me think of a rubber mask. His suit is no longer white, but yellow-looking. He needs a shave, and his wheat-coloured hair sticks out at one side. He sways slightly when, in his cut glass voice, he says, "Hulloa." For a second, I experience a terrific rush of disappointment.

"Well, well, well ... " the General says. He's looking

at College and smiling. "Look what the cat dragged in."
He takes a pull on his cigarette. When the smoke has
cleared, he says, "From the look of you, I'd say you
were up all night."

College gives a rueful sort of grin. "Yes," he says,
"I'm afraid I've been rather naughty. An all-night party
followed by drinks with a few of my Billingsgate
chums."

"And afterwards?"

"And afterwards back to my place for more drinks.
Very naughty."

College must've seen the disappointment in my eyes,
because he says to me, "I'm afraid I look somewhat
Hogarthian."

"If you mean you look like shit, you're right, you
do," the General says.

College sighs and says, "The price we pay for our
stolen moments of pleasure ... "

"Moments?" the General says and lays a quick wink
on me. Then he says, "I think you'd better get some sleep."

College shakes his head and says brightly, "C'est
impossible, mon General: I've a client at two." He looks
at me, and smiles. "Unless of course Simon here would
care to stand in for me. I must say, I *do* feel rather
drained." He sniffs the tips of his fingers. "What I
simply *must* do is have a shower. I have a distinct cod-
ish aroma."

I look at the General. "It's okay with me," I say.
"Standing in for College, I mean." Although I don't let
it show, I'm all nervous excitement: my first trick under
the General's command ...

"What's the sell?" the General asks.

"Penetrative," College says. He turns to me and adds, "but nothing to worry about, Simon. He's very slightly made."

The General gives me a questioning look.

"That's okay," I say. I'm surprised at how eager my voice sounds.

"Okay," the General says to College, "make the introductions, then go home and get some sleep."

College places a hand on the General's shoulder. "I'll be back on duty at five, five-thirty," he says. "You're an absolute prince, General."

The General says to me, "You got skins?"

"No," I say.

Saying this, I feel like a kid caught out.

The General digs into a leg pocket of his fatigues (What's with this camouflage? I wonder) and produces a small square-shaped pack. "Here, take these," he says.

Mates.

Mint flavoured.

* * *

Outside on the street College says, "You know, Simon, the General really is the nicest of people. A gentleman."

"He says the same about you," I say.

A look of surprise comes on College's face. "He does? How sweet." He looks me over. "By the way, you look extraordinarily smart, extraordinarily handsome, if you don't mind my saying so."

"The outfit's the General's idea," I say. I can feel my neck reddening; for some reason his words have embarrassed me. "You always wear white?"

College smiles. "It makes me look virginal," he says.

I laugh, and College says, "I think we're going to be good friends, don't you?"

Hearing him say this, something swells my chest, some special kind of happiness. "Count on it," I say.

We walk at an easy pace, College with a hand on my shoulder, and come – in no time at all, it seems to me – to a wide main street clogged with traffic, its pavements crowded with people in summer clothes – men in lightweight suits, and women in dresses of all colours: pinks ... blues ... greens ... Every colour you can think of. A big parade of colour.

At a busy intersection we wait at traffic lights, College with his hand on my shoulder still.

Across the road, facing us, gleaming in the sunlight, is a broad white building with tall, gold letters fixed to it. Massingham Hotel, the letters spell out.

* * *

The Massingham has a wide marble staircase with a golden handrail, a thick wall-to-wall moss-coloured carpet, tall glass cabinets displaying china and crystal ornaments, deep couches and armchairs, and long, low tables made from honey-coloured wood. Facing the staircase is a curved reception desk, and to one side of the desk, just inside the entrance, a restaurant. Facing the restaurant is a dimly lit bar. There are lifts with chromium doors, and a line of telephone booths. Milling around are people wearing expensive-looking clothes and jewellery, some speaking with a foreign accent. Money written all over them. Standing here and seeing all this richness, seeing College fix a cigarette into his ebony holder, I feel – even though I don't look it, even though I look like a young Hollywood star – dirt poor. More than that – I feel inferior.

But the feeling soon goes.

College lights his cigarette, and when he's inhaled and blown smoke at the ceiling, says like he owns the place, "Let's get your key, shall we?" He looks like shit but the style's still there. If you've got it, it doesn't go away. How d'you get it in the first place, though?

We go to the reception desk, and a small, thin guy with dark patches under his eyes comes up and says to College, "Good afternoon, sir."

"Good afternoon, George," College answers. "This is Mr – " College looks at me and says, "I'm most awfully sorry, Simon, but your surname seems to have escaped me. Or perhaps I wasn't given it."

"Sixsmith," I say.

"This is Mr Sixsmith, George. I believe you have a key for him."

George looks at me and says, "Good afternoon, sir. We've been expecting you."

Sir! I'm fazed.

George goes away and returns a few seconds later with a key with a circular metal disc attached to it. "Room nine, first floor," he says. "I'll let my colleagues know you're here."

"Thanks," I say.

"Thank you, George," College says.

Thank you, George ... I look forward to the day when *I'll* say that. Or would I say, 'Thanks, George'? There's a difference, you know.

As we leave the reception desk, College says, "My sister Poppy would have the most tremendous difficulty with your name, Simon."

I look at him. "Yeah?"

College says, "She lisps." He pauses. "Thimon Thixththmith." He smiles to himself, then lightly grips my arm. "Now, what say I show you the residents' bar and then we have a drink?"

"Okay," I say, and laugh. The Thixththmith has tickled me.

"What?" College asks, meaning what's funny?

"Thixththmith," I say.

Smiling, College says, "You'd like Poppy. A wonderful girl. Full of life. You must meet her."

I try to get a picture of Poppy in my head, but can't.

The residents' bar is at the far end of the foyer; a very airy-looking place done in pale yellow and greens and laid out with low Regency-style tables and Regency-style chairs. Everything that can be polished has been polished to a high shine.

College introduces me to the barman – a small Spanish-looking guy named Louis – and after he's asked him, "What time did I leave here last night?" and received the reply, "We didn't see you last night", we move to the non-residents' bar.

This is the bar facing the restaurant and, while not as elegant as the bar we've just left, is not bad. The carpet is blue with a gold coronet pattern, and the wallpaper blue with gold stripes. The tables are glass-topped and the chairs tubular steel with padded backs and seats. At the windows, which are frosted glass, hang long blue-velvet curtains, and hanging from the ceiling on heavy brass chains are brass parrot cages containing trailing ivy. The lighting comes from yellow and blue spotlights fixed to the walls and ceiling and from yellow lights sunk in the bar-counter's overhang. There are about a dozen people present, all guys, all middle-aged.

"Not exactly the Ritz," College says, "but tolerable. What will you have to drink?"

I ask for a vodka and tonic, and College says, "Good idea." To one of two barmen – a youngish, slimly-built guy with dark curly hair and a thin moustache – he says, "Michael, this is Simon, who, as the General will have told you, will be having sexual congress here. Two large vodkas and tonics and something for yourself and Terry."

I glance at the other barman (Terry?), who is small and stocky with straight red hair, and as I do, Michael reaches across the bar-counter to shake my hand. With an Irish accent he says, "Hello there, Simon."

"Hi," I say back.

"Should you find yourself without funds," College says, "Michael will allow you drinks on tick, and when boredom sets in provide you with reading material. Michael is something of a bibliomane. Is that the right word, Michael – bibliomane? Perhaps not. Bookworm, then. Michael is something of a bookworm. Personally, I find book-reading an ordeal; though I have just finished reading *In Cold Blood* and found it hugely exciting. If you haven't read it, Simon, you rarely (really) must."

All this is said very quickly, and I think, If this is College 'drained', what's he like when he's on Full?

"I'll ask the old lady to get it for me from the library," I say.

"The old lady?" College says.

"My mother," I explain.

"Oh, yes, of course," says College. "Stupid of me." After a little pause, he says, "Your old lady reads does she? *My* old lady hasn't read a book in her life. The only thing *my* old lady reads is tomorrow's weather. Ignorant as they come. I do congratulate you on having a mother who reads books." He sighs. "Yes, *In Cold Blood*. Superb."

"Right," I say. It's all I can think of to say.

"Written by an American, of course. American writers are the only writers I can read these days. Updike. Roth. People like that. Not so tedious as British writers." He touches his tie, which is a bit skew-whiff. "Whom do *we* have? Anthony Powell – I believe he pronounces it Po-el. Anthony Po-el … Does he pronounce 'bowel' bo-el', do you think? Baden-Po-el … Enoch Po-el … General Po-el … Tro-el … " He shakes his head. "Extraordinary."

"What about *you?*" Michael says.

"Me?" College asks.

"You pronounce off 'orf' and really 'rarely'," Michael says.

College raises his eyebrows. "I do?"

"Yes," Michael says.

College says, "Oh, dear", and grins – sort of sheepishly. "I had no idea." He looks off for a bit, still grinning, and then says, "Where was I? – Oh, yes, Anthony Powell, or Po-el, and A.N. Wilson. Not my cup of tea, Simon. Rather dated. They never seem to get beyond Oxbridge and names like Biffy and Cordelia. The only near-to-decent writer we've got is Martin Amis. On second thoughts, Michael, I think I'll have a bloody Mary. Will you have a bloody Mary, Simon?"

I love it that he keeps speaking my name: it makes me feel special.

I tell him I'll stay with vodka and tonic, and he says to Michael, "One bloody Mary, Michael, and a vodka and tonic." To me he says, "With ice, Simon?" He's smiling. I give him a, "Yes, thanks", and he says, "Yes, of course. It makes sense, doesn't it?" Holding the smile, he says to Michael, "Both with ice, Michael. Large ones of course."

As Michael makes the drinks, College says to him, "Have *you* read any of Amis the Younger's work, Michael?"

All this book talk is making me feel a little out of my depth. I make a mental note to take up reading.

"*Money*," says Michael.

"And what did you think of it, Michael?" asks College.

"Not bad," says Michael.

"What about *Success*?"

Michael shrugs like he's saying it didn't do much for him.

"Of course, Simon, being Irish, Michael tends to favour Celtic penmanship. Isn't that so, Michael? James Joyce, etcetera."

Michael sets our drinks on the counter. "He was the best," he says.

"Do you think so, Michael? Truthfully?" College says this like he'd give anything in the world to believe Michael.

Michael says, "I'll lay you a hundred to one there's not a writer living who wouldn't give an eye to write *half* as well – a writer of serious fiction, that is." He looks at me and winks. "Isn't that so, Simon?"

"You bet," I say. Who the fuck's James Joyce? I think.

"Michael is also something of a betting man, Simon," College says. "Loves the horses." Quickly he adds, "By the way, Michael, that horse you gave me for the Bunbary finished stone last. Electric hedgehogs move faster, as a racing chum of mine would say. But returning to Joyce: did you know he was a shit fetishist? He was what is known as a coprophiliac." He pauses. "Coprophiliac – lovely word that. He had his wife send him her shitty drawers and write him shit-stained love letters."

Michael looks at College like he doesn't know if he should believe him. Eventually he says, "Ah, get away with you", and moves off down the bar.

In a loud voice, College calls after him: "If I'm not speaking the truth, Michael, may my balls fester and drop orf (off)."

Over his shoulder, Michael calls back, "They did that years ago."

College laughs. Half to himself, he says, "Lovely chap, Michael", and then looks around the bar, kind of disinterestedly. I don't know why, but I feel kind of sorry for him..

A silence develops between us, so I break it by saying:

"Tell me something – why does the General wear camouflage?" Not brilliant, but it breaks the silence.

College takes a mouthful of bloody Mary, swallows and says, "He's extremely interested in militaria, particularly World War Two militaria. His flat is a veritable weaponry. Pistols, rifles – he even has a rocket launcher complete with rocket. His dress is an extension of that interest." He smiles. "Rather sweet, really."

"And that's why he's called 'General' – because of his interest in guns and stuff?"

"Plus his surname happens to be Montgomery."

"And you're called 'College' because of your cockney accent?"

College chuckles. "We'll have to find a name for *you*," he says. "That's if the chaps at the Roll-In haven't already done so. It's my guess they have. Like to know what I think it is?"

"I'm all ears."

"Ya-ya."

"You're kidding."

"You shouldn't have worn that rather fetching top on Sunday." He looks at his watch, and, as he does, a guy comes up behind him and taps him on the shoulder.

The guy is tall and slim and aged about forty-five. He's wearing a double-breasted grey suit, a white shirt, and a plain, red tie. His face is longish, with prominent cheekbones and a straight nose. His hair is black-going-grey, wavy, and combed back without a parting. Plenty of hair. Not a bad-looking guy.

"Ah, Brian," College says, "I was beginning to wonder what had happened to you."

Brian gives a small smile. "I'm afraid my taxi got caught in traffic." His voice sounds tired, a little dreamy. I notice his eyes, and they look the way his voice sounds. Put him in beat up jeans and trainers and you'd think he was on something.

College says, "Brian, I'd like you to meet Simon." He touches my arm. "Simon – Brian."

I give Brian a sunny smile. "Hi," I say.

"How do you do?" Brian says, and offers me a hand.

I shake it, and College says, "Brian, may I have a word with you?" To me, he says, "Do excuse us, Simon. Won't keep you a tick."

Won't keep me a what?

College takes Brian to the end of the bar – the bar is L-shaped, incidentally – and, after he's called, "Harold! How nice to see you!" to a guy in a bowler hat and an old-school tie, gets into a huddle with him (Brian).

They're back in about a minute-and-a-half, College saying, "Well, I'll leave you two together", and Brian (my trick, obviously) hitting me with a big smile.

"I'll see you what time?" I ask College.

"Five, five-thirty," College replies. "I'll meet you here, and if you're not otherwise engaged, take you on a tour of the Connaught."

"Fine," I say.

"Right, see you later then. See you in a week or so, Brian." And, with a happy half wave, College cuts.

Now it's just me and Brian – a *nervous* me, I can tell you. I mean, here I am with a guy I've never seen before, in a hotel I've never been in before, and pretty soon I'm gonna take this guy to a room in this hotel and there commit what some people would call an immoral act, what police would call an illegal act. Oh, I'm nervous all right. But at the same time I'm excited. I've a feeling there's a light of excitement in my eyes!

"Would you like a drink?" Brian asks. He's looking at me the way Roy Rogers looked at Trigger.

"Thanks," I say, "a vodka, if that's OK."

Brian orders drinks – a scotch for himself – and says, "Just *one* drink, I'm afraid. I've rather a lot on today."

I smile to myself. *A lot on, eh? You soon won't have, Brian!*

"Sure," I say.

"College tells me this is your first time. You must be nervous."

I shrug. "A little."

Brian smiles. "Don't be," he says, and then, very discreetly, without – I hope – being noticed, feels me up. At the bar! And wow! I immediately get a hard-on.

(A few questions here: What is it with me? What's with these queer excitations I keep experiencing? Is it normal for a guy my age to experience queer excitations? I'd like to find out. I'd like to see some research carried out on this subject.)

"You took my mind off my Shakespeare there for a second," I say.

* * *

The room has a single bed, a bedside table with a lamp and an ashtray, two easy chairs, a chest of drawers, and a wardrobe with a mirrored front. The walls are papered in light blue, and the carpet is dark grey. Brian's cock has no foreskin, is very thick, and is ropily veined. Looking at it, these words come into my head:

Holy shit!

CHAPTER 26

Me: By the way, I thought you said he was slightly made.

College: You didn't think so?

Me: I was expecting something kind of – well – pathetic.

College: I'd say you were in for a few surprises, Simon old chap.

College is looking Hollywood again. His face has tightened up and his hair is immaculately groomed. He's wearing an ivory-coloured double-breasted suit, a cream silk shirt with long collar points, a beautiful dusty-pink tie, and lightweight suede brogues the colour of tap rust. I catch a whiff of the aftershave he has on and it's not Aqua Velva. We're seated at one of the Massingham's glass-topped tables and I've just been telling him about my session with Brian. Seated at a table a dozen feet away is a guy who can't keep his eyes off me – an elderly guy with sleek silvery hair, black flaring eyebrows and a clipped moustache. I've already given him a lot of balls-play and was just about to lay some arse on him when College came in. If I hook him he'll by my third trick of the day, Brian being my first. My second was a short, bald guy with a round, pink face; a very chatty little guy. Gerald his name was. *I* blew Gerald, and Gerald blew *me*; a double blow, in fact. It was OK. Well, the receiving was; the giving turned my stomach – for no other reason than that

Gerald's dong was as white as a Tesco chicken. As you may've gathered, white dongs gross me out.

Of course, for a *double* blow the take is a hundred; which means I've made two hundred pounds – a hundred from Brian and a hundred from Gerald.

Two hundred pounds ...

Not bad, eh?

Not bad? It's fucking terrific

But back to Gerald for a second:

During his blowing of me – listen to this, you'll like this – during his blowing of me he looked up at me with goo-goo eyes (he was on his knees at the time) and said, "Tell me I'm a dirty cow."

That's what he said – Tell me I'm a dirty cow. So I did. "You're a dirty cow, Gerald," I told him. Gerald smiled and went back to what he was doing.

I tell College about Gerald (incidentally, when I told Gerald what my terms were, he had to go to a cash dispenser), then tell him about the guy at the table. I've got this really good feeling inside my head. I feel sort of ... I dunno ... full of optimism ... about the way my life is going. I see myself as someone being propelled – not propelled, hurtled – towards a golden future. I feel like giving a big, glad shout.

"Splendid," College says. "In that case, I'll leave you to it." He gets to his feet. "I'll be in the residents' bar. Meet me there when you've finished and we'll toddle along to the Connaught." He shoots a look at the guy at the table, then, leaning over me, says, "From the cut of him I'd say he wants to be fucked. These military-looking types usually do."

It turns out College is right.

CHAPTER 27

The Connaught's about the same size as the Massingham, but where the Massingham glitters the Connaught glows – a totally different atmosphere. The foyer has wood panelling, a wooden staircase, square wooden tubs planted with ferns, and a polished wooden floor protected by Turkish-looking carpets. The lighting comes from wooden wall lights with apricot shades. The reception desk looks to be solid mahogany and's manned by a guy whose name, so College has told me, is Albert – a tall, bony-faced guy with sunken eyes and hair the colour of strong tea. Handing me a key, he says, "Room 16, sir." To College, he says, "Mrs Harrison arrived this morning, sir."

"Rarely," College says, meaning 'really'.

That's all he says – Rarely.

The Connaught's residents' bar has plum red wallpaper with a tiny gold leaf pattern, plum red carpeting and plum red chairs and sofas. The curtains, too, are plum red. Everything's plum red – the exact same colour as the lipstick Mrs Fisher once painted my nob and her nipples with.

What a day that was.

The barman in the residents' bar is named Morris – a small, chunky guy with a square head, who shakes my hand with thick, hairy fingers. Not including College and me, the bar has six customers.

The non-residents' bar has about twelve customers

and looks pretty much how I imagine a stockbrokers' or bankers' club to look. Deep, leather armchairs (some with winged backs), low wooden tables, and hessian wall covering. On the walls in slim gold frames are oblong prints of old London. The barman here, I soon discover, is named Lionel. He's tall, blond-haired and anaemic-looking. He looks as if he could stand a pint-and-a-half of blood.

We, College and me, chat with Lionel for a while, then, at College's suggestion, return to the residents' bar, where College orders drinks – a triple brandy for himself and a lager for me ("Are you quite sure you wouldn't like something a little stronger, Simon – a drop of gin, perhaps?")

We carry our drinks to a table near a window and are just about to sit down when a voice from the door calls, "College darling!"

She's got to be crowding seventy and's as thin as a pencil. Her hair is jet black and short and her face long and creased. Her face makes me think of a slack sail. She's wearing a black dress that shows her shoulders, and very high-heeled riot-red shoes. Against the plum red of the carpet the shoes look like open wounds.

"Noreen, you old reprobate," College calls back, "I thought you were in India."

Noreen comes up to us, sort of swaggers up to us, and says to College, "I couldn't stand the heat and the humidity, darling. And the smell …! It was like living in a Chinese wrestler's jockstrap." Her accent is Australian and her voice is cracked and high-pitched.

She kisses College on the mouth, and goes on, "I must have a drinky, darling. What will *you* have, or are you all right for the moment?" She looks at me, and smiles. Still looking at me, she says: "Who's your beautiful friend, College? You *must* introduce me."

College, when introductions have been made and we're all seated – Noreen with a large Johnnie Walker in front of her, tells me that Noreen (the Mrs Harrison referred to by Albert the receptionist) is from Sydney and that thanks to a string of brothels she owns is "frightfully well orf."

"Don't take any notice of him, Simon darling," Noreen says. "They're not brothels, they're massage parlours." She sighs and, glancing at College, says, "My God, you're beautiful boys. So sexy."

"Noreen likes to fuck, Simon," College says. "At *her* age, would you believe? It makes one's blood run cold."

Noreen pats College's arm. "Darling, you're never too old to fuck." She takes a big swallow of Johnnie Walker. "When are *you* going to fuck me, College?" she asks. She turns to me, dabbing her lips with a handkerchief that's just a bit bigger than a postage stamp. "I keep asking him, Simon, but he says he can't get it up women. I don't believe him."

"It's true, lightness," College says. "My predilection is for males. I couldn't fuck you for the name of next year's Derby winner – as much as I would like to, of course. Now Simon here ... Simon could fuck a hole in a wall. Isn't that so, Simon?" He's looking at me with his eyebrows raised, Noreen with a bit of tongue showing.

"Well – " My voice trails off. Suddenly I'm embarrassed. By the language. I've never heard anything like it – not even on Albion Street. I look around me, expecting to see faces with tut, tut written on them. But no: every face has a smile on it. Which tells me something about the fat-wallet crowd.

Noreen reaches across the table and places her hand on mine. "Is it true, Simon darling?" She looks at College. "Oh, God, isn't he beautiful, College?" Not waiting for an answer, she says, "Simon, why don't I meet you here at eleven (it comes out iliv'n) and we go to my room? I've friends to meet for the theatre now, but if you'll be here at iliv'n ..."

"We go to your room?"

Noreen leers at me. "For rumpy pumpy, darling."

I cut a look at College, who's smiling.

I ask Noreen: "Are you serious?"

"Simon darling, I want you to fuck me. On my grandchildren's lives."

Her *grand*children's lives.

I'm still not convinced. I ask College: "Is this a wind-up?"

College answers: "If Noreen says she wants you to fuck her, she wants you to fuck her."

"And no French letters, darling," Noreen says. (It comes out Frinch litters.) "Just a plain, honest-to-goodness fuck."

In a voice that won't be heard by the whole bar, I say, "If you're serious, Noreen, I have to tell you: it'll cost."

"Oh, I know *that*, darling." She glances at College. "What *is* it these days, College, a hundred and fifty?"

College smiles. "Plus VAT," he says.

As if not hearing this, Noreen finishes her drink in a lump, stands, and says, "I must tear (it comes out teer). Be here at iliv'n, darling," she flips me a wink, "with a hard-on." She kisses me on the mouth, kisses College on the mouth, and leaves the table. As she passes through the door she looks back at us over her shoulder, grins, and cocks a hip.

I give a big laugh, and, when she's out of sight, say, "Is she for real?"

College reaches for his glass. "Will you be able to accommodate her, d'you think?"

"I'll give it my best shot," I say. (For a hundred and fifty quid, you can bet I will.)

"Rather you than me, old chap," says College.

"She's not exactly Playmate of the Month," I say. I take a sip of lager and, after a longish pause, say, "Tell me something – is it true you can't make it with women?"

College drains his glass. "It's a fact of my life, Simon old chap. I've never had the slightest interest in the female gender – as sexual beings, that is. I think it must have something to do with Nanny. As a child I was made to watch her rub orf – a truly horrible sight, one from which I never recovered."

"Nanny?"

"Our nurse."

"She made you – "

"Yes."

"Jesus." I let a second go by. "How old was, uh, Nanny?"

"She must have been getting on for sixty at the time; a *frightful* old thing; quite hideous. She always had this disgusting smell hovering around her. My father wouldn't allow her near him. Poppy, my sister, on the other hand, wouldn't let her out of her sight. The smell seemed not to trouble her."

I think about this for a while, then say, "I get the impression you and Poppy are very tight – like, very close."

"Extremely close," College says. "She's quite possibly my dearest friend."

Over another drink he tells me about Poppy.

She's twenty-three and works in a publishing house, where she reads manuscripts sent in for publication. Her sole qualification for the job is an A-level in English Literature – plus she's the publisher's niece. Most of the manuscripts she gets to read are "tripe", she reckons. She can tell if a manuscript is tripe or not just from reading the first page. The first page has to seduce her, she once told College. If it doesn't, she tears a leaf from her memo pad, writes "Tripe" on it, pins it to the manuscript, and sends it – the manuscript – back to the person who gave it to her to report on. Sometimes she makes a mistake. For example: two years ago she pinned a "Tripe" note to a manuscript which later won the Whitbread Prize.

When Poppy's not pinning "Tripe" notes to manuscripts, she's dining and drinking with her friends. Most of Poppy's friends don't work, so Poppy is frequently left holding the bill. However, Poppy doesn't mind this; she's a very generous person – and very beautiful. She has blonde hair, is tall, and very slim. She should take up modelling, College thinks. Very occasionally she gets drunk and when this happens, she dances. Once, she was arrested for dancing on top of a parked car and spent the night in a police cell.

Does she have boyfriends?

"Oh, good heavens, yes," College says. Her current

boyfriend is a captain in the Household Cavalry and is named Henry Cunningham-Brown. Poppy knows about College's lifestyle and thinks it 'rather fun'. In fact, when College fucks with his Billingsgate chums at his house in Chelsea, she sometimes joins in.

"That's another splendid thing about Poppy," College says, "she's frightfully broad-minded."

Morris the barman comes up and changes our ashtray.

When he's gone, I say, "She sounds sort of... interesting ... Poppy."

College says, "Oh, she *is*. Desperately."

I wait for him to continue, but he doesn't, so I switch the conversation back to Noreen. "No shitting me, College," I say (it's the first time I've addressed him as College and I hope he doesn't think I'm being familiar), "is Noreen one hundred per cent serious about having me screw her tonight?"

"Oh, absolutely, old chap," says College. "Come eleven she'll be waiting at that bar with her tongue hanging out." He touches the knot of his tie (he has a habit of doing this, I've noticed.) "As I said, rather you than me."

"I'm up for new experiences," I say.

"Spoken like a true libertine," College says. "Now; what say we finish our drinks and make tracks for the Roll-In. I've a feeling the General will want to know how you've been getting on – or orf, as the case may be."

"Okay," I say, "but first I wanna call in at a chemist's."

"Why not?" College says.

The reason I wanna call in at a chemist's is I wanna get Pebbles something for his zits.

CHAPTER 28

It's a half hour later and I'm seated with the General and College in the Roll-In, a tube of Clearasil in my pocket, the General with twenty-five per cent of my take in *his*. ("Well done," he said after counting it off; then, joking, "Keep it up.")

I swallow some coffee and say: "Maybe he found himself a twenty-four hour trick."

I'm referring to Pebbles. According to the General, Pebbles hasn't been seen all day. The last person to see him was Titch. Titch saw him leave the Leisuredrome with a weasel-faced guy in a blue parka. This was around ten p.m. yesterday.

The General shakes his head no. He looks worried. "He would've let me know," he says.

"Perhaps he's sick," College suggests.

"I called at his pad," the General says. "He wasn't there."

The General looks at me with serious eyes. "Give me a minute with College, will you, Simon," he says.

I nod. "Absolutely," I say. I finish my coffee in one, get to my feet, and start towards Stick and the twins, who, when I came in with College, gave me a cheery greeting ("Ya-ya!" one of the twins called. "What did I tell you?" College said).

They're seated at a table near the door, their heads in sunlight that comes through the transom. With them, but separated by the aisle, are Tits and Titch, Tits banging down a cheese roll like he's only got a minute to go before he gets lockjaw, and Titch pulling on a cheroot. The twins are dragged up in hot-pink turtle-necks and flesh-tight jeans, and Stick is wearing a Reebok tennis shirt and very short pale blue shorts with inch-wide turn-ups. Tits is wearing a yellow T, with LAST EXIT TO BROOKLYN stencilled on it in red, and Titch is in his school gear, his cap tipped on the back of his head.

I join Stick and the twins in the middle of a conversation, Stick saying, "Okay, France is out, how about Switzerland?"

Twin Paul – or it could be Twin Pat – pulls a face. "Switzerland?" he says. "Oooooo no-o-o-o, I'm not going *there* … all those fucking views!"

When the laughter dies down, the second twin says, "Ya-ya, how've you been doing?"

"Yeah, Simon," Stick says, "how've you been making out, man? What tricks you turn?"

I tell them, and the first twin says, "How was the blow job?"

"Strictly sickroom," I answer.

"Not as sickroomy, I bet, as the one *I* had last night – eh, Paul?" says Twin Pat.

Twin Paul closes his eyes and shivers. "Don't," he says.

Twin Pat says, "It was like blowing an ear plug. Honestly, it was so sma-a-a-a-l-l. I kept losing it!"

Over more laughter, Twin Pat asks, "How's your bum, Ya-ya? Is Brian big?"

"In College's book, no," I say. "In mine, yes."

"College'd say an elephant's was small," Twin Paul says.

"He must have a ring like Rotherhithe Tunnel," says Twin Pat. He turns in his chair. "Isn't that right, College darling," he calls.

"Is what right?" College calls back.

"That you've got a ring like Rotherhithe Tunnel."

"If you mean, does it get plenty of traffic, the answer is yes; which is more than can be said of yours, duckie."

The twins put on shocked expressions and look at each other. "Oooooo," they say together.

Because it's something I think might interest them, I tell them of my deal with Noreen.

"Lucky thing," Twin Pat says. "Noreen, I mean, not you."

"You swing both ways, Simon?" Stick asks.

"I suppose I do," I say. There's a note of apology in my voice.

Tits must've been listening, because he says, "You had any with a woman before, Ya-ya?"

I look across the aisle at him and, by flashing a demon grin and making my eyes big, tell him yes.

"What's it like?"

"It's OK. Pretty nice."

Titch, through a cloud of cheroot smoke, says, "A hole's a hole, same as a hand's a hand, or a mouth's a mouth."

I get his drift and say, "I can't argue with that."

And who can?

Twin Pat can. "Yes, but there are holes and there are holes," he says.

"How would *you* know, you've never been in one," Titch says.

"With this I have," Twin Pat says. He's holding up

his middle finger, which has a long almond-shaped nail painted pink.

"How many stitches did he need afterwards?" Titch asks.

Twin Pat smiles. "It's my bot scourer," he says; and as our laughter splits the Roll-In's cruddy air – Tits laughing so hard he sprays Titch with a mouthful of the cheese roll he's eating – the feeling comes over me that I've never been so happy in my whole life.

* * *

Some time later, about twenty minutes later, on the steps of the Massingham, College says, "Where would you prefer to trade, old chap, here or the Connaught?"

"Seeing that I'm meeting Noreen at the Connaught, I'll take the Connaught," I say.

"Eminently sensible," College says, and after he's wished me, "Good luck", we part.

I don't go straight to the Connaught, I take a taxi to Pebbles' pad.

He's not there.

CHAPTER 29

Noreen comes towards me smiling; and boy, am I pleased to see her: apart from turning one trick – a hand job – all I've done all evening is read a newspaper: I can use some company.

The guy I tricked with was about fifty and insisted on wearing a skin. He was scared of catching AIDS – from my hand! What really knocked me out about him, though, was the size of his balls – really massive balls. I weighed them in my palm and they weighed about the same as a grapefruit – or two large peaches. Unbelievable.

After tricking with him I went to the residents' bar, where I found a copy of *The Times*. It was lying on a chair. For something to do, I read it. Normally, the only newspaper I get to read is the *Mirror*, which the old lady buys. The old lady is very big on socialism, so she buys the *Mirror*. To give you an idea of how big on socialism the old lady is: hanging on a wall in our living-room is a poster with these words printed on it: *Government is for the people's progress and not for the comfort of an aristocracy. The object of industry is the welfare of the workers and not the wealth of the owners. The object of civilization is the cultured progress of the mass of workers and not merely an intellectual elite.*

Words, the old lady says, to put air in your lungs.

Also hanging on a wall in our living-room is a piece of linen embroidered with rosebuds and the message:

From each according to his abilities, to each according to his needs – *Karl Marx*. The old lady got it from a charity shop, and, because she liked it so much, I made a frame for it – from a nice piece of wood I found on a skip. Carpentry is something I shine at – excel at, if you like. When I was at school, I once made a cigarette box that earned me an A-plus. The carpentry teacher, a guy called Sams (this guy was a real weirdo; like, to punish a kid, he'd rub his facial hair – he always needed a shave – over the kid's face. He did it to *me* a few times and I tell you, it hurt like a bastard), said it was one of the finest pieces of joinery he'd seen by a student in fifteen years of teaching.

No shit, that's what he said.

Where was I? Oh, yeah, *The Times*. *The Times* gave a lot of space to the Maastricht Treaty, which, I have to say, is not a subject that knocks me in a heap. It also gave a lot of space to wars. In case you haven't heard, there are wars all over the place. Cambodia, Armenia, Somalia, Angola. Everywhere wars. What *I'd* like to know is who starts 'em. It's not *us*, the people on the street, who starts 'em. No – it's gotta be the politicians and fat cats. They're the only ones who get anything out of 'em. The politicians get more power and the fat cats get to be fatter cats, the fat cats being the industrialists who produce the war machinery – paid for by the taxpayer, who gets killed by it. Of course, the politicians and the fat cats, they don't fight in the wars. No, they're too smart for that. They stay at home and wait for the power and money to roll in.

Am I right, or am I right?

What we need is a war on fat cats and politicians.

OK, I get Noreen a large scotch, and over it she tells me about her massage parlours, which, she says, are the genuine article (no hand jobs and stuff), and of her home overlooking Sydney harbour.

"You'd like Sydney, Simon," she says. "You'd have a lovely time there."

"I like England," I say. "I like the place where I live."

"Of course you do, darling," she says. "Now – let's go up."

She wants it badly, no question.

We go up stairs and along a corridor and into a room with fat chairs and sofas, and rugs you lose your feet in. Air conditioning, a drinks cart, long drapes at the windows, a giant TV... Definitely a comfort zone.

"Would you like a drink?" Noreen asks.

I tell her no thanks, I've had enough, and Noreen says, "Well, make yourself comfortable while I freshen up. Take your jacket off." She flips switches, and the ceiling light goes off and rosy wall lights come on. She looks around. "How's that?" she asks.

"Fine," I say.

"Like a Peruvian brothel," Noreen says, and laughs. "Sit down," she says.

I take off my jacket, lay it on a fat sofa, and sit in a fat armchair.

"Good," Noreen says. She's looking a lot of affection at me. I don't know why, but I feel about twelve years old.

Noreen flashes me a smile, crosses to a tall doorway and disappears through it.

A short while later I hear water running and, over it, singing. It's Noreen. "Waltzing Matilda", she's singing.

She returns wearing a white terrycloth bathrobe.

The robe is a couple of sizes too big for her, and in the rosy light and without her high heels and with her hair wetted back she looks – even though, as I've said, she must be crowding seventy – like a little girl.

She stands a few feet away from me and after a moment or two and with her eyes shining out happiness she unties the bathrobe and shrugs it off.

Her tits are flat and her ribs stick out; but she doesn't give a fuck: she spreads her arms wide like she's got the most beautiful body in the world and says, "Come and love me."

* * *

Afterwards, lying side by side on a king-sized bed, with a single wall light burning above our heads, Noreen says softly, "You know, that wasn't the real me you saw in the bar earlier; I'm not *really* like that."

"I didn't think it was," I say.

"It was just a show, a silly show."

"It's okay," I say. "We all put on a show. I try to come off being cool, but I'm not."

"Oh, Simon," Noreen says, "how I wish you'd known me when I was sixteen. How I'd love to be sixteen again and meet you. I was beautiful then. You wouldn't think so to look at me now, but I was beautiful."

"I bet you were," I say.

Noreen places a hand on my leg. "You've got such a beautiful cock," she whispers. "If I were younger I'd do so many wonderful things with it."

"You did okay," I say. "In fact, you were great."

218

Noreen takes hold of my cock, which is now limp, and says, "Will you do something for me?"

"What's that?"

"Very soon I'll go off to sleep. I'm very tired. Will you stay with me and let me go off to sleep holding your cock? It's been such a long time since I've done that."

"Sure," I say.

"The money's on the shelf in the bathroom," Noreen says.

This touches me, and I say, "That one was on me."

"You're making me cry," Noreen says. Then, "Promise me something."

"What?"

"Promise me you'll squeeze all you can out of life ... all the fun and laughter and all the love."

"You've got it," I say.

"Good boy," Noreen says, and after a short while and with her hand cradling my dick and with a tiny snore, she drifts into sleep.

* * *

Next day Albert the receptionist hands me an envelope. In it are three hundred pounds and a note written on hotel notepaper. The note says:

Simon my dear,

By the time you get this I'll be winging my way back to Australia. I've decided to leave England quickly, before I make a fool of myself and perhaps embarrass you – something I should hate to do.

You know, my dear, you made a beat-up old broad very

happy last night. You put love back into this ancient heart of mine, and it felt so good. Oh, my dear, dear boy, it felt so good.

With a tender kiss,

Noreen

P.S. Remember your promise to me.

It's my first love letter as an adult. And I'll keep it.

CHAPTER 30

Titch wipes tears from his eyes, looks at the General. The General shakes his head. There's a big silence. We're so numb with shock we can't speak.

Pebbles, so Titch has just told us, is dead. His body was discovered two days ago – four weeks to the day of his disappearance – on a golf course six miles north of London. A guy walking his dog discovered it half hidden by bracken. A few yards from where Pebbles' body was discovered lay a second body. Both bodies were naked and badly decomposed, the second body – that of a young male – little more than a skeleton. The only clothing found was a nylon sock stuffed into Pebbles' mouth.

Titch got his information, he's explained, from two dicks. They approached him in the Leisuredrome, flashed I.D. cards, and asked him if he knew of any kids who'd disappeared. Titch gave them a yes.

Later, at the mortuary, after he'd identified Pebbles, he gave the dicks a second name – that of the guy Pebbles told me about when we first met. Did he wear a skull's head ring? the dicks wanted to know. Yes, he did, Titch told them. Over coffee, the dicks told Titch about the discovery and state of the bodies, etcetera.

The General has a terrible look in his eyes. Finally he says, "The cops have any idea who did it?" His voice sounds as if he's drowning.

"No," Titch says softly.

Stick comes alive and says, "It's got to be those snuff fucks we've been hearing about."

The General nods quietly, looks at the Roll-In's stone floor.

"The cops want to see me again," Titch says.

The General looks up. "What about?" he asks.

"I dunno," Titch says. "They just said they might have some questions for me."

Twin Pat who's sitting next to me puts his hands to his face and bursts into tears. "Oh fuck," he sobs. "Oh fuck."

I place an arm around his shoulders to comfort him.

I don't feel embarrassed doing this.

"What about the guy you said you saw Pebbles leave the Leisuredrome with – the weasel-looking guy?" the General says to Titch.

"What about him?" Titch asks.

"You think you'd recognise him?"

"Definitely," Titch says.

"Did you tell the cops about him?"

"No."

"Didn't the cops ask if you'd seen Pebbles with anyone?"

"Yes," Titch answers.

"So?"

"I didn't want to get too involved. I didn't think you'd want me to."

"You thought right," the General says. Then, "Don't tell them *anything*. This one's mine." He clears his throat slowly and says, "I need a volunteer," he looks at *me* when he says this, "somebody to work the Leisuredrome and act as bait for the bastard or bastards who killed Pebbles. I'd like to get to them before the cops do."

Tits puts a hand up and says, "I don't mind." It's like he's volunteering to chop wood or something.

The General gives him a gentle look and in a kind voice says, "I don't think these people are chubby chasers, Tits."

Tits shrugs.

"I'm your man, General," Stick says. Stick's all energy.

The General thinks for a moment, then shakes his head. "You're too heavy-duty, Stick. They wouldn't go for you; they'd be scared you'd give them muscle. They'll want someone they can handle."

"I'd give the mothers muscle all right," Stick says.

There's nothing else for it: I raise my hand. I try to look zero cool doing this.

The General looks a lot of quiet at me. He clears his throat again and looks away. After a while he looks back at me. "Okay," he says, "here's the plan."

CHAPTER 31

The General's plan: it goes like this:

Monday to Friday I'll work the Massingham and Connaught hotels and on Sunday evenings play sprat at the Leisuredrome (it was a Sunday evening, remember, that Pebbles went missing; similarly the other guy. The other guy, I've learned, was aged sixteen; a softly spoken guy – Les his name was – who didn't mix much.)

My Leisuredrome wear will be T-shirt, jeans and trainers (rough trade threads). I will arrive at the Leisuredrome at five and remain there until it closes. With me, mobilephone at the ready, will be Titch, who, as soon as he sees me – or *anyone* – leave the Leisuredrome with weasel-face, will call up the General, who'll be in wheels parked in Break Street, a narrow side street exactly opposite the Leisuredrome's front entrance.

After making the call, Titch will follow weasel-face and me at a "discreet distance" and every ten seconds or so report our whereabouts to the General. Weasel-face, the General thinks, will have transport. This being the case, he, the General, will expect from Titch a full description of same – colour, make, licence-plate number, and so on. Once he has it, he will pick up Titch and together they will tail us – weasel-face and me – to weasel-face's destination. Weasel-face's destination, the General reckons, will be a house. I will enter the house with weasel-face and wait for the General to make his move.

That's the General's plan. Pretty hairy, but I'm happy to be part of it. I'd be happy to be part of *any* plan that'd help nail Pebbles' killer. Pebbles mattered to me. Okay, I didn't know him that well, I wasn't heavily connected with him, but he mattered to me. I felt towards Pebbles the way I feel towards – well, towards Wally, say: protective.

To stay too long with Pebbles, to have brought to mind the pain he must have suffered, the fear he must have experienced, chokes me up, so I'll move to a lighter subject – that of myself. In the four weeks I've been with the General I've had some pretty interesting experiences; experiences you'll want to hear about.

I'll start with a drag ball I attended with Twin Pat and Twin Paul.

I was their escort for the evening; they asked me to be their escort, and I agreed. "Why not?" I told them. Twin Pat wore pink chiffon and Twin Paul lavender tulle. Very beautiful. I was dressed in a dinner suit hired from Moss Bros. "Oh, sleeeeeeeek!" Twin Paul said when he saw me. I shot him a wink. "You know me," I said, "sleek, cool, and easy to take."

Twin Paul loved that.

The ball was held at the Hammersmith Palais and was attended by a lot of big showbusiness names. Eric Clapton was there, as was Elton John, John in his new hair looking like William in the Just William books. Pathetic. I don't know about you, but my tendency is to think of elderly pop and rock stars – the Johns and Jaggers and Cliff Richards of the world – as pricks.

The purpose of the ball was to raise funds for AIDS research, a worthy cause, in my opinion (this AIDS thing is getting out of hand). The price of a ticket was £50, which now that I'm rolling in money (I'm now trousering, on average, £2,000 a week) is pigeon shit. I tell you, I've got so much money I don't know what to do with it, and this is after paying for two two-way plane tickets (Club Class) to Las Vegas and a night's stay at a top Las Vegas hotel. Las Vegas is where you have to go to get to the Grand Canyon. I didn't know that.

Music for the ball was provided by two bands – a regular dance band and a jazz band. The dance band was really something – a really big sound that made your heart swell with excitement. As soon as it struck up, Twin Pat asked me to dance ("Dance with me, Ya-ya,"), and, not wanting to hurt his feelings, I agreed. However, before we could get to the dance-floor we were surrounded by a bunch of queens. There must've been a dozen of them. They were friends of the twins. Each of them held a drink and took quick sips from it, sort of pecked at it, the way a bird would, and they kept touching and leaning against each other. "Have you seen Gloria?" I heard one of them ask. "She looks like the Queen of the fucking Dew." Introducing me, Twin Paul said, "This is Ya-ya, everyone" – and a very tall, hook-nosed, sleepy-eyed queen wearing a slinky black number with feathers round the neck, flapped a hand and said, "Oo-ya-ya!" A little while later, I heard him say to a pudgy queen in a gold-spangled cat-suit the colour of cocoa, "Don't keep fucking looking at me like that."

"Looking at you like what?" the pudgy queen asked.

"As if I was The Nightmare on fucking Elm Street," the tall queen said.

"Don't be so phobic," the pudgy queen said.

The queens of course were all over me – like, I really turned their keys – and I spent most of the night dancing with them. One, whose name was Bernice, told me he'd just got out of prison. "I tried to mug a karate expert, didn't I, silly cow," he said.

I asked Bernice what it was like in prison, and he said, "Fabulous, I was fucked rotten."

Then there was this really weird queen called Vivienne, who kept crying. Somebody'd only have to look at him and he'd burst into tears. He was about forty and looked a real mess. His hair was dyed pink and black and stuck out in all directions, and his lipstick looked as if it'd been put on with a knife. He wore a short green dress that flared at the waist, yellow silk stockings and red-satin pumps. A really terrible sight.

"Why'd's he keep crying?" I asked the pudgy queen.

"It's her change, dear," the pudgy queen said.

The last I saw of Vivienne, he was pummelling the back of a bouncer, who had him thrown over his shoulder like he was a sack of potatoes. It seemed he'd gone nuclear on the dance floor – creamed two guys who'd poked fun at him.

The pudgy queen, I discovered, was called Melissa, and the hook-nosed queen – the tall queen in feathers – Georgette. Every time I looked at Georgette I was reminded of a sleepy vulture. Towards the end of the evening Melissa and Georgette were joined by a short, porky guy called Freddie. Freddie, so Twin Pat told me, was a stockbroker with a million-pound house in Buckinghamshire. It was obvious from the way Georgette looked at Freddie that she (he) hated him, and when Freddie asked her (him) to dance, told him to fuck off. Georgette's actual words were, "Fuck off, you silly old sod." This made Melissa feel sorry for Freddie, so what she (he) did, she sat in Freddie's lap and fed him tiny sips of drink. A really hilarious sight. Everyone had a lot to drink. *I* was so smashed I couldn't see straight.

I spent the night with the twins at their pad in Hampstead, a really nice pad with views of the Heath. Twin Pat wanted me to dick him, but my head was spinning and I couldn't get a hard-on.

I could the next morning, though!

Twin Pat is really hot for me and wants us to be a pair.

I'm thinking about it.

* * *

Another of my experiences involved College and his sister Poppy.

Late one evening at the Massingham College and I (I'm working on my grammar) got drinking with Michael the barman, and before we knew it it was the next day; like, it was *seriously* the next day – 5 a.m.

"What say we have a drink in the market?" College said, meaning, I supposed, Billingsgate.

Michael wasn't keen, but I was all for it. To drink in a pub while most people slept, would, I thought, be sort of exciting, something to remember.

And it was. Try to get the picture:

Early morning with the sun coming up; a crowded bar smelling of fried sausages and Captain Morgan rum; College in a white suit being slapped on the back by tough-looking fish porters with raw hands; the sound of someone singing *L'il Ol' Wine Drinker Me*; somebody coughing his socks up; glasses clinking; laughter and loud voices all around. Then sunlight flooding the bar and painting everything gold – bottles, tabletops, faces … everything.

That's how it was. It was as if we were the only people alive and having a big party to celebrate the fact: a sort of celebration of life and the love of it.

While College was being slapped on the back, I found myself a table and sat down.

Before long I was joined by a guy whose name, I discovered, was Eddie; a big, handsome guy with grey-blond hair, who, after we'd chatted for a while, told me all about Billingsgate – its history and everything. Being a porter, Eddie stank of fish, but with the beauty and adventure of the day it didn't matter.

After telling me the history of Billingsgate, Eddie told me the history of the pub we were in (he knew his history, did Eddie), and then he told me about some of the characters he'd worked with. He'd just finished telling me about somebody called Ron the Shoe when College came up. His eyes were extra bright and he was swaying slightly. He was holding a pint glass half filled with what looked like whisky.

"Simon," he said, "I'll be taking a couple of the chaps back to my place for drinks. You'll join us, of course?"

"Sure," I said.

"And you, Edward?"

"Not me, College, mate," said Eddie. "I need some kip."

"You can rest at my place," College said.

Eddie chuckled and said, "Yeah, I'd get some rest all right." Then, "No, College, it's nice of you, but I've got to get home – the missis's got a breakfast waiting for me."

"Ah, Edward," College said, "and I did so want to see your membrum virilis. I'm told it's positively elephantine."

"Do what?" Eddie said, and laughed.

A little while later Eddie left, but not before he'd presented me with a huge cooked lobster he'd pulled from the duffel bag he was carrying. His parting words to me were: "You take care, son."

A really nice guy – the kind of guy you wouldn't mind having for a father.

The two guys College invited for drinks were named Terry and Vic. Terry had dark, tightly-curled hair receding at the temples, and Vic dark, combed-back hair that looked as if it'd recently been cut. Terry had a roundish face and a blunt nose, and Vic a narrow face and a long, sculptured nose; two good-looking guys. Both were in their mid thirties and, like Eddie, smelled strongly of fish. In the taxi taking us to College's place (for some reason College was without wheels, so we were cabbing it), the smell was overpowering and I couldn't help but feel sorry for Vic's and Terry's families. I mean, imagine living with someone who smells like a piece of haddock the whole time. Personally, I couldn't stand it.

College's place was in a cobble-stoned mews not far from Sloan Square Station; a little white-painted place above a garage (formerly a stable, I found out later), its front featuring two hanging baskets containing trailing geraniums, and two tubs each planted with a standard red rose. When I saw it, saw it in its mews setting, I got vibrations of women in crinoline dresses and a guy with a handbell shouting, Oyez! Oyez! That's how olde worlde it looked.

"It's somewhat diminutive, I'm afraid, chaps," College said, "but comfortable enough." And then he collapsed. He just went limp and collapsed.

When a person has a heart attack – which is what I thought College'd had – you do something. I knelt at College's side to give him mouth-to-mouth, and at that moment a voice said, "Oh, for heaventh thake!"

I looked up and saw this tall, very haughty-looking fem standing in the doorway, smoking a cigarette. She wore blue-satin short-sleeved pyjamas and blue-satin mules. Her hair was ash-blonde and straight and she had a small pointed chin and heavily-mascaraed eyes. Her nose was slim and upturned and her mouth small and pouty. A really stunning-looking fem. Poppy. It *had* to be.

"Take him into the houthe, will you, pleathe," she said.

"He just kind of collapsed," I said.

"Yeth," Poppy said. You'd think I'd said, Nice weather we're having.

Vic and Terry got College to his feet and half-dragged, half carried him into the house, Poppy looking on as if Terry and Vic were delivery men and College a crappy piece of furniture.

"It'th too tabloid of him," Poppy said. She closed the door and led us – College now needing only Vic's support – up stairs to a room which, apart from a huge painting of a field of buttercups under a blue sky, was all white. Walls, sofa, armchairs, rugs, bookshelves, drinks cabinet, piano, table, standing lamp … everything was white. College in his white suit looked like the Invisible Man.

"Where shall I put him?" Vic asked.

"Oh … on the thofa … anywhere," Poppy said. "I'll make thome coffee." She glanced at a white clock on a white mantelshelf. "Oh, dear, I thall be late for work," she said, and, as she said this, College growled.

That's what he did. He growled, twisted himself free of Vic, who was still supporting him, lurched across the room to the drinks cabinet, pulled open the cabinet's glass doors, reached inside, took out a full bottle of gin, swung around, steadied himself, growled again, and ran from the room. A second later there was the terrible sound of someone falling down stairs, and a few seconds after that the sound of a door flung open. After that, silence.

I was kind of dumbstruck – and scared. I mean, to see somebody – a friend – suddenly and without warning behave like an animal is pretty frightening. I looked at Poppy for some sort of, you know, direction, and in a casual voice she said, "Let him go … *he'll* be back."

"He might need help," I said.

"No, honethtly," Poppy said, "he'll be all right."

"He was growling," I said, "he might hurt someone." Growling! I couldn't get over it.

"He often doeth that when he'th had a drink," Poppy said. "It doethn't mean anything. He'th ath gentle ath a lamb." I noticed that when she spoke, she very slightly tilted her head to the left and for the first two or three words of some sentences closed her eyes. I found this very sexy.

"I'm going after him," I said, and left the house.

And didn't return until two hours later. That's how long it took me to find College.

I found him seated under a tree, his back against it, in a fenced-off square east of King's Road. His eyes were half closed, and between his legs was the bottle of gin he'd grabbed from the cabinet, the bottle now four fifths empty. The collar of his jacket was turned up and there was a black mark the size of a kid's hand on the jacket's breast pocket. A few feet away from him, asleep on his back, was a long, skinny guy with matted grey hair and a face that looked as if it belonged in a tool bag. His trousers were filthy and open at the fly, and his shirt bloodstained and torn. A pretty sight, both of them. Gin and chronic.

"Simon, old chap, how nice to see you."

I was amazed at how sober he sounded.

"Do sit down. Do join me. This by the way," College indicated the down-and-out-looking guy, "is Jock, a dear friend of mine. Jock's a former sergeant in the Scots Guards. A twenty-year man, silly bugger. Fallen on hard times. From a dizzying height. Haven't you, Jock, old chap? Why anyone should ..." His voice trailed off and he rested his head against the tree.

I knelt beside him and gently touched his shoulder. "Hey, come on," I said, "let's get back."

"Back?" College said.

"Home," I said.

"Oh, home," College said. Then he shivered slightly and got to his feet – very steadily. No falling about or anything. I supposed he must've drunk himself sober. "Why not?" he said quietly and laid one of his beautiful smiles on me, and for a second I thought I might do something stupid – like hug him or something. "Jock, you old bastard, get up," he said. He gave Jock a couple of taps with his foot, and Jock opened his eyes. "Jock, old chap, we're going to my place for a small libation. Come along – chop, chop."

"Wha' the – " said Jock, and looked at College with a fierce expression, as if College had kicked him in the balls.

"Hadn't we better get him zipped up?" I said. I didn't want Jock getting arrested for indecent exposure.

"The zip's broken," College said. "It broke when I undid it. A Freudian zip, you might say."

Jock stood up, and we left the square, Jock holding on to my arm and occasionally taking wild swings at things that weren't there. "Wha' the fuck – " he kept saying. "Wha' the fuck – " Those were the only words he spoke.

As we waited for a taxi, I said to College, "Why'd you run off like that? You scared the shit out of me."

"Run orf? Did I run orf?"

"Yes," I said. "Growling."

College looked at me with his eyebrows raised. "Growling?" he said. "My dear Simon, you must have been imagining things."

I was silent. I didn't want to embarrass him. "Wha' the fuck – " Jock said.

Back at College's, this is what we found:

Poppy on her hands and knees being serviced by Vic and Terry – Terry at one end, Vic at the other. The air was thick with cannabis smoke and Rod Stewart was croaking from a radio. On top of the piano was one of Poppy's blue-satin mules.

"How delightfully informal!" College said, and stripped off.

Then a kind of orgy developed, with everybody servicing everybody else; a really wild orgy. Old Jock had the time of his life. We all did.

Later, when everyone except Poppy and me was asleep, I got talking with Poppy in her bedroom and she told me about College's drink problem. He started drinking at the age of fourteen and by the time he was twenty was being treated for alcoholism. He refuses to join Alcoholics Anonymous because he enjoys drinking. Occasionally he dries out, but for no other reason than to get fit for a big binge. He once went on a binge that lasted three weeks. He started drinking in Chelsea, at his local, and wound up in Amsterdam. Another time he found himself travelling through Germany on the Orient Express. Two years ago he started having psychiatric treatment, but for some reason gave up on it. He has the most tremendous capacity for drink, sometimes drinking as much as a litre of whisky at one sitting.

"He'th one of thothe people who can look and thound thober while practically in a thtate of collapthe," Poppy said. She giggled and said, "He'th hopeleth, abtholutely hopeleth." And then she went down on me.

A weird and wonderful day that I'll never forget.

CHAPTER 32

And I've a feeling I won't forget *this* day, either.

It began with a call from the General. A client, he said – a watcher – wanted a black-on-white; I was to meet up with Stick at the Roll-In at 2 p.m; transport would take us to an address at Hyde Park Gate. As soon as Stick's name was mentioned my heart started to beat fast; like, the idea of making it with him excited me (I have to admit: I'm hot for him). "I'll be there," I told the General.

I guess my voice must've sounded eager, because the General, smiling over the phone, said, "Stick seemed pretty keen, too", and hearing this, knowing that Stick wanted to make it with *me*, my heart beat even faster.

As fast as it's beating now as I head for the Roll-In.

* * *

Stick is outside, waiting for me. He's wearing a pale blue denim shirt open to the waist and tight-fitting dark blue jeans that bulge at the crotch. This giant bulge. "Hi," he says, and ducks his head, the way a person who's shy might.

For something to say, I say, "The General said there'd be transport", and try not to look at his bulge.

"It should be here any minute," Stick replies, and at this moment a chauffeur-driven Rolls draws up. This beautiful Rolls Royce. Banana yellow with white-walled tyres. A really terrific-looking car.

The chauffeur rolls down his window and sticks his head out. "Stick and Simon?" he asks.

"Yeah," we say together.

"Get in," the chauffeur says.

We get in and sit far apart on the seat. We're nervous of each other. Not nervous of each other, shy of each other. I've caught Stick's shyness.

The car pulls away and 15 minutes later we're parked outside a large white house with a pillared entrance; the sort of house that makes you think, 'How the other half live', or, 'It's all right for some.'

The chauffeur turns in his seat. "Press the intercom button and wait," he says.

We get out and as we walk to the door I say to Stick, "How the other half live ..."

"You heard that Billie Holiday number, *God Bless the Child*?" Stick asks.

I catch his drift. *God Bless the Child* is a song about – you probably know this – about the haves and the have nots of the world – people with houses like the one we're approaching, and people with nothing but the clothes they stand up in. It was written by Billie Holiday herself, back in the forties, I think. I know this because I'm a big fan of Billie Holiday. She's a kind of hero of mine. (My tendency is to make heroes of tragic figures. We all do, right?)

"You kidding!" I say. "Check this out", and in my best voice, the voice I use at Karaoke nights at The Castle on Albion Street when I wow customers with my interpretation of that great Tina Turner number *Simply The Best*, sing: *Them that's got shall get/Them that's not shall lose/So the bible says/And it still is news/Mamma may have/Poppa may have/But God bless the child that's got his own/That's got his own …*

"A-r-i-i-i-ght!" Stick says when I've stopped singing. Then, "Hey, man, that's a voice you've got there!"

"It's not bad," I say.

At the door I press a button above a grill and almost immediately a voice says, "Yes?"

I put my face to the grill and say, "I believe you're expecting us – the General's men."

"Come up," the voice answers, and a second later there's a whirring sound, and a second after that the door swings open.

We go up a wide silver-handrailed staircase and are met at the top by a small Indian guy in a red silk dressing gown patterned with orange dragons. He must be about sixty; a big-gutted guy with thinning black hair combed sideways to hide his scalp. His face is round and sagged.

"This way," he says, and leads us into a room the size of a volleyball court.

The room is papered in silvery blue and bathed in a sort of trembly light. I get the impression of being on the deck of a giant ship, looking out to sea. The furniture – and there's not a lot of it, not for the size of the room – is positioned against the walls. There are four sofas with rounded corners, and an assortment of very delicate-looking chairs and desks and tables, some of which are decorated in gold leaf. On one of the tables is a stuffed toy tiger. The carpet is dark blue and very soft underfoot.

"I'm ready whenever you are," the guy says, and sits on a sofa. "I suggest you go to the centre of the room."

He leans back and crosses his legs.

I look at Stick and he lowers his eyes. You'd think it was his first time.

"Come on," I say and we go to the centre of the room.

"I'd like you to undress each other," the guy says. "I'd like you to be undressed first." He nods at me when he says this. His voice is very matter-of-fact.

Stick doesn't move a muscle. Nor do I.

"Begin, please," says the guy, and then Stick very tentatively, as if I've been sprayed with plutonium or something, removes my jacket.

He loosens my tie (I've left my crew-neck off because of the hot weather and am wearing a shirt and tie) and as he does, I breathe through my nose and mouth to smell him. He smells of just-rained-on earth.

He gets my tie and shirt off, then moves to my belt. While he's unbuckling it I have an urge to touch him, so I place my hands on his shoulders. My heart is thundering against my ribs and I'm breathing very heavily; I've suddenly become very sexed up, very hormonal.

My trousers drop to my ankles, and Stick kneels and eases off my loafers. As he rises, he brushes my dick with his mouth.

I kick away my trousers, and, looking Stick dead in the eye (our shyness of each other has gone now), move close to him and remove his shirt. I notice his solid neck and powerful biceps.

His jeans have a metal-buttoned fly that is difficult to undo. I undo it and lower his jeans.

When I see his dick, see its size and its erectness and

the sheen of its head – like black satin – I feel pure lust flow through me.

I remove his tennis shoes – he's wearing Reebok tennis shoes; a really nice set of shoes – and pull his feet through his jeans.

I stand up and look into his face. Then, mouths parted, we move close to each other.

CHAPTER 33

"When *I* go, I want to be buried," says Twin Pat.

"Face or arse upward?" Titch asks.

"Do you mind!" says Twin Pat.

We're at Golders Green Crematorium for Pebbles' funeral. When I say 'we', I mean all the guys from the Roll-In. Also present are Pebbles' landlord – a loose-limbed guy with rich coppery skin and a big peaceful face – and shit-chuter Harry, Harry of the Savoy, Savoy Harry, as he's known. Here's Savoy Harry:

Smallish, slim, with a long, thin nose and short black hair parted in the middle and brushed back. His complexion is pasty-looking, and his mouth a gash. You can't see his eyes because they're hidden behind round, steel-framed shades. He's wearing a black-silk shirt and tie, a black double-breasted pin-striped suit, black built-up shoes, and skin-tight black leather gloves. A very Underworld-looking character. I wouldn't be surprised if he had an ice-pick taped to his leg.

Why the funeral is being held in Golders Green and not in Pebbles' home town of Hastings is because – you won't believe this – is because none of Pebbles' relatives was prepared to claim his body. "I don't want it," his mother told the authorities. An aunt and two uncles said the same.

We got this from a police source – a dick the General knows, who's in the General's pocket.

"That's okay," the General told the dick, "*I'll* claim it."

And he did. Then he called at an undertaker's, where he ordered a satin-lined coffin with brass handles, a marble urn to put Pebbles' ashes in, a hearse, and cars for the mourners. The next day he fixed up a service – here at the crematorium. If it wasn't for the General, poor Pebbles'd be in an unmarked grave somewhere. I tell you, I've got a lot of time for the General.

We assemble outside a small chapel, and after a while a guy in a porter's uniform comes up and asks us to go inside and "take our seats".

The chapel has a grey stone floor, white walls and two lines of yellow pews. Facing the pews is a yellow wooden lectern, and behind the lectern an altar, on which sits a large piece of electrical equipment. Behind the altar, dominating the scene, so to speak, is Pebbles' coffin. It rests on a platform of sorts and points, narrow end on, to a wall that has a small red-velvet curtain fixed to it.

I choose a pew one up from the front and am joined by Twin Pat and Twin Paul. Both are wearing black organdie and have large squares of black lace covering their heads. They look like something out of a Mafia film. Seated in the front pew are the General, Stick and Tits, the General wearing a navy suit and black tie (out of camouflage he looks kind of helpless), and Stick and Tits light grey suits with black armbands, Tits's jacket breaking at the seams. Behind us are College (white suit, purple armband), Titch (black school outfit), and Savoy Harry. The rest of the guys, all suitably dressed for the occasion (not a navel or bicep to be seen), have taken places across the aisle.

A minute or two goes by, then a priest comes in and

stands at the lectern. He's youngish, bearded and has alien-blue eyes. "Let us pray," he says. "Please stand."

We stand, and the priest leads us into *The Lord's Prayer*, which I never can remember.

After *The Lord's Prayer's* been said we sing *Abide With Me*, and when we've sung *Abide With Me* listen to the priest say a lot of nice things about Pebbles – things the General must've told him. Then we recite the *23rd Psalm* – my favourite piece from the bible. Whenever I hear the *23rd Psalm* I get all choked up. I can't help myself.

After we've recited the *23rd Psalm* the priest suggests we close our eyes for a minute and think of Pebbles, and I think of him in his pad and of the hopeless smile he gave me and the Clearasil I bought him that he never got to use.

The minute comes to an end, and the priest turns from the lectern and moves to the altar, to where the electrical equipment is positioned. He reaches out a hand and all at once Simon and Garfunkle are singing *Bridge Over Troubled Water* and Pebbles' coffin is moving towards the wall with the curtain on it and big tears are filling my eyes.

CHAPTER 34

"I don't want it," the old lady says and pushes away the £300 I've placed in front of her. I've taken a day off from tricking and am spending it with Jimmy and the old lady. The three of us are seated at the table in the kitchen.

I push the money back. "Take it," I say. "Buy something for the house with it." In the background the fridge is twittering, making cracking sounds. "A new fridge, for instance."

"Where did you get it?" the old lady asks.

"I told you. I earned it."

"Doing what?"

This is iffy.

"Selling."

"Selling?"

"Yeah."

"Selling what?"

I shoot Jimmy a look that says "Jesus!"

"Flowers," I say. Well, it's better than Encyclopaedia Brittanicas.

"Flowers?" the old lady says.

"Yeah, flowers." I can't help myself, I make a private joke: "Golden Rod ... Stuff like that."

"Where are you selling them – these flowers?"

"Leicester Square. I met this guy who has a flower stall. He asked me would I like to work for him. A really nice guy."

The old lady gives me a funny look. "Three hundred pounds?... You must sell a lot of flowers."

"We do. Leicester Square. Prime spot."

The old lady gets to her feet. "As long as you're not selling drugs."

This hurts.

"Drugs? Hey, come on!"

"I'm sorry," the old lady says quickly. She softens her eyes. "I don't know why I said that." After a pause and in a quiet voice, she says, "It's just that I worry about you, Simon. I get these silly ideas come into my head." She reaches out and touches my face. "I'm sorry."

"I'm just trying to get some money together, that's all," I say. I sound like a sulky kid.

The old lady brushes hair from my forehead. "I know," she says. She looks into my eyes for a long while, then moves to the door.

At the door she turns. "Thank you," she says. She smiles. "For the money."

When she's left the room, Jimmy says, "I've got a message for you."

"Yeah?" My mind is on the old lady and the drugs bit. She really hurt me.

"Mrs Fisher would like to see you."

"Mrs Fisher? What about?"

"I don't know. She came up to me on the street yesterday and asked me to ask you to call in at the shop. She said it was important."

I glance at the clock on the wall. Six thirty. Mr Fisher will have left for his Chamber of Commerce meeting. For a second I see myself being led up stairs, Mrs Fisher running her hands over her hips.

I stand up. "Look, bro," I say, "I'm just going out for a minute. When I get back, what say we all go for a drink somewhere? You, me, and the old – " I correct myself " – and Mother."

* * *

Mrs Fisher is alone in the shop.

"Thank you for coming," she says.

"Jimmy said it was important."

"It's about Benjamin."

I feel panic. *He's found out, Mr Fisher's found out!* I see a headline: *Husband kills wife's young lover*.

"He's got to have an operation."

"Benjamin?"

"I thought you ought to know. He has a hole in his heart."

My panic turns to fear. "A hole? What d'you mean?"

"A small hole. It's not serious."

"The *doctors* say it's not serious?"

"Yes. He goes into hospital on Monday. He'll have the operation on Tuesday."

"It's *essential* he has the operation?"

"Yes. To stitch up the hole."

"Poor kid." I start flashing on guys in green masks and gowns standing over Benjamin, who's on an operating table. I feel a chill.

"It's not serious. He'll be out in a week."

"Can I see him?"

"Of course. He's upstairs."

Mrs Fisher locks up, and we go upstairs.

Benjamin is on the floor playing with building blocks.

I squat beside him, and he raises his head and looks at me. "Hi," I say.

Benjamin smiles and says something foreign. I look up at Mrs Fisher and crack a corny joke: "He's not been taking his English tablets."

Mrs Fisher laughs and picks up Benjamin; and when I'm standing she asks me if I would like to hold him. And this time I do. I actually hold the kid. For about a minute.

A little while later, downstairs, I say: "Let me know how he gets on. You can reach me at the Massingham Hotel in London."

"The Massingham Hotel?"

"I've got a job there."

There's a tiny silence, then Mrs Fisher says, "You seem to have grown up all of a sudden."

I smile. "I don't drink 7-Up anymore, if that's what you mean."

Mrs Fisher goes to the door and unlocks it. She turns and looks at me. Her face is full of quiet. "You don't hold it against me?"

I look a lot of affection at her. "Why would I do that?"

Mrs Fisher's voice is very soft, saying, "It was special, wasn't it?"

"It was more than that."

Mrs Fisher's eyes grow misty. "Yes, it was," she says. She pauses. "Much more."

* * *

Five days later and shortly after tricking with a client

who calls himself Bubbles, I get a call from Mrs Fisher. Benjamin, she tells me, is fine.

I can stop worrying.

CHAPTER 35

It's my tenth Sunday at the Leisuredrome and I'm standing with Titch beside a *Death to the Invaders* machine, and feeling very uncomfortable. Titch is rummaging in his satchel. A second or so ago he nudged me in the leg. "There he is!" he said, and motioned with his head towards the door.

I looked. "You sure?" I asked.

"That's him!" Titch said. "Fucking weasel-face! Where the fuck's my mobilephone?"

Weasel-face is about forty-five and has – well – a weasel's face: black glittering eyes; a silky untrimmed brownish moustache; a long, sharp nose; a wide, thin mouth above a receding chin. His hair, which is the same colour as his moustache, looks as if it's been cut with a broken dinner plate. He's wearing a grey jacket that's too short in the sleeves, bottle-green jog pants, and black and white trainers. You wouldn't put him on your wish list.

At last Titch finds his mobilephone and after he's pressed a few buttons holds it to his ear. "General? Titch. Yeah. Our man's shown. Yeah." A longish pause. "Yeah." Another longish pause. "Okay. Right." Titch lowers the mobilephone and presses its Disconnect button. He looks up at me – sort of expectantly. I look again at weasel-face, who's moved to a slot and's feeding it money, all the while looking around. For a split second our eyes meet.

I take a deep breath. "Okay, Titch," I say, "this is it. For fuck's sake don't let me out of your sight."

"I won't," Titch says. He touches my arm. "Good luck."

Good luck! You'd think I was about to take a geography test or something.

I make my way, heart beating fast, to a slot that's two along from the one weasel-face is playing. It's the Leisuredrome's oldest model, and the only person I've seen collect from it is Titch. I slip it five 20 pence pieces.

I'm between two players. On my left is an old bookish-looking guy in brown tweed and half-moon glasses, and on my right a guy of about thirty wearing a busman's uniform. (You get all types in here – draughtsmen, systems analysts … Intelligent guys, some of them. And they play the slots. Unbelievable.)

After a minute or so the guy on my left, the bookish-looking guy, moves off, and quick as a flash I take his place. Now I'm next to weasel-face. I can smell him. He smells of machine oil and metal shavings. I glance at his hands and see that the nails are rimmed with black. It's not body dirt, the black; it's more like grease. Whatever it is, I wouldn't like him to peel me an orange.

I shoot him a look. "Hi."

For an instant he looks surprised. Then he smiles. "Winning?" he asks.

I run a hand through my hair. "Nah."

I feed my slot a few more coins and, with weasel-face watching me – his eyes are all over me, I can sense they are – thumb the Play button. Once, twice, three times. At the third spin, two triple-line bars and a bell come up. A second later the Nudge One light starts flashing. Seeing this, Weasel-face crouches at my side and tries to see what's above and below the bell. He doesn't know that I *know* what's above and below the bell; above it is a single-line bar and below it a lemon. I also know what's above the single-line bar and below the lemon; I've been playing these slots every Sunday for ten weeks, remember.

"Nudge down," weasel-face suggests. He's putting the moves on me, no question.

"You think so?" I say, and nudge down.

"Bad luck," weasel-face says.

I start to say, 'That's the way the piss-pot cracks", but check myself and instead say, "That's the way it goes." Not so tough-sounding. Toughness might scare him off.

"Here, try again," weasel-face says, and feeds the slot a thick one. "You come from round here?" he asks.

I tell him no, and try to think of a place that's pretty far removed from London. I want him to think I'm a lost soul in a big city, that I'm – what's the word? – vulnerable. The name Hertfordshire comes into my head. "Hertfordshire," I say.

"What, you're down for the day, are you?"

I shake my head no. "I've left home."

There's a silence between us while I play my slot.

"You got somewhere to stay?"

"No – I'm sleeping rough."

A lot more silence. Then, "You can stay the night at my place if you like. It's not much, but it's better than sleeping rough."

I shoot him a look. "Where d'you live?"

"Not far from here." A pause. "I've got a car."

I give him a heartbreaking smile. "If it's not too much trouble."

"No, no trouble at all. Finish your game, and we'll get a coffee; there's a McDonald's up the road."

* * *

Outside, the pavements are heavy with people. Everywhere you look, people. And traffic. A big movement of life.

"Look," weasel-face says, "instead of a coffee, why don't we have a beer at my place?" He can't wait to get his dirty paws on me.

I shrug. "OK." I feel amazingly calm. I *shouldn't* feel amazingly calm, but for some reason I do. "Where's your car?" I ask.

"A ten-minute walk away," weasel-face says. "If that." His voice is light, very reassuring. I imagine Pebbles being taken in by it; being led, as I am, past brightly-lit shops and eating houses; seeing young couples with their arms round each other's waists; catching the scent of an exciting perfume; glancing at a particular window display; weaving and side-stepping; turning into a narrow side-street that midway along shows a glowing pub sign; passing the pub – The Blue Boar – then rounding a corner and hearing weasel-face say:

"The grey Cortina."

* * *

The springs of the front passenger seat are broken and there's an old-clothes smell in the air. On the floor, digging into my ankle, is an unidentifiable object.

We move off, and suddenly my calmness goes and a terrible panic overtakes me. What if Titch couldn't keep up with us? Or there's interference on his mobilephone and he can't get through to the General? Or the General is caught in traffic? What then? An expression of the old lady's comes into my head: The terrible destiny of some people.

We drive down back-streets and stop when we come to an intersection. Ahead of us and to our left is a road sign with an overhead light. Edmonton 6 miles, the sign says.

When we're moving again, I say, "Edmonton ... that where we're headed?"

Not taking his eyes off the road, weasel-face gives me a yes.

After that there's a long silence, about a five-minute silence. Then I ask: "That your first time at the 'drome? I've not seen you there before." I'm doing a little detective work here.

"I've been there a few times," weasel-face answers. (A *few* times. Does that mean there's a *third* body; a fourth, even? Jesus!) He slows as a yellow light comes on and asks, "Why'd you leave home?" He looks at me.

I think quick. "To get away from my old man. He kept beating up on me."

Weasel-face nods. "My father was the same. Couldn't keep his hands off me. One day I tore my jacket and he blacked both my eyes. I was only twelve. Another time he knocked three of my teeth out."

"Why'd he do that?"

"He caught me playing with myself."

Uh-oh, here comes the dirty talk.

"There's nothing wrong with that – playing with yourself."

"My father thought there was."

The lights go to green again and we pull away. Glancing at me, weasel-face says, "Do you play with yourself?"

An Esso petrol tanker rockets past.

"All the time."

"You do?"

"Sure – all young guys do."

"You think so?"

"Of course. It's a natural thing to do."

"How often – do you play with yourself?"

"I dunno. Every day." I'm not enjoying this.

"More than once a day?"

"Sometimes."

"What's the most you've ever played with yourself in one day?"

"Five, six times." Let him get his head round that.

"Where d'you do it?"

"In my room. In the bathroom." My imagination gets the better of me. "In a pot-hole once, when I was big on potholing. Once on top of a bus."

"People around?" From the way he's gripping the steering wheel I can tell my words are having a serious hormonal effect on him.

"No, the bus was empty."

"You got it out, eh?"

"No, I had a hole in my pocket."

"What, you came in your trousers?"

"Right." I pause. "Another time in a cinema." I'm getting into this.

"What was the film?"

"*Home Alone.*"

"I saw that."

Yeah, I bet he did. That Culkin kid. Fancied him, I bet.

"Anywhere else?"

"In a library – the reference section where nobody gets ... In a lift – I was stuck between floors ... On the back of a moving pick-up truck ... In a launderette ... On deck of the Woolwich Ferry ... In a swimming pool – the deep end ... In a telephone booth. Anywhere you care to mention. Battersea Dogs' Home."

"Battersea Dogs' Home?"

"I once took a dog there I didn't want. There was this vacant plot at the back of some kennels ..."

"Ever do it in a church."

"Never in a church. In a graveyard."

"Over a grave?"

This is a number one psycho I've got here, no discussion.

"Not far from one."

"Any *other* places you can think of?"

"Let me see ... In a booth in a music store while listening to a Beethoven number ... In a doctor's consulting room – the doctor was called to an accident outside his surgery. I was in his consulting room at the time, so while he was away ... At the top of the Monument ... Behind a stack of timber in a Texas DIY store ... In the grounds of the insane asylum where my mother stayed for a while ... In my aunt's greenhouse ... In her sun lounge ... In her linen cupboard – she has this giant linen cupboard ... At the back of the Benefit

Office ... In a Chinese take-away .... In an *Indian* take-away ... At the end of Brighton Pier." I pause. "That's about it."

Weasel-face lays a smile on me that's not exactly alluring. "I thought you might have done it over a grave." He pauses. "Wouldn't you like to?"

I look out the window. He's pissing me off now. "It's not one of my goals in life."

In a sort of remote voice, he says, "I'd like to do it over my father's grave. Do it over *him*, if he was alive. Tie him up and do it over him."

"That's not very nice," I say.

"*He* wasn't very nice," weasel-face says. He makes this last point like he's describing something that crawled out of a dead cat. He crashes the gears and says, "I'd like to dig him up and come all over him."

"I don't think the world'd be a better place for knowing that," I say, and then wish I'd kept my mouth shut, because weasel-face shoots me a really heavy look.

In time we leave the main drag and move along a road lined on both sides with small shops, most of them unlit. There's nobody about. Not a soul.

At the end of the road, we make a right. Now we're in a street of houses. The street is very long and wide and the houses tall and drab-looking; every house seems to have red curtains with a 50-watt bulb burning behind them.

"Not far now," weasel-face says.

I glance in the left rearview mirror and see the yellow light of a London cab. "I could use that beer," I say. My voice is flat-sounding, and there's a trembling in my left leg. I'm developing a lot of nervousness. I say a small prayer: Please don't let the General screw up.

We turn into another long street of houses and weasel-face says, "At the end of the road."

* * *

We halt under a yellow streetlight and get out of the car.

The house is a corner house and, unlike those on its left, detached. It's square-shaped and has four steps leading to the front door. In the downstairs front room a light burns behind drawn, orange curtains – across which a figure is moving.

"You got company?" I ask. What I'd like to do now is go home and have a nice cup of tea with the old lady and Jimmy.

"A friend of mine," weasel-face says. "He drops in from time to time. He has a key."

We go up the steps of the house, weasel-face leading, and as we do, I glance to my left and right for a sign of the General.

Nothing. Just a lot of quiet. This is very bad shit, I decide.

The front door is ajar, which puzzles me. "After you," weasel-face says and stands aside to let me enter.

Now I'm in a narrow, dimly lit hall that has a linoleum-covered floor, cream-painted walls and a staircase part-carpeted in red. There's the smell of cat piss. What am I doing here? I ask myself. How can I be having anything to do with this shit?

Weasel-face closes the door – with a kind of finality, it seems to me – and says, "This way."

He leads me to a door a few yards along the hall, and

opens it. "By the way, what's your name?" he asks.

"Simon," I answer.

"Mine's Ron."

There are four guys in the room. The eldest is about sixty, and the youngest about thirty. All are seated – two on a sofa, two in armchairs, the armchairs set side by side facing the sofa – and all are in what newspapers like to call a state of undress, the youngest, a slimly-built guy with bleached-blond hair, wearing only jockey pants. The others are wearing singlets and trousers. None is wearing shoes or socks. It's obvious that a lot of sexual activity's been going on. The guy in the jockey pants, the bleached-blond guy, is seated on the sofa with the sixty-year-old, who's ruddy-complexioned and has a full head of white hair. This guy, the white-haired guy, is very big. Popeye arms. He looks as if he could tie a knot in a scaffolding pole. In the armchairs are a chunky dark-haired guy with zits on his shoulders, and a fat-ish, unwashed-looking guy with a wispy, yellow moustache.

The room is about 15-feet square and has a carpet that I'd like my old history teacher to see. The wallpaper is pink with a white rose pattern and is faded and grease-marked. Facing a yellow-tiled fireplace is a beat-up chestnut sideboard, on which sits a six-pack of Long Life. A second six-pack, opened and two thirds empty, sits on a straight-backed chair placed next to the door. In one corner of the room is a TV on legs. In another, a plastic clothes horse with a white nylon shirt draped over it. The light comes from a single bulb that hangs from the ceiling beneath a yellow pyramid shade. It's the ugliest room I've ever been in, and the hottest.

"This is Simon," weasel-face announces. "Simon's from Herefordshire." He moves away from me and stands near the TV.

"Hertfordshire," I say. I brighten my voice: "Hi."

Silence. They're all staring at me, scoping me out. You've no idea how scared I am. Eventually the chunky guy says, "Like a beer, mate?" and gets to his feet. I see the unwashed-looking guy look at the big guy and give a slight nod, coupled with a slight pouting of his mouth and a widening of his eyes. In anybody's language he's saying, "Not bad."

"No thanks," I say. I'm too tensed up to drink. A single bead of sweat is sliding down from under my armpit.

"*I'm* having one," the chunky guy says, and goes to the sideboard. "You want one, Ron?"

"Thanks," says weasel-face.

"Get us one while you're there, George," the big guy says. Then, patting the middle cushion of the sofa and looking at me: "Here you are, son, sit down."

I hesitate for a second, then go to the sofa and sit down.

The chunky guy, George, passes around Long Life and returns to his chair. I've just noticed that he walks with a slight limp.

"Sure you wouldn't like a beer?" the big guy asks. He's wearing Brut aftershave.

"Certain," I say.

Weasel-face opens his Long Life, sets it down on the TV and leaves the room. He's back in a few seconds in shirtsleeves, his hair combed. He makes a big point of closing the door, and when he's holding his drink again, says, "You comfortable enough there, Simon?"

"Fine," I say. I'm about as comfortable as a fly in a spider's web. These are not sweet, simple people.

"*He's* all right, aren't you, pal?" the big guy says and puts an arm round my shoulders. And for a second my heart stops. I'm so scared I can hardly breathe. He squeezes the top of my arm, and then starts to stroke it. I don't make resistance; I pretend not to notice what he's doing.

After what seems a long time but probably is only a few minutes, the unwashed-looking guy says, "How you doing there, Len?" He's addressing the big guy, who still has his arm round my shoulders.

Len doesn't answer. He places his drink on the floor, straightens up, whirls on me, grinning, and shoots a hand under my crotch.

"Hey," I say, "cut it out." I make to stand, but he grips me by the back of the neck, his fingers digging into the veins and cutting off the blood supply. This is not a delicious moment.

"Come on, son," he says, "let's have a bit of fun." He yanks my belt undone and starts tearing at my jeans.

"Cut it out," I yell. I try to push him away, but there's too much of him. I see the guy on the other side of me, the bleached-blond guy, slip his jockey pants off, and a second later see the two guys in the armchairs get to their feet and, along with weasel-face, start to undress.

The bleached-blond guy stands, and the big guy says to him, "Watch him for a second." He hauls himself up, and the bleached-blond guy takes his place on the sofa. "Here, get hold of this," he says, waving his dick.

"Get hold of it yourself," I tell him.

"Go on, boy, get hold of it," the big guy says. "It's lovely; it'll do you good." He's ripping his clothes off like his life depends on it.

The bleached-blond guy locks an arm around my neck and says, "Fucking get hold of it."

"No," I say. I feel a tear roll down my cheek. I'm coming apart.

"Do as you're fucking told," the big guy says. He pulls me to my feet and punches me in the stomach.

I fall on the floor on my knees, and the big guy grabs hold of my hair, jerks my head back and shoves his dick in my face. "L-u-u-u-u-vly," he says. They're all around me, all naked. I fill my lungs with the room's cruddy air. "General!" I scream.

And at this very moment I hear heavy blows on wood, and then wood splintering, and seconds later hurrying footsteps in the hall. Then the door is thrown open and there in the doorway are the General and Titch. The General has his face blacked up and is holding a sledge-hammer slantwise across his chest. From a belt around his waist hang hand grenades. No shit, hand grenades! Titch is holding a horror-movie knife. It's Rambo and The Mighty Atom.

"You bastards!" the General yells, and lunges forward. There's a sort of animal gleam in his eyes.

The sickos fall back.

"You dirty bastards!" The General takes a swing at them with his hammer. He glares at them. "You dirty rotten bastards." He kneels beside me and in a caring voice asks, "You okay?" As he asks this, the big guy moves towards us, and, quick as a flash, Titch sticks him with his knife. He more than sticks him with it, he pushes the fucking thing in up to its hilt. The big guy staggers back and slides down the wall, making little mewing noises. "Let's go," the General says and helps me to my feet. "Don't fucking move," he tells the sickos.

We back out the door, and, once in the hall, the General does this: he quickly unhooks a grenade from his belt, pulls the pin – Jesus! – and tosses the grenade into the room. Then he says:

"Run like fuck."

Out on the street we hear a terrific explosion.

* * *

The next day, this story appears in the *Daily Mirror*: *Three men, believed by police to be members of a terrorist bomb squad, died in an explosion in a house in Edmonton last night. A fourth man suffered severe head and chest injuries and is critically ill. Detectives investigating the blast are working on the theory that a home-made explosive device was set off accidentally.*

* * *

Incidentally, that taxi I saw ... . The General was driving it.

CHAPTER 36

When I was at school, I read something that gave me a good feeling through and through, so I memorised it. Here it is:

I feel drunk with the joy of being alive. I look at everything with a sense of wonder and see everything bold and clear. I have no malice or bad thoughts in me. I am honest and open; I can be trusted. I am sympathetic and will listen to you. I will not turn away from you. I will praise you and expect no praise in return. I am strong; I will protect you. There is nothing I will not do for you. I am your friend. I am a friend of the world.

CHAPTER 37

It's Saturday, 8 p.m., and there's a party going on at the Roll-In. The party's for me. On Monday I'm off with Jimmy to Arizona and I doubt I'll be returning – to the meat rack, that is. The guys know this and are throwing this party for me, or, to be more accurate, the General is. Which is nice of him – a nice, friendly gesture. Since our Edmonton escapade the General and me – and I – have become really tight. It's true what they say: Danger makes for close relationships.

Inflated coloured condoms hang from the ceiling, and streamers of coloured paper are taped to the walls; a space has been made for dancing. Some of the guys are dancing now – Titch with Twin Pat: a hilarious sight. The music comes from the Roll-In's beat-up radio. The room is hot and smoke-filled and there's a lot of loud laughter. For no special reason, I'm looking at College, who's talking with Twin Paul and Stick. Beyond them, near the door, deep in conversation, are the General and Savoy Harry, Savoy Harry occasionally sipping milk from a plastic glass (he has an ulcer, I've been told). To my left, pigging out on kedgeree, is Tits.

There are faces here I've never seen before. One belongs to a skinny, dark-haired guy who keeps throwing looks at me. Twin Pat must've noticed this because every now and then he looks daggers at him. Twin Pat is crazy for me. Stick is too. Twin Pat's so crazy for me he even offered to trick for me, like work for me, but I said no. I'm no pimp. When I told him I was going away, he broke down, cried his eyes out. When I told Stick, he said, "Hey, man, don't say that. Don't say that, man", and went very quiet. We were at his pad. I'd spent the night with him. It was his turn to – well – sleep with me. I've got myself into a situation where I'm being shared: Stick one night, Twin Pat the next. Pretty tiring. Anyway, Stick at his pad: "Don't say that, man. Don't say that." I put my hands on his shoulders and looked a lot of quiet at him. "My brother's gonna need my help," I told him. Which is not what I believe – Jimmy could manage without me, I know he could. But I want to be with him. I just do.

Abandoning Titch, Twin Pat comes over to me and says, "Dance with me, Ya-ya." He looks tearful.

I bow. "Your wish is my command," I say.

Corny.

As we dance, I catch Stick's eye and lay a wink on him.

"Keep it loose, Bruce," he calls. But sadly.

I was feeling insecure
You might not love me any-m-o-o-o-ore

Bryan Ferry's *Jealous Guy*. A favourite of mine.

"You'll keep in touch, won't you, Ya-ya?" Twin Pat says.

"Count on it," I say.

He starts to cry.

"Hey, shape up," I tell him.

* * *

Around midnight the General calls for quiet. When he's got it, he says, "Before we go, boys and girls, I've a few words to say concerning Simon."

If a pin dropped you'd hear it.

"As you know, Simon has been with us for something like four months, and in that time has made many friends."

Murmurs of agreement.

"And made a lot of johns happy."

A loud "Whoo-ee!" from someone.

"The johns are going to miss him as much as we are."

I hear Stick say, "A-r-i-i-i-ght."

"Especially Wallnuts." (Wallnuts is the name we've given to a Member of Parliament on account of he has these wrinkled-up balls.)

Laughter.

"When I told Wallnuts Simon was leaving, he said, 'Not counting my wife's chihuahua, he was the best fuck I ever had.'"

Loud laughter.

"Which didn't do much for my ego. Because at one time, Wallnuts was screwing *me*."

Shouts and cheers.

"But seriously, Simon," the General turns and faces me, "I'm certain I speak for everyone present when I say, 'I wish you all the luck in the world.'"

Applause. Twin Pat, I notice, is dabbing his eyes.

"You're a terrific guy and it's been a pleasure having you on the team."

I find this moment embarrassing, but I handle it cool. "Keep going, General," I say, "you're getting there", and everyone breaks up laughing.

After a few more jokes, the General says, "And now, Simon, we come to the presentation."

I give a look of surprise, and the General, grinning, says, "You didn't think we'd let you leave here empty handed, did you?" He looks at College, who's standing behind the counter. "If you'd be so kind, College?" he says.

College lays one of his beautiful smiles on me and says, "Certainly, General."

He disappears into the kitchen and returns a few seconds later with something that makes my eyes fill and a lump form in my throat.

He returns with a golden labrador, complete with harness.

CHAPTER 38

We stand together on the ridge. The earth is cool beneath our feet and the early sun warm on our faces. And there in the distance, coming in low, its blades cutting through air that gleams and sparkles like water, is the helicopter.

CPSIA information can be obtained at www.ICGtesting.com
Printed in the USA
LVOW071448090911

245617LV00001B/16/P